CASE
OF THE
BLEUS

CASE
OF THE
BLEUS

A Cheese Shop Mystery

BY

KORINA MOSS

St. Martin's Paperbacks

First published in the United States by St. Martin's Paperbacks, an imprint of St. Martin's Publishing Group.

CASE OF THE BLEUS

Copyright © 2023 by Korina Moss.

For information, address St. Martin's Publishing Group, 120 Broadway, New York, NY 10271.

www.stmartins.com

ISBN: 978-1-250-89389-5

Our books may be purchased in bulk for promotional, educational, or business use. Please contact your local bookseller or the Macmillan Corporate and Premium Sales Department at 1-800-221-7945, ext. 5442, or by email at MacmillanSpecialMarkets@macmillan.com.

Printed in the United States of America

St. Martin's Paperbacks edition / October 2023

10 9 8 7 6 5 4 3 2 1

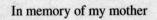
In memory of my mother

ACKNOWLEDGMENTS

Once again, I have to start by thanking my agent, Jill Marsal, and the entire team at St. Martin's. I feel incredibly lucky to have my series guided by Madeline Houpt, a puntastic editor who cares about my characters as much as I do. Thank you to John Simko, who teaches me so much with every book he copyedits; to the immensely talented artists, Danielle Christopher and Alan Ayers, who design and illustrate my beautiful covers; my publicity & marketing team, Sara LaCotti and Allison Zeigler, who keep my calendar full; and John Rounds, who herds all the cats so my books make it out into the world. I'm very proud to be a St. Martin's author.

An enormous thank you to my first reader, Caitlin Lonning, who I ask too much of, yet still ends up giving me even more. You're a rock star editor. (And a "just because" shout-out to her mom, Elizabeth, my longstanding BFF.)

To my cheese gurus at Spread Cheese Co. in Middletown, CT—Jamie, Lindsey, and Nina. I appreciate your generosity in sharing your passion for and knowledge of cheese with me. If I get anything cheese-related wrong, it's solely my mistake. I'm just a mystery writer—these women know cheese.

My books are all the better being narrated by Erin Moon, who elevates every scene with her talent, passion, and dedication.

The mystery community is truly the most supportive, friendly writing community I could hope for. As I fangirl over my fellow authors, those same authors lift me up. A special shout-out to Sisters in Crime and Mystery Writers of America.

To those people who are first in my heart—my son, my family, and my friends—who aren't reserved in their show of support and pride, I appreciate you. Thanks, Dad, for reading all my books twice.

Thanks to reader Nancy Novacek, whose clever name for the new bicycle shop in town, The Kick Stand, was chosen from hundreds of entries. My sincere appreciation goes to all my readers, including the bloggers, booktubers, and bookstagrammers, who share their excitement about my series with their followers and with me. You make it fun to be a cozy mystery author. #TeamCheese!

"There's never a wrong favorite when it comes to cheese."

—Willa Bauer

CHAPTER 1

"Church Bleu. It's bound to be the highlight of this weekend's invitational—Max Dumas's one-of-a-kind bleu cheese." Behind the counter of Curds & Whey, I held my phone out so my cheese shop crew, Archie and Mrs. Schultz, could admire the photo of the special cheese wheel. Its ivory-colored rind only hinted at the pronounced blue-green streaks within that gave it its complex piquant flavor. This wasn't their first time seeing the extraordinary cheese, but we couldn't help but take another peek at it. We'd be viewing a wheel in person in a few hours at the Northwest Cheese Invitational, which was held annually to showcase cheesemakers' custom creations. This year, they'd be posthumously honoring my former employer, Max Dumas, at the new conference center right here in Yarrow Glen. "It's amazing the amount of attention it's garnered in only seven years," I added. "It won Best in Show its first year out and then the next two years after that until Max stopped entering it."

I stuck the phone back in my Curds & Whey apron pocket and took up the broom I'd left leaning against one of the turned-leg display tables. I'd been neatening the shop for my former colleagues from Church Cheese Shop, the last place I'd worked before moving to the

Sonoma Valley to open Curds & Whey. They were coming by any minute and would be seeing it for the first time. I was excited to show it to them. I finished sweeping and took a last look before deciding if I was satisfied that it was perfect.

My shop's aesthetic was inspired by my brief time working at a *fromagerie* outside of Lyon where my passion for cheese blossomed. I wanted to bring the color, warmth, and romance of France into my Sonoma Valley shop. We sold charcuterie boards, cheese lovers' cookbooks, and anything you'd need for a cheese-perfect picnic: picnic baskets, engraved cheese knives, and plenty of sweet-and-savory cheese accompaniments. Of course, there was also cheese, and plenty of it. Distressed tables held stacked wheels of aged cheeses from all over the world, while the front windows displayed wrapped wedges. The shades and textures revealed inside their casings lured customers into the shop to inhale their heady fragrances.

Archie, my twenty-year-old cheesemonger-in-training, wanted to know more about Max's Church Bleu. "Had there ever been a three-peat winner before?"

"Never," I replied.

Archie and Mrs. Schultz teamed up to cut, weigh, and wrap an online order while we talked about the special cheese.

"I bet the other cheesemakers were relieved when he withdrew his cheese from the competition," Mrs. Schultz commented. The retired high school drama teacher's wheat-colored apron was livened by a summer scarf that complemented a colorful flared dress cinched at the waist, her usual attire. She and Archie had been with me since I opened the shop last spring, and I'd yet to ask why she preferred to be called Mrs. Schultz.

"Just the opposite, Mrs. Schultz. They wanted their custom cheese to be the one to finally best Church Bleu. Max was of the 'keep them wanting more' school of thought. He kept the location where it was made and aged a secret, so batch sizes were small, and his Church Cheese Shop was the only place that sold it. That fit his personality perfectly—Max loved puzzles, riddles, mysteries . . ." I stowed the broom away. "He was protective of his cheese, but he also really enjoyed his Church Bleu being enigmatic."

"A mysterious cheese! That's cool," Archie said. The only thing Archie liked almost as much as cheese was solving a mystery, which he'd taken part in several times, along with me, Mrs. Schultz, and my best friend, Baz, when the necessity had arisen.

I noticed him repeatedly glancing out the large picture windows at the front of the shop. As we didn't close for another couple of hours, my Church Cheese friends had volunteered to take Archie to the invitational ahead of me and Mrs. Schultz. I'd spent a couple of hours there this morning, but I couldn't leave my shop all day. I knew he was excited to attend his first invitational, although he tended to be enthusiastic about most things. He was often like a human Tigger.

"Max thought it was cool too, but the threats he'd gotten over the years weren't," I said.

Mrs. Schultz's toothy grin vanished. "Threats?"

"Just because he wouldn't disclose the secrets to making the Church Bleu. There can be a dark underbelly to a popular custom cheese. Thieves have been known to steal cheese and sell it on the black market. In one year, almost seven hundred blocks of Saint Nectaire were stolen in France."

"Cheese can be *that* valuable?" Archie said.

I moved on to fussing with the displays. "A wheel of the Spanish Cabrales was auctioned one year for twenty-two thousand dollars."

"No way!"

"With the right hype and a supply that can't meet the demand, some people will pay up."

"What did Max do about the threats?" Mrs. Schultz asked.

"Nothing really. He didn't take them seriously. He'd gotten a kick out of the fact that the FDA inspectors were occasionally bribed to give up its location. To their credit, they never have. I don't think it affected him too much. Like I said, Max always had a mischievous streak. He liked the cloak-and-dagger aspect of keeping it to himself and driving to the secret location solo. Although, it made our jobs a little harder because he never told us ahead of time. We'd open the shop and find a note that would say *I've left under the dark of night*." I chuckled at the thought. "Then a handful of days later, he'd be back."

"I've seen you pick apart cheese, Willa, and tell me exactly what's in it and how it's made. Why couldn't that be done to this special blue cheese, so others could figure out how to make it?" Mrs. Schultz asked.

"It has been. Some have even tried to replicate it but couldn't get it exactly right. There are so many variables that go into making cheese—timing, aging, temperature and humidity, where the milk comes from . . . even the type of grass the cows graze on. We can only come up with educated theories, kind of like paleontologists. The consensus is that Church Bleu's uniqueness comes from where it's aged."

The order done and packed, Archie removed his gloves. "What's your guess?"

"Well, since his cheese shop is in a renovated church,

Max would say the difference between his cheese and others is divine intervention. It's ironic, really, since he had such a devilish streak." I smiled thinking about crazy Max.

"Willa!" Kendall Waterstone walked into the shop and wrapped me in a hug. "Long time, no see."

"Too long," I replied.

We looked each other over. I hadn't changed much except maybe for some extra worry lines around my eyes that had developed since opening my own shop. She noticed my shorter hair. It was easier to deal with, although I still had to pluck the stubborn premature grays that stood out like neon signs against my jet-black color.

She looked just as I'd remembered her. Her highlighted brunette hair was out of its work ponytail and flowed past her shoulders. She wore a short denim jacket over a well-fitting crew neck and dark jeans with loafers. She didn't try to outshine anyone, but often did anyway. She was one of the best cheesemongers I knew and among the hardest working. Yet, unlike me, no matter how long of a day she'd had, she still always managed to look incredibly put together.

Behind Kendall, I spotted Claire Ingram, another Church Cheese colleague. She left the doorway to give me a hug. "Hi, Willa. Good to see you." Not surprisingly, I hadn't noticed her walk in with Kendall. I recalled how, as a staff member and not a certified cheesemonger, she seemed to prefer to blend into the background at the shop. She had Kendall's brunette hair and hazel eyes, although they seemed dulled a bit.

Archie bounced slightly on the balls of his feet in excitement. I introduced him and Mrs. Schultz to Kendall and Claire.

"I'm sorry we're running late," Kendall said. "We just

drove in and got our rooms at the inn. Pepper and Freddie wanted to wash up before we go to the invitational, but they'll be by tomorrow morning after the reading of Max's will." Pepper was another cheesemonger from Church Cheese, and Freddie was hired after I'd left.

Of the group, I'd felt closest to Kendall when I worked at Church Cheese Shop in southern Oregon before moving here to Yarrow Glen. She'd talked about coming to see my new shop, but I wasn't surprised when she hadn't. It's one of those things you say to people you've had extended work relationships with. We were close work friends only, unlike her and Claire. Having spent the eight years prior to opening Curds & Whey employed in roughly as many cheese shops across the country, I was used to work friends. In fact, I'd preferred them. It wasn't until Archie, Mrs. Schultz, and I were brought closer together by investigating the murder of a magazine critic shortly after I opened my shop that our work relationship turned into much more.

"That's fine. I understand," I said.

Kendall's gaze swept the room. "Look at this shop! It's divine!"

I blushed with pride. "Thank you."

"It really is beautiful, Willa," Claire concurred. She was drawn to the Italian cheeses by one of the front windows. She picked up a wrapped wedge and put it to her nose. "Mmm. I know I should have more sophisticated favorites by now, but to me, nothing beats Parmigiano Reggiano."

"There's never a wrong favorite when it comes to cheese," I said.

"Kudos to you for having the guts to open and run your own shop." Kendall stuck her hands on her small waist and continued to take it all in.

It's everything I hoped it would be, and I've got a great crew," I said. Archie and Mrs. Schultz beamed.

"We might have to ask you for some advice after we buy Church Cheese," Claire said, leaving the window display.

"You two are going to buy Church Cheese Shop?" I asked. This was the first I'd heard of it.

"The four of us—Pepper and Freddie too—so we can continue Max's legacy," she replied.

It was a nice sentiment, but knowing Kendall and Claire's bumpy relationship with Pepper, it surprised me.

I ignored my reservations about it. "That's wonderful. Congratulations."

"There's a lot of moving parts to make it happen. We'll see." Kendall didn't sound as enthusiastic about it as Claire.

A trill sounded and we all checked our phones, except for Mrs. Schultz, who kept hers stowed in her purse.

Kendall's phone seemed to be the source. She rolled her eyes after glancing at the screen. "It's Pepper. She wants to get going to the invitational. We drove together."

"You should. It's getting late."

Archie removed his apron, ready to go.

"But I've barely seen your shop," Kendall said, looking past me to see what she missed.

"You can take more time tomorrow," I replied.

"I'll walk to the inn with Archie and hold Pepper off for a bit longer," Claire offered.

"Thanks, Claire," Kendall said.

"It was nice to see you, Claire. We'll catch up with you at the invitational tonight," I said, directing that last bit to Archie too.

Archie nodded, and he and Claire left the shop to walk up the street to the inn.

Kendall walked over to our refrigerated cheese case. I began to point out some of the blue cheeses we'd just gotten in, like the popular Point Reyes Original Blue, a bold farmstead cheese good for snacking or salads. She responded politely but seemed preoccupied. I finally took notice of the difference in her—there was a sadness in her eyes that hadn't been there when I'd known her before. I dispensed with the cheese talk.

"Are you okay?" I asked her.

I could imagine how raw Max's death was to Kendall, who had been working with him all this time—three times as long as the thirteen months I'd been with him. Max was easy to love and quite a character—we used to call him the Willy Wonka of cheese.

Mrs. Schultz stepped away, allowing us to talk in private.

"I'm sorry I didn't tell you that Max was sick. I meant to. We thought he had more time," she said, hugging herself. She was shaken.

I put a hand on her arm. "Nobody could've predicted that he would die from a car accident instead of his illness." I was sorry to have let the chaos and pressure of opening my own shop keep me from being in touch with him more over this past year. Perhaps if I had, he would've told me himself.

"It was awful. The news of it, I mean. It's not the way he should've gone." After a few moments, she seemed able to put the thought aside. "I know you two were close when you worked with us."

"He was the one who pushed me to finally take the leap and open my own shop. I owe him a lot."

The thought of Max, a playful, passionate mentor and grandfather figure, made me smile. I pushed away the thought that he may have suffered when his car veered off the road and barreled down a short embankment. My brother Grayson had died in a car rollover on the weekend of his college graduation. I purposely never listened to or read any details of Grayson's accident. His friend was driving, the SUV rolled over on a turn, and he was pronounced dead when paramedics reached him—that's all I know. I didn't want to see images of the car or skid marks on the road. I didn't want to keep wondering if he was scared in those final moments or if he suffered before succumbing. When I think of Grayson, I focus on his twenty-one years of life, not his moment of death. As difficult as it was, I'd do the same with my memories of Max.

"He believed in you. He was always so full of exuberance, even after he got sick." Kendall sighed.

"I hope I can take after him and still have the joy for the job when I'm in my seventies like he did."

Silence passed between us as we thought of Max.

Eventually, I asked, "Should he not have been driving in his condition?"

"You think anyone could keep him from his Church Bleu?" she replied with a brief smile. "He was a little frailer, but he seemed all right to me." She looked away and was quiet for a moment, the same worry on her face as before. "I wonder if he was distracted thinking about his brother."

"His brother? I didn't even know he had a brother."

"He died just a few months ago from the same blood disorder Max had."

I shook my head, the shock of it leaving me in disbelief for a moment. "I feel terrible that I didn't even know that."

"Well then, hold onto your cheese curds—he had a daughter too."

"What? How did we not know this?"

"They've been estranged for like twenty years, pretty much her whole adult life, ever since his wife died. They recently reconnected, though. She'll be at the invitational."

"What could have caused that? I bet she's glad they made amends before he passed." Once I digested the news, guilt again set in. "All that extra time I spent with Max and all I was ever concerned about was learning how to run my own cheese shop. I should've asked him more about himself."

"Don't beat yourself up about it. He kept it private from everyone." Another trill from Kendall's phone sounded. She glanced at it. "Pepper again."

"We can catch up more tonight. I'll be there in time for the presentation of the Church Bleu," I assured her.

"I'd better go, then. See you later." We hugged again, and she said goodbye to Mrs. Schultz on her way out.

I continued to think about what Kendall had just told me. I thought it was just his Church Bleu that was shrouded in mystery, but apparently Max held onto a lot more secrets than any of us had realized.

CHAPTER 2

The Northwest Cheese Society chose a different city in the northwestern United States each year to hold its invitational, and this year Yarrow Glen held the honor, thanks to our new convention hall on the edge of town. Mrs. Schultz and I were running late for the big Church Bleu presentation, but once we arrived at the hall, it was difficult to pull myself away from the cheesemakers' tables. I wanted to look at, hear about, and try each and every custom cheese. It seemed most people were abandoning their tables, anyway, in favor of attending the ceremony, which was to begin shortly.

We only had to follow the stream of people through the wide hallways to find the ballroom. There was a sprinkling of chairs in the back, but the rest was standing room only. I picked up snippets of conversations as we wove our way through the crowd, each one talking about Max and his cheese. Most people had their phones in hand, ready to take photos or video when the Church Bleu arrived. We worked our way toward the front where we spotted Archie, Kendall, and Claire.

"This is amazing!" Archie said when we reached them. His cheeks, freckled with a port-wine stain birthmark across his left one, crinkled from his huge smile.

"You're having a good time?" I asked, already knowing the answer.

"Claire and Kendall have been great!"

"We love an enthusiastic future cheesemonger," Kendall said, smiling at Archie.

"There's so much cheese here, but all anybody's been talking about is Max and the Church Bleu. It's like it's the holy grail or something," Archie said, still marveling at the event.

I laughed to myself at the analogy. I looked to the front of the ballroom and noted the velvet rope, behind which a lone table draped in blue cloth stood on a riser. Atop the table, a simple elevated platter would hold Max's custom cheese for all to admire.

Pepper Sheffield came up from behind and joined our group. "Look at us. All together again," she said in her *Pepper* way that left you wondering whether she was happy about it or not.

"Good to see you again, Pepper," I said.

"Sure it is," she replied, unconvinced. She extended one arm, which barely touched my shoulder in a weak half hug before she retreated. She was keeping it real, as always. She had a disarming directness about her and a biting edge to her sarcasm, if it was sarcasm. "This is Freddie Yang. He was hired after you left. Freddie, this is *the* Willa Bauer, second only to Kendall in Max's devotion when she worked at Church Cheese."

Freddie waved from beside Pepper. I guessed him to be in his early thirties and was slim like Archie, but with scruffy chin whiskers and enviably thick black hair, slicked back. His high energy also reminded me of Archie. He seemed revved up to be here.

"It almost feels like you never left, Willa, as often as

Max bragged about you opening your own cheese shop," Pepper continued.

The year and a half since she and I had worked together obviously hadn't done much to dull her lukewarm feelings toward me. Pepper, still wearing heavy bangs cut straight across her forehead and favoring bold eyeshadow as I'd remembered, was in her early forties—older than Kendall and me by about a decade. She always resented that Max treated the three of us cheesemongers equally, even though she had the most experience. She was a hard worker with a lot of cheese knowledge, but she wasn't great with customers. I had to admit, she could be fun when she wasn't being snarky. She and I got along okay when her perception of Max's favorites didn't get in the way.

"Willa's shop is beautiful," Kendall said, trying to sweeten Pepper's bitterness a touch.

"She knows I'm teasing. I can't wait to see it tomorrow," Pepper said, finally stowing her sarcasm and bringing me in for a second hug.

I brought Archie and Mrs. Schultz into the fold and introduced them to Pepper and Freddie. As hellos were exchanged, I realized none of them was carrying the Church Bleu. "Which one of you brought Max's cheese?"

"Maxine is bringing it," Kendall said lightly, although her forced smile didn't match her tone.

"Even though *we* were the ones who saved the last wheel to honor Max today," Freddie said. He pursed his lips, his prior enthusiasm dampened.

"She never showed any interest in him or the shop until she found out he was dying. Perfect timing, huh?" Pepper said with a raised eyebrow.

"When you find out your dad is dying, you could have

a change of heart. It might not be about inheriting the shop," Kendall said.

"Except it worked. He told you just weeks before he died that he was leaving the shop to *her*, didn't he? Anyway, the shop is secondary. What she really wants is the secret of the Church Bleu," Pepper insisted.

"Let's be honest, we all do," Kendall fired back.

Pepper and Freddie's silence implied they couldn't deny it.

Claire finally spoke up. "But we cared about Max and his cheese shop. We deserve to get the Church Bleu handed down to *us*."

Freddie waved his hand as if shooing away a fly. "What Maxine wants doesn't matter anyway. Max already told us he was leaving the cheese's secrets to Kendall."

"No, he didn't," Kendall countered, looking embarrassed.

"Okay, he said he was leaving them to his 'favorite cheesemonger,' but we all know that's you, Kendall," Pepper said.

"We shouldn't be talking about this now. We're here to honor Max," Kendall hastily replied.

Pepper wasn't letting it go that easily. "Of course we are, but let's be practical. The will reading is tomorrow. Once you find out the secret location where the Church Bleu is made and aged, we can bid on the shop."

Mrs. Schultz, always the peacemaker, broke in. "It's wonderful that you're all continuing his legacy this way."

"It's what we'd like to do. If he really left his shop to Maxine, we don't know if she'll be willing to sell it to us for a reasonable price," Kendall said, once again demonstrating her skepticism about it.

"She has absolutely no interest in cheese. She's said so

herself," Freddie said. He stood on tip toe to look over the heads of the crowd. He seemed anxious for the cheese to get here—he was over this conversation.

If Mrs. Schultz thought she was going to stop their arguing with one nice sentiment, she was mistaken. Claire was still invested in it. "Maxine doesn't have to be interested in cheese, just money. The Church Cheese Shop name is worth a lot."

"Not as much without the Bleu. Max could've changed his mind and left its secret to his daughter," Kendall said. Her furrowed brows demonstrated her concern at this possible outcome.

Pepper shook her head in doubt. "No way. He respected the cheese too much to give that kind of information to just anybody. Even though she's family, she knows nothing about cheese."

I found myself agreeing with Pepper. "I know I haven't been around in over a year, but I think Pepper's right. I know he never wanted the Church Bleu to get into the wrong hands."

"The wrong hands? It sounds like you're talking about nuclear codes or something," Archie said.

"He was protective of it. I think most cheesemakers dream of creating a perfect cheese that will define who they are. After a lifetime of trying, he finally managed to do that. He was never in it for the money, and I don't think he'd leave it to someone who would view it as only that," I explained.

"That's why I'm sure he's left it to us—well, to Kendall, I mean," Claire said.

"Will you continue to keep how and where it's made a secret?" Mrs. Schultz asked the foursome.

"Of course we will," Freddie said. The others nodded in agreement.

"The mystique is what makes the cheese and Max's shop worth so much more," Pepper said.

"We'll do it for *Max*," Claire corrected.

The noise level suddenly heightened just before a hush fell over the crowd. Heads swiveled toward the back of the room.

Pepper tapped Freddie's shoulder. "There's Hugo and Maxine. It's here. Our cheese is here." She pulled him toward the velvet rope at the front of the ballroom where the cheese would be showcased.

Hugo Potts, a short man in his early fifties, recognizable by his spiky platinum blond hair and Hawaiian shirts, was the president of the board of directors of the Northwest Cheese Society, the NWCS. Hugo and I knew each other from the cheese community and the many invitationals I'd attended.

All eyes were on Hugo, and he knew it. He took slow, deliberate steps toward the front of the room, holding the plate of the last Church Bleu at chin level in front of him as if he were delivering the crown jewels to the king. The sinewy, fit woman behind him must've been Max's daughter, Maxine. She was a bit plain with cropped hair, and looked, not surprisingly, solemn. One of the invitational volunteers, wearing an NWCS polo shirt, unclipped the velvet rope for the two to go through to the riser where the lone table awaited the cheese.

"It almost feels like Max is in the room," Claire said, her eyes becoming glassy. "I'm going over."

Kendall nodded in acknowledgment, and Claire followed Pepper and Freddie's path to the table.

"I gotta see this up close," Archie said. He and Mrs. Schultz hurried over to the cheese at the same time the crowd surged toward it like a breaking wave.

Kendall and I stayed put. She looked contemplative.

She didn't seem to be able to push aside Max's death to partake in any excitement about the Church Bleu as the others had.

"I think Max would be happy that you want to continue Church Cheese Shop," I said, hoping to make her feel better.

Kendall glanced at the front of the room where Pepper, Freddie, and Claire were now behind the velvet rope with Hugo and Maxine. "I think Pepper and Claire are a little more optimistic about the four of us being co-owners than I am."

"If Max means to leave the Church Bleu to you, then you have the deciding vote. That can't be easy."

Her head bobbed slightly in agreement. "I hate to be the one to crush their dreams of taking over Max's shop. We've agreed that I'll get the biggest share of the profits."

"What about Freddie? I don't know him at all. How does he feel?"

"Freddie and Pepper are as thick as thieves. He goes along with whatever she says, which is something else that makes me a little wary about the whole thing."

I chuckled, understanding implicitly. Pepper, alone, was enough to handle.

"I'm not as confident as the others that he's leaving his Church Bleu to me, anyway. He said he'd leave it to his favorite cheesemonger, but I always figured that was you."

I was surprised she thought so. In fact, I was surprised he declared any of us his favorite. He'd never done that when I was there. "I wasn't listed in his will, so it's definitely not me."

Kendall sighed. "He'd been in business long before either of us worked there. Who knows who his favorite really was?"

"I have to say, I'm relieved not to be in contention. I couldn't handle that responsibility. He gave me exactly what he knew I'd want before I left—his knowledge about running a cheese shop," I said. Then with a chuckle, "And his copy of *Rebecca*." I smiled at the memory.

"Rebecca?" Kendall asked, confused.

"The Daphne du Maurier book? I've seen the Alfred Hitchcock movie countless times. Max knew about my obsession with it and gave me his copy of the book when I left, which was really sweet of him. I was telling Mrs. Schultz about it just a week before he died."

"Did you have some kind of premonition?" Kendall's eyes widened at the thought.

"No, it was just a coincidence. I was going through my boxes of books to donate to our used bookstore's charity sidewalk sale and came across it."

"That's quite a coincidence. It could've been a sixth sense." She held fast to the thought.

"Huh. Maybe." I considered how occasionally the universe did things like that to you, and goose bumps skittered down my back.

I shook it off and focused on the cheese. Organizers had gotten the crowd into somewhat of a line, albeit several people wide, to stream past the cheese like a processional. The invitational was always popular, but even more people had come for this special occasion honoring Max, which was possibly the last time Church Bleu would be featured here.

As my gaze wandered over the crowd, I saw a man staring at Kendall. He was one of the few not focused on the cheese. I'd caught a flash of him earlier, taking notice because of his dashing good looks—tall with a cleft chin, dark hair, and a muscular body underneath the preppy clothes. I pretended I didn't notice him, but each time I looked back, he still had his piercing blue eyes on her.

"That man over there has been staring at you, Kendall. Do you know him?" I nodded over her shoulder in his direction.

She turned to look. He immediately walked away, blending into the crowd.

"Which one?" she asked.

"Drats, he just left."

"What did he look like?"

"Tall, dark hair, broad shoulders. You're going to laugh at me, but he reminded me of the actor, Henry Cavill."

"Superman?"

"I was thinking of his Sherlock Holmes role in *Enola Holmes*, but yeah, the actor who played Superman."

"That doesn't sound so bad. I don't know the guy, unfortunately."

"A secret admirer?"

We giggled like schoolgirls about the possibility.

"Let's go up front. Hugo should be speaking soon. Pepper, Freddie, and I are supposed to stand up there with Maxine. You should too," Kendall said.

"That's okay. I'll stay on this side." I loved Max, but I wasn't a part of Church Cheese Shop anymore. I preferred to be among the spectators.

We were jostling our way toward the front when raised voices caught our attention. There was a commotion near the cheese. We made it to where Mrs. Schultz and Archie were standing in the front row.

"What's going on?" I asked them.

Mrs. Schultz was happy to relay the spectacle. "Hugo and Maxine are arguing about which one of them is keeping the cheese until the closing ceremonies on Monday. Maxine took the cheese and said she was leaving."

It looked like Pepper had gotten in on it and was giving Hugo and Maxine a stern talking to, as Hugo's face got redder and redder in anger. I thought his spiky bleached hair was going to turn red too, like a flame sparking from his head. The chatter and shocked reactions from the crowd kept us from hearing more than a word here and there. Now Maxine was pointing her finger at Pepper's chest and giving her an earful through clenched teeth. They looked equal in age, but Pepper was a lot taller than Maxine, although Maxine was physically more fit. I'd never seen anyone stand up to Pepper like that. I didn't think Kendall had either.

"Uh-oh." Kendall left us and breached the velvet rope to break things up.

Before Kendall could reach them, Hugo grabbed the plate of cheese out of Maxine's hand and ran with it. Unfortunately for him, there was nowhere to go. He was roped in with a sea of people blocking his path to the exit at the back of the ballroom. With panic on his face, he stuck his knee on the table and pulled himself onto it. He managed to stand upright on the table while holding the plate of Church Bleu precariously above his head. The others ran over to him. Maxine extended her arms toward the plate of cheese, but it was out of reach.

Archie, Mrs. Schultz, and I looked at the spectacle in disbelief.

"What is he doing?" Mrs. Schultz said. She had both hands to the sides of her face like the kid in *Home Alone*.

"Maybe it's a stunt, like *Mission Impossible*, and he'll leave through the ceiling," Archie said, looking up.

I stayed silent in disbelief.

"It's mine!" Hugo declared, unsteady atop the wobbly table.

"Give me that, you greedy jerk!" Maxine yelled. She

grabbed the hem of Hugo's untucked Hawaiian shirt to pull him down.

Pepper stood underneath him and grabbed him at the calf, pulling his leg out from under him. His other knee buckled, and he lost his balance, sending him backward. His flailing hands dropped the plate. Maxine grabbed for it, barely catching hold of it, bobbling it as the cheese slid off. Freddie dove under her and caught the Church Bleu before it hit the floor, like a touchdown catch in the end zone. Nobody caught Hugo.

CHAPTER 3

Several volunteers in NWCS polo shirts, who'd been frozen in place during the melee, now ran to help Hugo off the floor. He'd managed to fall onto the table, which collapsed under his weight, sending him rolling off the riser. He pushed the volunteers away and stood on his own.

"Where is it?" Hugo said, looking around.

Freddie held up what was left of the Church Bleu, some of it having come off the wheel in the fracas. Hugo's face crumbled, much like the cheese. He turned his attention to Maxine.

"Look what you've done!" he cried.

"All you care about is this stupid cheese. You're an awful man, Hugo Potts," Maxine barked back.

"That's not true. I cared about Max. And it was because of this invitational that Max Dumas's blue cheese is even on the map. Max knew that. That's why he left *me* his secret to Church Bleu."

"He did?" Claire cried.

"You're lying. He wouldn't have," Pepper said, looking like she was ready to clip him at the knees again.

"Why else would I have gotten a notice to attend the reading of his will?" Hugo said with his nose pushed in the air.

"So you don't already know the secret?" Kendall clarified. She stared at him, awaiting his answer.

"I told you he was lying," Pepper said.

"It's just a matter of time," Hugo declared.

"Don't be so sure. The secret may very well have died with him," Maxine said. "And maybe that's for the best."

Hugo's eyes widened in horror. "How can you say that? Do you know what's at stake here?"

Maxine huffed. "This memorial is a farce. I'm taking the cheese and leaving, and this time you won't stop me." She held out the plate to Freddie, who reluctantly stuck the broken wheel onto it.

Kendall cut in. "Maxine, your father's life's passion was cheese and we're all here to honor that, regardless of how Hugo behaves."

Hugo's face scrunched in a sour expression at Kendall's words.

Maxine stopped focusing on Hugo and looked out at the crowd.

"Please, let us say a few words about your father," Kendall pleaded.

The muscle in Maxine's clenched jaw bulged as she contemplated this, saying nothing. Finally, she relented. "I'll allow it to continue for my father's sake, but then I'm leaving . . . *with* the cheese."

Archie leaned toward me and whispered, "What does it matter who leaves with the cheese?"

I whispered back, "That's the last wheel of the Church Bleu, for now anyway. Maybe for good if Max didn't leave the secret location where he made and aged it in his will."

Our attention went to Freddie. "What about Monday's closing ceremonies?" he asked Maxine, referring to the cheese.

"I'll bring it back then. It stays with me for now," she replied.

Hugo didn't have a choice but to give in. He finally worked his way over to the podium, giving the side-eye to Maxine who remained holding the cheese. Kendall moved the others—Claire, Pepper, and Freddie—off to the side with her to await their turn to say a few words about Max.

Now recovered from the spectacle, the crowd settled into the room to hear about Max Dumas and his Church Bleu from those who knew him best. Hugo straightened his Hawaiian shirt and gently patted his short, spiky hair, before taking to the podium first. I looked out into the standing-room-only audience. My gaze landed on Kendall's handsome secret admirer, who still seemed to be fixating on her. I looked across to Kendall to see she was staring back.

CHAPTER 4

The following morning was a busy one at Curds & Whey. A lull in customers hit just before the afternoon farmer's market began, which was a good time to prep the cheeses we were bringing to the park. This week's farmer's market was also a charitable one. Each business was soliciting donations for a California farmland conservation charity.

Because Max was so much on my mind, I chose a blue cheese to bring to the park that wasn't nearly as pricey as Church Bleu, but was delicious, nonetheless. I decided on the tangy, spicy, and nutty Huntsman from England. Its contrasting layers of golden, firm Double Gloucester cheese with white, crumbly Blue Stilton makes it look like a decadent layer cake of cheeses.

I wanted to give Archie and Mrs. Schultz the lead on the remainder of the cheese choices for the market while I started a plate for my picnic with Kendall, Claire, Pepper, and Freddie. The Church Cheese group and I had planned to meet at the park for lunch after the will reading that was taking place this morning with Max's attorney at the Inn at Yarrow Glen.

Archie was restocking some of our cheese accompaniments, but I'd noticed there was a lot less pep to his step this morning. It had been that way for the last couple of months shortly after he moved in with his girlfriend. I called them to the counter and noticed Archie yawn as he sauntered over.

"Did last night's craziness at the invitational wear you out?" I asked.

"No. It was awesome," he replied.

"You just seem tired lately. That's not like you."

"Nah, I'm fine." A stifled yawn didn't do much to convince me.

Mrs. Schultz and I glanced at each other and she said, "I've noticed it too, Archie. We're just concerned about you. Are you taking care of yourself at Hope's?"

"I know you both think moving in with her was a bad idea." He cast his gaze to the floor to avoid any disapproving looks.

"You're twenty years old. You can make your own decisions. It just seemed a little hasty," Mrs. Schultz said gently.

I concurred with Mrs. Schultz. "It was only three months ago that you two had your first date."

"It's not like we're living together because we want to get married or anything. I couldn't keep living at home with my mom, and all the apartments are too expensive. Baz offered to let me room with him, but he uses his second bedroom to do his wood carvings. When Hope said she had a spare room I could rent out, it seemed like a good solution. It's right down the street from here. What could be easier?"

Hope had inherited Rise and Shine Bakery on her twenty-first birthday from her mother who'd died when Hope was a young girl. When Hope came of age last year, she took over the successful bread bakery from her aunt and ran it with the help of a manager while she took cake decorating classes. The bakery was attached to the cottage she—and now Archie—lived in.

"Why don't you get into your costume for the farmer's market? You can go over early. Maybe the fresh air will wake you up," I suggested.

"Good idea." Archie ambled to the back of the shop and through the swinging door into the stockroom, where my office was, to change clothes.

I asked Mrs. Schultz to choose the market cheeses on her own.

"To be young and in love." She sighed and perused the choices.

"I'd take being old and in love," I kidded.

"You're thirty-four. You're hardly old. Wait until you reach my age." Mrs. Schultz was "smack dab" in her sixties, as she liked to say. Vivacious, smart, and talented, she would be a catch for any lucky guy.

"I hope what happened with Frank didn't sour you on dating again," I said. Frank, one of Mrs. Schultz's former teaching colleagues, had started courting her around Valentine's Day, but it had ended disastrously.

"I used to tell my drama students that as long as you take something away from a bad experience, it was worthwhile. Of course, I was talking about performing on stage, not dating, but I suppose it still applies." She shrugged. "I can thank Frank for showing me that the part of me I thought had died along with Mr. Schultz is still inside me." Mrs. Schultz was referring to her husband who'd died unexpectedly about five years ago, just after Mrs. Schultz retired. "Having said that, I'm just grateful to have had one love of my life and I feel lucky for it. I hope you have a great love, too, someday, Willa."

"Oh, I do, Mrs. Schultz. Cheese!"

She laughed with me, then changed the subject. "Why

aren't you at the reading of Max's will? I hope it's not because you didn't want to leave the shop."

"You know I trust you and Archie to be here without me. I wasn't on the list of beneficiaries, but I didn't expect to be."

"Really? It sounded like Pepper thought you were one of his favorites when you worked there," Mrs. Schultz said, cutting and weighing a few wedges of Milton Creamery's 4-Alarm Cheddar to sell at the park. A creamy cheddar packed with a blend of chipotle, chili, jalapeno, and ghost pepper, the fiery cheese was a great conversation starter.

I dismissed Pepper's assessment. "They all say Kendall was his favorite, but I always thought Max loved us all the same. He paid attention to who we were. To Pepper, it may have seemed like he was giving me more attention, but it was only because I was always hounding him for information about how he ran the shop. When Kendall, Claire, and Pepper went out together after work, I stayed behind to ask Max questions about sales and storage and inventory."

"Do you think they're ready to run the shop together?"

"I don't think it's something Kendall wants to take on by herself, especially a shop that's as well-known as Max's."

"I'd think inheriting an already successful shop would be easier."

"In some ways, but it was successful because of how Max ran it. People always want to put their stamp on things—that makes four competing stamps! And because the Church Bleu has made it such a destination, customers already have high expectations. It takes a lot to keep a successful shop running the way it's always run. On the other hand, whenever Max went on his Church Bleu excursions, he'd leave the shop in our hands, so Kendall, Pepper, and I got a feel for it. Claire's been working there for a long time and Freddie seems to fit right in. I think they'll do fine if they get along, but that's a big *if*."

The very people we were talking about appeared through the picture window on the brick-lined sidewalk dotted with crepe myrtle trees, newly bloomed a brilliant pink in the May sunshine.

"They're here," I said.

I found myself suddenly nervous to have them see my shop. Guernsey, our cow scarecrow mascot, was stationed outside, helping to hold open the teal door.

I greeted them as they walked in, but they appeared downtrodden. I'd figured the morning would be an emotionally taxing one.

Everyone forced a smile and said hello.

"Was it a tough morning at the will reading?" I asked, already knowing the answer. Their faces didn't hide their distress.

"To say the least," Pepper replied.

"Max didn't leave Kendall the secret to the Church Bleu," Claire said glumly. She ran her hand over the jams and relishes on one of the tables without interest.

"He didn't?" I said, surprised.

"He gave us each a nice bit of cash, and he left the shop to Maxine like he said he would," Kendall told me.

"But no mention of the cheese?" I asked.

"The secret went to someone else," Freddie said, shaking his head as if he couldn't believe it.

Archie's entrance through the swinging stockroom door at the back of the shop interrupted us. He was outfitted, horns to hooves, in a black-and-white cow costume with only his face and hands showing. He must've been wearing some kind of pack on his stomach to fill out a belly where the udders were positioned. He walked across the shop to us, his uddered belly bouncing in step with his strides.

"I'm ready for the farmer's market," he announced with a smile. As his former high school's mascot, a good costume always energized Archie, even today. Now that he was closer, I noted the triangular cheese wedge, with Curds & Whey on it, stitched at his chest above the udders.

"Wow! This is new. I hope Guernsey doesn't get jealous," I kidded.

"Guernsey is a standout, regardless, but I made Archie a Holstein costume so as not to detract from her." Mrs. Schultz went along with the joke. I was lucky Mrs. Schultz was adept at making costumes from her days overseeing high school plays.

"Mrs. Schultz and I figured more kids might want to take a picture with a cow than a wedge of cheese. We might get more donations this way," Archie said, tugging at his horns. He didn't look like he was quite used to the costume yet.

"Good thinking. You look great." It made me a little weepy how much Archie and Mrs. Schultz cared about my shop. They always put just as much effort into representing it as I did.

I turned my attention back to my former colleagues who had seemed to put aside their own disappointment and were now browsing Curds & Whey. Pepper had her nose in the refrigerated display case. "You've got some great cheese choices here," she said, sounding impressed.

Freddie stroked the textured walls that gave the illusion of ornate wallpaper above the butterscotch-colored wainscoting that ran along the lower portion. Rich mahogany raised paneling made up the feature wall behind the counter. The crimson faux Aubusson rugs warmed the hardwood floors. "It's a nice-looking shop," he said.

"It's so cozy and . . . French," Claire remarked, taking a closer look at the finely detailed botanical tablecloths.

"Thank you. That means a lot. I'm sorry for the reason you're all here, but I'm glad you're getting a chance to see it," I said.

"Why did you decide to go with French-inspired? Was it Max's influence? That's why he gave his cheese the French spelling, as an homage to his French Dumas family heritage," Pepper said.

"Don't you remember, Pepper? She told us she spent a college semester in France. That's where she decided to become a cheesemonger," Kendall answered for me.

Kendall was always one to remember details, and she'd gotten this one right. In college, I'd been exhilarated by the idea of spending a semester in a city like Lyon, completely different from the farm where I'd grown up. But three weeks in, I found myself searching out the quieter areas that felt more like home. One excursion to a nearby village led me to a small cheese shop and to its owner, Genevieve, a stoic, even-tempered woman who reminded me of my mother. I began taking frequent jaunts out to her shop, learning more about cheese, and eventually I worked out a sort of apprenticeship with her, and the seed to my dream was sown.

Pepper squinted her green-shadowed eyes as if that would enable her to visualize our old conversation about it better. "Nope, I don't remember."

I chuckled and didn't bother to refresh her memory. Kendall rolled her eyes, then continued toward the back of the shop where the kitchenette was. With its teal cabinets and white marble counters, it was where we held special events and cheesemaking classes.

"We have almost an hour before lunch. Anything you suggest checking out around here?" Claire asked.

"Read More Bookstore is having a sidewalk sale with their used book donations. The profits are going to the same charity today's farmer's market is contributing to," Mrs. Schultz offered

"That reminds me, Archie, we have to grab those books I boxed up from my apartment. I keep forgetting," I said.

"I ran upstairs yesterday morning and brought them over when you were at the invitational. I hope you don't mind," he said.

"Mind? Thanks! I guess that's what happens when I complain three mornings in a row that I've forgotten them. You want to head over to the park?" I handed him the donation can and Curds & Whey flyers. "You can hand out flyers and pose for photos for donations until we get there."

"Will moo," he said, laughing. "Get it? Will do, will moo?"

Mrs. Schultz and I laughed along with him.

"You're sure to be a hit," she said.

He lumbered out of the shop and up the sidewalk in his bulky cow costume.

"Forget the bookstore. Where's the best place to get some wine for our picnic? After the morning we had, we're going to need some," Pepper said.

"You can get some nice wine at the Golden Glen Meadery across the street," I answered. "I suggest the Riesling."

"There's a meadery here? Cool. That's what I want to check out," Freddie said.

"What's mead?" Claire asked.

"It's delicious," I told them. "It's kind of like a cousin to wine and beer. Beer uses malt as its base, wine uses grapes, and mead uses honey. It's brewed and fermented like beer, but its taste is reminiscent of wine."

"Count me out. I'd rather keep my EpiPen in my purse than have to put it to use," Kendall said.

"That's right, you're allergic to honey." I recalled how she had to stay away from it when we did pairings at the shop. "Do you still keep your EpiPen in a purple glitter case?"

"You bet." Kendall unclasped her purse and took it out to show me. "I might've had to use it this morning at the reading when Constance brought in honey tea for everyone. Lucky I always know to ask before drinking anything from anyone else."

"You can feel confident about the wine you end up getting from the meadery. My . . . uh, friend Roman owns it. It's from his family's winery." I tripped over the word *friend*.

It wasn't long ago that Roman and I had been more than friends. We'd dated for four months but broke it off after some hard truths were discovered just as we were becoming serious. However, we were friends before we'd started dating so we'd been trying to work our way back to something like that over the last few months. I got the feeling his meadery manager, Gia, preferred this awkward gray area Roman and I were currently navigating where we basically just avoided each other.

"Let's head over to the meadery now," Freddie suggested. "Maybe we can get a tasting."

"You guys can go. I'm going to look around Willa's shop some more," Kendall replied.

"See you later at the park?" Claire said to me and Kendall.

"We'll be there," I replied.

Kendall nodded her agreement and the three wandered

across the street toward the meadery. She continued browsing the shop, but I could tell she was preoccupied.

"How are you feeling, Kendall?" I asked now that the others were gone.

"It hasn't been the easiest weekend so far. I just wish I could reminisce with my friends about Max without them being so focused on the Church Bleu."

Mrs. Schultz stepped forward. "If you and Kendall want to have a little time to yourselves, I can manage the shop until we go to the farmer's market."

Kendall perked up. "Are you sure you wouldn't mind?"

"Not at all. I think most of the customers are probably already at the park, anyway. It's slowed down considerably."

"My apartment is right above the shop," I added, liking the idea. "If anything comes up, Mrs. Schultz knows she can call or text me and I can be back in no time." I walked behind the counter and, from the bowl underneath, grabbed my keyring that held my shop and apartment keys. I jingled the keys in my hand. "We'll be back so I can lock up before we leave for the park," I told Mrs. Schultz.

"I'll hold down the fort," she said.

Before Kendall and I could walk out the door, a group of four couples streamed in.

"We've been reading about the big cheese event over at the conference center and a blue cheese that's supposed to be the best. Do you have any here?" one of the women inquired.

"I don't have the cheese you're talking about—no one does at the moment—but I do have some I think you'll enjoy," I answered.

"What brand of blue cheese dip should I buy for my

hot wings? Phil loves his hot wings, but he's not crazy about the dip," another woman in the group said, patting the arm of the man beside her, presumably Phil.

I looked at Kendall apologetically and returned the keys to their bowl under the counter before pulling up my recipe file and printing out instructions to make my Cool and Creamy Dolce Dip.

I handed Phil the recipe. "Making this blue cheese dip is easier than going to the store to buy it. And much better." I showed him a Gorgonzola Dolce, its creaminess and comparatively milder flavor making it perfect for the dip. He nodded and handed his wife the recipe.

A few from the group fanned out among the shop, where Mrs. Schultz aided them. A question about the different names for blue cheese caused me to gather the others around the kitchenette's island as I brought over three wedges to demonstrate.

"This beautiful white cheese with veins of blue is Roquefort from France and it's made from sheep's milk. The Gorgonzola is made in Italy from cow's milk and most closely resembles Roquefort in robust taste and crumbly texture, although this Dolce I recommended for the dip is creamier and milder. Stilton is British and is also made from cow's milk, but it's creamier like the Dolce and has earthy hints of mushroom. Danish Blue is a smoother blue cheese, as well. Here, try the Dolce."

As I handed out samples of the Gorgonzola on crisp crackers, my eye caught someone making a beeline for me. It was Hugo.

"Have you seen the others?" he said, without preamble or an apology for interrupting.

"Hugo, I'm in the middle of—"

His attention left me and searched the shop, spotting

Kendall, who seemed to be trying to hide behind the front counter. "There you are." He reversed course to the front of the shop.

Kendall did not look happy to see him. I left the customers with their samples and headed over to help.

"Hugo, it's already been a long day," I heard Kendall say.

"I need to talk to you while the others aren't around. Come on. You and I can work together. You're the reasonable one. Maxine won't budge and you know how Pepper is," he pleaded. "If they know anything about who Max left the cheese to, they're not telling."

"I told you, Hugo, I don't know anything more than anyone else. I don't know why everyone thinks I know something," Kendall insisted.

"But you must."

"See you at the park, Willa," Kendall said, sounding exasperated. She headed for the door and away from Hugo.

Hugo wasn't letting it go. "Wait! Kendall!"

Hugo started to follow her out, but I had an idea. "Ladies and Gentlemen, this is Hugo Potts, the president of the board of directors of the Northwest Cheese Society. He can answer all your cheese questions."

They swarmed Hugo, who seemed gratified by the attention, but looked wistfully out the window as Kendall made her escape.

A moment later, the Henry Cavill look-alike passed by the window, going in the same direction Kendall went, looking like he was on a mission. Was he following her?

I extracted myself from the customers surrounding Hugo and stepped out the front door to see where he was going. A customer exited Carl's Hardware next door, blocking my view for a moment. Beyond the customer, farther down the sidewalk, I saw Lou sweeping around people coming in and out of his market, and a small crowd browsing the sidewalk sale tables in front of Read More Bookstore. There was no sign of the handsome stranger. He seemed to have vanished.

CHAPTER 5

Although my intention in keeping Hugo at the shop was for Kendall's sake, he turned out to be a hit with the customers, and they left with lots of cheese by the time Hugo eventually made his way out. I was helping a new customer, and Mrs. Schultz was cleaning up the kitchenette, when Kendall returned. She stepped inside with some hesitation, scanning the shop, I assumed for Hugo. I smiled at her in greeting from the rear of the shop and returned my attention to the woman who had been picking up some banana jam to pair with her Brabander Gouda, when she decided she also needed one of our lovely cheese boards—my favorite kind of customer. I couldn't help but brag to her that the cheese board she was considering was made by my best friend and neighbor, Baz, who carved as a hobby. She loved it even more knowing it was made by a local, and decided to buy it.

When the customer left, I met with Kendall where she'd been waiting by the sampling counter up front. She apologized for departing earlier in such a hurry.

"I understand completely," I told her.

"Thanks for detaining Hugo so he couldn't follow me. I don't know why everyone still thinks I know something about Max's Church Bleu."

"Without it, do you think you'll still try to buy the shop from Maxine?"

"I don't know. I'll have to talk about it with the others."

"We've been so busy, I haven't finished the cheese board for our picnic yet. It shouldn't take me too long."

"I'm going to go on ahead if that's all right?" she said.

"Of course. Let them know I'll be there shortly."

"I will. Thanks again, Willa." Kendall left the shop in better spirits than when she'd first arrived an hour ago. The shock of not getting the Church Bleu from Max must've worn off.

Mrs. Schultz helped me with my cheese selection.

"I wish I knew which wine or mead they're going to be drinking so I could pair it properly."

"You can always call Roman to see what they bought," Mrs. Schultz suggested.

"I *could* . . ." I hesitated. It was something I would have done in a heartbeat a few months ago. But now, it gave me second thoughts. "Hopefully, they'll get the Riesling I suggested. Kendall won't drink the mead, so I'll do a light wine pairing and keep my fingers crossed."

Mrs. Schultz didn't comment on my refusal to call Roman, but the expression on her face did.

"I don't want him to think I'm making an excuse to talk to him," I explained.

"Maybe you *should* make an excuse. You've barely spoken in the last three months. I'm sorry if I'm overstepping. I just hate seeing you two at odds. You were such close friends."

"You could never overstep, Mrs. Schultz. You're right, I want to be friends again. I needed some time, but now I'm not sure how to approach him."

"Asking about the wine could be a start."

I sighed. "All right, fine. I'll call him about the wine."

I plucked the phone out of my pocket and tapped his name. One ring . . . two rings . . . three rings . . . *oh no* . . . voicemail. I tapped the red button to end the call. "He didn't answer. Do you think he didn't want to answer? Maybe I should've left a message. What if he thinks I called to like, *talk*? Oh, huckleberry!" Baz's childhood curse word was a good replacement for what I really wanted to say.

"Maybe you're overthinking it? Our farmer's market Saturdays are even more chaotic than regular Saturdays. He's likely too busy to even look at his phone. Should we do some stress exercises?" Mrs. Schultz was known to emote vigorously in her efforts to rid me of my stress. This time her voice resounded in deep-throated foghorn bursts: "Ooohaaaaa. Ooohaaaa."

"That's okay, Mrs. Schultz," I rapidly assured her.

Thankfully, she stopped.

"I'm sure you're right again," I said. "He's probably hauling his mead to the park, which we should also be doing with our cheese, since we're running late. I'm going to throw together this cheese plate for my picnic and then we can go."

I started with Pecorino Fresco, a young, pliable cheese, more sweet than sharp. Next, I cut an aged Asiago, salty and pungent, then finished with an intense semihard goat's milk cheese, Semistagionato. I added a jar of pear preserves and chipotle jelly, double-checking to make sure neither were made with honey. I packed crispy crackers and sliced crunchy Italian bread Archie had brought from Rise and Shine Bakery this morning.

Once Mrs. Schultz finished with the last customer, we closed the shop with a note on the door: Find us at the farmer's market.

I brought out the wagon I'd purchased from the thrift shop and loaded the coolers of cheeses and accompaniments we'd sample and sell. We trekked one block up Pleasant Avenue and took a left onto Main Street where the town hall building was located. Its working clock tower rose higher than any other building downtown, even the neighboring church steeple. Most of the government offices remained in the old town hall building, except for the police department, located across the street at the newer public safety complex, which also housed the fire department. The town hall and the church were separated by a parking lot, their two properties taking up the entire block. Behind them was the town park.

The park was casual, no fancy arched entrance or fencing, just a beautiful sprawling lawn edged in wildflowers, including yellow and white yarrow, currently in full bloom.

As we crossed the parking lot, we were greeted by a friendly German shepherd/golden retriever mix we knew.

"George!" I greeted him in return and scrunched his floppy ears.

He belonged to Everett Trumbull, who owned The Kick Stand bicycle shop, which shared an alley with Curds & Whey. George had barely gotten the chance to sniff all the goodies in our wagon when a sharp whistle caused him to retreat. He bounded to the edge of the park, where Everett was stationed with almost a dozen bikes from his shop. George rubbed his snout against Everett's leg and Everett gave him "good boy" pats.

We sidestepped one of his potential customers pedaling in circles in the lot.

"Hey, neighbors!" Everett said hello with his usual greeting. His shorts and The Kick Stand logo shirt showed off his tanned, fit physique. Everett was around my age, early thirties, and had just opened his shop two months prior.

"How's it going?" I asked, pausing to give George proper pats.

"Really well. We've had so many rentals today, I had to get more bikes from the shop," he said. "I see a lot of out-of-towners today. I think we're getting some extra folks from that big event at the conference center. My mother's going to be happy to hear that." Everett's mother was the mayor of Yarrow Glen and was instrumental in the construction of the town's first conference center. Some didn't like the idea of hordes of strangers pouring into town for large events, while others, like myself, appreciated the extra business it would bring. "How come you're not there? Isn't it some big cheese convention?"

"I was there for a little while yesterday, and Archie and Mrs. Schultz went later in the evening to experience some of it. I knew I'd be needed at the shop this weekend. You can tell your mother business has been good."

Everett noticed Mrs. Schultz eyeing the wrapped desserts on a table behind him. "I recommend the lemon muffins. Ginger made them for the charity. She's doing double duty at the bookstore's table." Ginger worked at Read More Bookstore's café as their barista. She enjoyed vegan baking and concocting healthy smoothies. "She figured bike riders might get hungry, so she made these vegan desserts."

"What a nice idea. You're certainly making the citizens of Yarrow Glen healthier." Mrs. Schultz stuck some bills in the donation tin and took a muffin.

We continued into the park with our wagon of cheese. The walk to the park had sounded like a good idea, but there was no respite from the brilliant afternoon sun, which made temperatures in the seventies feel a lot warmer. We'd had the choice of renting just a table or one with a canopy, and I was now glad we'd splurged on the canopy for our two hours here. Mrs. Schultz carried one of the totes to lighten the wagon's load as I maneuvered it on the grass.

Table after table represented almost all the downtown businesses, as well as local gardeners and some crafters and hobbyists who regularly sold their homemade wares. It wasn't hard to spot Archie—he was the only cow in the park. Three moms and their small children waited while Archie took a picture with another child. He happened, not coincidentally I was certain, to be standing by Hope's table of cupcakes. This week, Hope's pixie-style blonde hair had streaks of neon pink in it, which I was sure matched her nails, as her varying color choice always did. Her cupcake towers looked spectacular. We waved to her and Archie as we walked by.

We passed the produce stand for Lou's Market. I didn't hear as much as I *sensed* Lou grumbling at customers who were already trying to pick through his crates of fresh avocados while his employee, Trace, finished setting up the stand. Lou, in his fifties, was nearly always grumbling about something. However, Trace—a high school senior, who for some reason took to Lou—was perpetually unaffected, and counterbalanced Lou's personality at the market.

As soon as Lou saw us passing, he changed his demeanor and scurried out from under their canopy.

"Do you need help with that, Mrs. Schultz?" He offered to take the tote from her and ignored me struggling with the wagon.

"Thank you, Lou. No, I'm fine. Our table's just down the way. Your plums look amazing," she said.

Lou plucked one from the bin and placed it in the tote she carried. "For later. On the house," he said.

"I'll enjoy it. Thanks, Lou."

It was apparent Mrs. Schultz had no clue that Lou had developed a crush on her. I'd noticed it during the time we all spent on the decorating committee for a community dance when Mrs. Schultz's attentions were on Frank. I'd yet to bring it up to her. She seemed content putting romance on the back burner for now.

We continued to our table. I noticed Roman and Gia at a table for his Golden Glen Meadery. I'd love to steal his phone and delete my call, but instead I pretended I didn't see him and made a beeline for our canopy.

It didn't take us long to set up. We kept the cheese in the coolers, except for the container I was bringing to my picnic lunch, and displayed signs listing what we had on hand. As we set out the samples, Archie made his way over to us with the donation tin. He was trailed by a flock of preschoolers enamored with him as a cow. I handed out cheddar cubes for the kids with their parents' permission, which brought the parents to our table. It was another twenty minutes before the crowd cleared and I realized I was late for my picnic with the Church Cheese Shop crew.

"We're good here. Go!" Mrs. Schultz shooed me away.

I started to collect my containers to assemble the cheese plate when I spotted Maxine.

"There's Maxine. I didn't get a chance to introduce myself to her at the invitational. I'd like to offer my condolences," I explained to Mrs. Schultz.

I left our canopy and approached Maxine, who was browsing the thrift store table.

"Maxine?"

She turned. Her eyebrows raised in question, creasing

the deep lines of her forehead further. She looked a little intense, although maybe it was just her abundance of taut muscles. Her tank top revealed a patch of sunburn on each shoulder but her sculpted legs beneath nylon shorts were tan.

"Hi. I'm Willa Bauer. I didn't get a chance to speak with you at the invitational to offer my condolences. I'm very sorry about your father's passing."

She eased. "Thank you. That's nice of you. I'm sorry you had to witness the spectacle last night with Hugo."

"I understand. Emotions were running high," I replied tactfully. "I used to work with your father."

Maxine stiffened. "I have no intention of keeping Max's cheese shop if you're wondering about your job."

I put my open hands in front of me in defense. "Oh, I left Church Cheese over a year ago. I own Curds and Whey here in town."

Maxine lowered her head, and when she looked up at me her demeanor had changed once again. "My mistake. I've been hounded by some of the others since my father's will was read this morning, so I assumed . . . sorry. His shop is the last thing I'm thinking about right now." She turned away and dabbed at her eyes.

"I didn't mean to upset you," I said.

"It's not you." She struggled to smile. "My father and I were estranged for practically my entire adult life. I only reconnected with him recently after my uncle became ill. I wish I'd seen him sooner. You always think you have more time." She looked heavenward.

"I'm so sorry," I said. "I hope this weekend gives you some comfort in getting to see what his Church Bleu meant to the cheese community."

Her expression soured. "It seems to have meant greed for some of them, like Hugo Potts. You must know Hugo."

"I've been acquainted with him for many years."

"He's been after me as if I know anything about my father's secret cheese. It's the reason my father and I had barely spoken to each other for the last twenty years. Cheese—not his family—was his life. That never changed, not even for me. I just wish I had accepted that better. Instead, I bounced all over so I wouldn't have to call anywhere home."

"I can relate to that." I spent the eight years after my brother's death working in cheese shops across the country, purposely keeping people at a distance, until I finally took a chance on Yarrow Glen.

"I don't know why I'm telling you all of this. The fact remains, I know nothing about cheese, not even my father's, and I have no desire to," she said firmly.

"He didn't share anything about it with you in his final months, knowing he was dying?"

"So you *are* interested in it." She crossed her toned arms. Any rapport I'd made with her vanished instantly.

"No, I'm really not. I'm curious is all, since I heard he left you his shop."

She studied me for a moment before deciding to answer. "Maybe he still held out hope that I would be interested in it, although he had to have known I would sell it. But that's not what he wanted for his Church Bleu. He was more secretive about it than ever. It didn't matter that I was his daughter. When it came to his precious cheese, I was just a layperson. So please pass along to Hugo that I don't have answers to any clue to the Church Bleu's secrets, because he's not accepting it from me."

"When I see him again, I'll do my best."

Her demeanor softened and she dropped her arms. "Thank you. What was your name again?"

"Willa Bauer."

"Willa. You're the nicest person I've met this weekend."

"Hopefully you'll meet some others too."

"I just have to stick it out until the invitational's closing ceremonies on Monday. I'd cut out now, but I'm afraid Hugo will follow me and haunt me forever." She let out a half-hearted chuckled. "Nice to meet you."

"Same here," I said.

As I watched her walk off, I thought she certainly wasn't the Maxine described by Freddie and Pepper. Speaking of, I was late to meet up with them. I headed over to the picnic area and thought I spotted Kendall by the big oak tree. I started over to see if it was her, but as I made my way around, I saw she was with the dashing stranger. I didn't want to interrupt—maybe he was a secret admirer, after all.

Instead, I continued to the picnic area, where I saw Claire seated by herself on the lawn with a cup in hand, away from the crowds gathered at the picnic tables. A colorful blanket was spread out before her with a cooler of wine. A small pile of personal items held down one of the corners—shoes, a backpack, and one of Lou's Market bags filled with snacks, presumably.

"Hi, Claire. Where is everybody?" I asked.

"Everyone scattered after we put down our stuff to check out the farmer's market. You want a glass of wine?" She got another cup from a stack next to the cooler where two wine bottles were burrowed in melting ice up to their necks. I noticed the same plastic cups dotting the picnic blanket. "Sorry, we already broke into it before you got here."

"That's okay. I'm working today anyway. I'm fine."

She poured more into her own cup and returned the bottle to the ice. She checked her phone for the time. "We were supposed to meet back here by now. Of course, I'm the only one who pays attention to what we're supposed to do. Let's go find them. I'm on my third classy cup of wine without lunch."

Claire and I left the picnic blanket to round up the others. As luck would have it, Freddie and Pepper were admiring the carved creations at my best friend Baz's table. Baz was about five years younger than me, not quite thirty, and was the handyman and carpenter in town. We'd bonded over discovering our first dead body together and had developed a close sibling-like friendship since then. We were also neighbors—I lived in the apartment above my cheese shop, and he lived above Carl's Hardware next door.

"I see you found the best table here," I said to Pepper and Freddie. Baz's table was filled with his hand-carved wine racks, bird houses, keepsake boxes, and cheese boards, one of which Pepper was in the process of buying. I made a proper introduction, and hellos went around the group.

"You know *everybody*, huh Willa?" Again, she spoke in that *Pepper* way of hers, where I wasn't sure if a nice-enough comment was meant to be nice.

"Not everyone, but it's a small town," I replied.

"You kept to yourself when *we* knew you. Maybe it was just us," she said more straightforwardly this time.

"Maybe the people here are friendlier than you, Pepper," Claire said. That third cup of wine was giving her some liquid courage.

"Everyone *is* oddly friendly," Freddie said, squinting at the clusters of people congregating.

Pepper muttered in his ear, "It's bizarre, isn't it?" They shared a quiet laugh.

"I'm starving. I'm going back and hitting the snacks whether anyone comes with me or not," Claire said.

"We're hungry too. Is Kendall at the picnic blanket?" Pepper asked.

"Not when I was there," Claire answered. "I hope Hugo isn't stalking her again." She turned to me, "After we saw him here, she told us what happened with him at your shop earlier."

"So nobody's watching our stuff? My backpack's over there," Freddie said. He started to walk away.

"I saw Kendall just a minute ago. I'll get her and meet you guys there," I offered.

Pepper took her newly purchased cheese board and thanked Baz. "Tell her we're starting without her." She caught up with Freddie.

"See you at the picnic blanket, Willa," Claire said, following her colleagues.

"They seem like an interesting bunch," Baz said diplomatically.

"You can say that again," I replied.

"They seem like—"

I put my hand up to stop him. "Very funny. Catch you later."

I left Baz's table and waved to my *friendly* fellow shop owners as I passed their booths. I didn't know why Pepper had to be so snarky all the time. I walked over to the large oak where I'd last seen Kendall, but she was on her way to the picnic blanket on her own. I trotted to catch up with her.

"So what's his name?" I asked her as we closed in on the group.

"Who?"

"Superman. Sherlock Holmes. You know, the handsome stranger."

"I don't know what you mean." She walked ahead of me and sat down on the blanket, purposely ignoring me. She reached for her cup and downed whatever was in it. "Who's in charge of the wine?"

I sat down too and dropped the subject. Maybe she didn't want to talk about him in front of the others.

Freddie refilled cups and offered one to me. I declined.

"Come on, Willa, we have to do a toast. We're all drinking. You can have a *sip*," Pepper said.

"For a toast, I will," I conceded, accepting the cup from Freddie.

"Here's to Max," Kendall said, plastic cup raised. "May he rest in peace in a heaven filled with cheese."

"Peace would bore him. May he rest in riddles," Claire corrected.

"So true. He was still playing his games to the very end." Pepper wore a slight grin, but her tone sounded a tad bitter.

As we took our first sip, Freddie went in for a second toast. "And may his jester spirit lead us to his Church Bleu."

Pepper took her cup away from her lips to call out "Hear, hear" before drinking again.

"After the morning we've had, I need to have more than a sip. Bring on the food and drink," Freddie said. He tipped his head back and drained the rest of his wine.

"Bottoms up," Pepper agreed, and did the same.

"We can sleep it off at the inn," Claire said. She and Kendall clinked cups again and also finished their wine.

I didn't go in for the bottoms up, but my sip was sweet and delicious. I was glad I chose the right cheeses for it.

The cheese! "I can't believe I forgot to bring my cheese. It's at my table. I'll be right back."

I hurried across the lawn to the Curds & Whey canopy. I was glad for the excuse to check in with Archie and Mrs. Schultz, and to make sure everything was running smoothly. Of course, they had everything well in hand. I quickly gathered my containers, and put the contents on a plate, which I covered in wrap.

As I trudged across the sprawling park lawns one more time, this time with my cheese plate, I heard yelling. It caught the attention of others in the park, and suddenly I was one of many heading to the outskirts of the picnic area. I picked up my pace. What could be wrong?

I saw a man running in that direction, and heard him yell "I'm a doctor!"

As I got closer, I realized it was our picnic blanket people were gathered at. The man who said he was a doctor was now hunched over someone lying prone on the ground. When I reached the blanket, I finally saw it was Kendall and she wasn't moving.

Claire was on her knees next to her, crying. "She needs her EpiPen. Who has an EpiPen?" she screamed into the gathering crowd.

"I still can't find it!" Freddie cried, shaking an empty purse in the air as Pepper hurriedly rummaged through its contents that had been dumped on the blanket. I dropped my cheese plate and fell to my knees on the blanket to help Freddie and Pepper sift through the items from Kendall's purse: a wallet, a ChapStick, a paperback book, a sunglasses case, aspirin . . .

"It's not here!" Pepper angrily shouted. Still, she stuck her hands into the pile for a last-ditch effort too. She was right—it wasn't there.

"I have one!" a woman's voice called.

The woman ran over to the doctor who was tending to Kendall and handed him an EpiPen. A crowd encircled us now.

The doctor took the EpiPen and jammed it into Kendall's thigh. Kendall still didn't move. I heard the sirens of an ambulance in the parking lot and saw EMTs racing over, but I knew it was too late. Kendall was dead.

CHAPTER 6

I felt sick as I stood there with my arms wrapped around Claire as she sobbed. We'd been shuffled off to the side when the EMTs came. I allowed myself a sliver of hope as they continued to work on Kendall and then rushed her away on a stretcher. If I hadn't been holding onto Claire, I might've allowed myself to believe it hadn't really happened—it was too overwhelming to comprehend. I sensed Freddie and Pepper near, although neither spoke a word. Eventually, Claire's sobs turned to sniffles.

I lifted my head to the activity surrounding us when Officer Shepherd, the local police officer everyone in town knew as Shep, was suddenly next to us. With a gentle arm, he escorted us to the shade of a nearby tree.

Claire pulled her face out of a handful of tissues. "Where's the hospital? I should be there for Kendall," she said to him.

Shep had a crooked nose beneath expressive eyes that crinkled in sympathy. I suspected what was coming when his thin face pinched. "I'm sorry. She never regained consciousness," he said gently.

An empty nausea throbbed at my stomach again.

"She's dead?" Claire cried.

This caught the attention of Pepper and Freddie, who'd been huddled near the tree.

"She's really dead?" Freddie echoed Claire.

"I'm afraid so," Shep replied.

Claire stuffed her face back into the wad of tissues.

Freddie grasped his own elbows in a hug.

"It's not a surprise, is it? She was already gone before they took her, as far as I could tell," Pepper said with her usual directness. However, her face belied her words—her steely eyes had the blank look of shock.

Shep's focus was elsewhere. The crowd continued to encroach. "Please stay right here until we can talk to you," he said before leaving us.

I watched the activity unfold around me, but still felt removed from it, as if watching it on a movie screen. Shep contained the crowd with the help of an imposing officer I'd been acquainted with during a previous investigation. His size coupled with his fixed, solemn expression brought to mind *The Addams Family*'s Lurch, which was how I referred to him in my mind since meeting him last time. It took a moment for my memory bank to extract his actual name: Officer Ferguson.

I finally came out of my mental fog when I noticed Baz, Mrs. Schultz, and Archie in his cow costume pointing in my direction, obviously trying to convince Officer Ferguson to let them through. Not surprisingly, he wouldn't budge. I gave them a slight wave and tried to gesture that I was okay. Shep's partner, Officer Melman, began unfurling that dreaded yellow crime scene tape and they weren't happy about having to stay behind it. Melman—a portly guy probably in his thirties, same as Shep—made a wide perimeter around the picnic blanket where I'd been sitting with my former colleagues.

I stared at the blanket, now in disarray with scraps of

the beginnings of our picnic—toppled over cups and my carefully curated cheese plate scattered near the contents of Kendall's purse. Why couldn't we find her EpiPen? She'd just shown it to us earlier. I saw her take it out of her purse and put it back. How could it have fallen out between then and now?

My gaze scanned the wine bottles, both still chilling in the cooler. Was one of them mead? I know Roman would've been careful not to sell them a wine with honey in it. I thought back to the little bit I had after we'd done our toast to Max. It was a sweeter wine than I was used to. In fact, it tasted a lot like mead I'd had in the past, but since I was told it was wine, my brain had agreed.

As Detective Heath came into view, the heaviness in my chest lifted just a little. I watched the handsome, dark-haired detective work. He unbuttoned the jacket to his well-fitted suit and crouched to get a closer look at the items on the picnic blanket. I knew his dark eyes were taking everything in. Shep was soon next to him, listening as Heath gave him direction before leaving his side. He looked my way and our eyes met. He immediately walked over.

Heath's sympathetic gaze lingered on me for a few moments before he gave his condolences to us about the loss of our friend. From his suit jacket pocket, he took out his mini notepad and a pen. He asked Claire, Pepper, and Freddie for their names and wrote them down before proceeding with some general questions.

Freddie seemed nervous. "I don't know what happened. We were drinking a toast to Max and then Kendall's face got weird. I thought she was laughing at first, but she was grabbing at her neck. She was all red. We looked for her EpiPen. Didn't we, Pepper? We looked."

Pepper nodded, quickly brushing away a tear.

I interjected, "I came over after she was already unconscious, but I looked too. It wasn't there."

"So you weren't present when it first happened," Heath confirmed.

"No. I was there when we toasted to Max and then I left to get my cheese plate. I was walking over when I heard Claire yelling at the crowd for an EpiPen. I don't know why it wouldn't have been in her purse. She'd just shown it to us a couple of hours ago."

"Why did she do that?" Heath asked in his steady tone.

I thought back. "I was telling them about the meadery, and she reminded us of her allergy to honey."

"Willa!" a voice called out.

We all looked toward the voice. Roman maneuvered around the crime scene tape and Officer Melman, and trotted over to us. "Are you all right?" he asked me.

"You can't be here, Roman," Heath commanded, putting an arm out, ready to shuffle him away.

"That's the guy who sold us the wine," Freddie said accusingly.

Heath changed his tune. "Is that true? Could their wine have come from your shop?"

Roman looked at the others with recognition. "They were in my meadery today. They purchased mead and a few bottles of Enora's Riesling."

Claire took her face out of her tissues long enough to accuse Roman. "You told us that wine was safe for Kendall! There had to have been honey in it from your mead! You killed her!"

A heightened murmuring of the nearby crowd made it clear Claire's cry had traveled and her accusation had been overheard. Roman's voice remained calm, but I saw fear in his eyes. "I make my mead here, and Enora's wine is made and bottled at my family's winery. There's no way there could be cross contamination. And my family doesn't use honey in any of their wines, besides."

"Roman, I'll question you privately later," Heath said.

"There must've been a way, because it happened," Claire kept up.

Roman was the most chill guy I knew. He didn't let too much faze him, but this time, he couldn't hide the hurt apparent on his face at the thought he'd harmed someone, even inadvertently. He looked to me for support.

"The wine that I had tasted was awfully sweet. Maybe you brought one of the mead bottles by mistake," I said to the group. Regardless of our current awkward relationship status, I had to defend Roman.

"We wouldn't be that stupid," Pepper growled. She took a step toward the blanket to prove her point, but Heath put an arm out to stop her.

"Everybody, hold up." Heath snapped his notepad closed with one hand and stuck it and the pen back in his suit jacket pocket. "We're going to have to take this back to the station."

"Whatever happened, it was just an accident," I said.

"We have to determine that," he responded.

He looked over at the crowd and let out a sharp whistle that pierced the air. All officers' eyes were on him. With one nod of his head, Officer Lurch strode over to us with wide, even steps. "Ferguson, can you escort this group to the station. Keep them separated when you get there." Heath added to us, "No more talking to each other for now."

Officer Ferguson nodded and gathered us like school children in a playground. With his height well over six feet, it was easy to feel like one.

I caught Heath before he was about to step away. "Can I have a quick word with you?" I quietly asked him.

He gave a nod of assent.

My relationship with the contemplative detective had progressed over this past year. He'd been a newcomer to Yarrow Glen not long before I'd moved here. We'd grown to trust and understand each other, while we simultaneously investigated a few of his murder cases. He didn't like it, but he seemed to accept my stubbornness in doing so.

I gave Roman a weak smile in support and waited for him and the others to walk off with Officer Ferguson, so they'd be out of earshot.

Heath had already stepped away again to speak to another officer. This one had a camera. Heath directed where he wanted photos taken then left him to his job. He returned to me.

"What do you think happened?" I asked him quickly, knowing he had a hundred other things to get to.

"It appears she died of anaphylactic shock from her allergy," he said.

"Yes, but do you think it was intentional?"

"We don't know. There's a lot of investigation to be done. By *me*, not you. But you can help me."

"How?"

"Did you see anything?"

"Just Kendall, lying lifeless on the ground. She had a cup near her. It was one of the red cups we were drinking out of. Her purse was already dumped out, but I helped to look for her EpiPen in case they'd overlooked it in their panic. She kept it in a glittery purple case."

"That's helpful. I'll tell the officers. We'll be scouring the area to see if it rolled into the grass unseen."

"Boss." It was Shep, walking up to Detective Heath, holding a clear plastic bag in a gloved hand. I could see the cylindrical purple object inside.

"You found her EpiPen! Where?" I asked. *How had I missed it?*

"It was in one of the garbage cans," Shep said to Heath.

"Why would it be—?" My brain latched onto only one possibility. "Someone threw it out on purpose. I bet there'll be traces of mead in her cup. Kendall was murdered!"

"Willa," Heath said with a warning tone, but it was too late. The train had left the station.

CHAPTER 7

Heath let me speak to Mrs. Schultz and Archie about the shop before I went to the police station. The two of them and Baz wrapped me in a hug as soon as I walked over to them. Archie was in shorts and a T-shirt, having taken off his cow costume.

"Are you all right?" Mrs. Schultz asked.

"I'll be okay."

"I heard them yelling at Roman. Kendall's not really dead, is she?" Archie asked.

"I'm afraid so."

"Whoa." Baz ran a hand through his brownish-blond hair.

"You two should take everything back to the shop and close for the day," I told Mrs. Schultz and Archie. "I have to go to the police station. I'll tell you everything when I get back."

"You want me to come with you?" Baz asked.

"Thanks, but there's no point. You'd just be waiting in the lobby. I'll be in touch when I'm done."

They nodded and gave me another hug before we parted. I was still in a daze as I began the short walk across the park lawn and the town hall parking lot to the station. My mind replayed the afternoon until I suddenly found myself at the glass doors of the security complex, a building I'd become familiar with through my connection with other investigations.

I entered, passing the uncluttered lobby with two vinyl sofas bookended by fake floor plants, to the bullet-proof partition that had POLICE stenciled across the top. Officer Ferguson was on the other side of it, speaking to another officer who was leading Claire, Pepper, and Freddie presumably to interview rooms. I didn't have to bother the security officer at the desk, as Lurch saw me and allowed me in. He brought me to a vacant interview room, which was even more spartan than the lobby. The happy yellow color of the bare walls didn't bring any joy to the space. Without windows, the only light came from two strips of LEDs attached to the ceiling, dispersing an unnaturally bright glow. The air-conditioning chilled me. I walked to the opposite side of the rectangular table and sat in the hard plastic chair.

"Coffee, tea, water?" Officer Ferguson said.

"Oh. Uh, coffee I guess. Black, please."

He nodded and left me, returning after a few minutes with tepid coffee in a plastic cup.

"An officer will be with you shortly to take your statement," he said.

I barely had a chance to thank him before he'd exited the room, shutting the door behind him. I waited alone. Out of habit, I checked my phone, but I knew there'd be no signal. I was left with only my thoughts.

Someone took Kendall's EpiPen from her purse while she was at the park, so she'd be helpless after drinking what I was pretty certain was mead. That meant it was a premeditated murder. I hoped Heath was able to get more information from the others. A stray email here and there had been my only contact with Kendall since leaving Church Cheese Shop. I didn't know about anything going on in her life this past year.

The reading of Max's will just this morning felt like more than a coincidence. Whoever knew Max's secrets to making the cheese had a financially lucrative future ahead of them. But they all admitted that Max didn't leave the information about Church Bleu to Kendall, so why would she be killed? I contemplated the question, but my memories of Kendall overtook my thoughts about her murder. I allowed myself to reminisce about our days together in the shop while I waited for Heath.

Heath. Our relationship was somewhere in that gray area between acquaintances and friends. We'd grown closer over the last year, learning tidbits about each other as talking about a case at times turned more personal. We chatted at community events and lingered over coffee after town hall meetings. Our connection had us wading into something that looked like it could grow into . . . something more. I couldn't deny my attraction to him. However, Heath was widowed, and I was still soured on relationships since my last one crashed and burned before it was able to pick up speed, so neither of us were great at being vulnerable. For now, I'd be happy if we could see eye to eye during this investigation into Kendall's murder. I knew some of the background of everyone at Church Cheese Shop who was connected to Kendall and Max's Church Bleu. Maybe this time, Heath would see the advantage of working together.

The door opened and my optimism about working this case with Heath sprang forward. I sat up straight. But it was Shep who walked in. I slouched back in my chair, feeling as deflated as a popped balloon.

"He's busy with the others. They were there when it

happened," he explained without my asking. He must've been able to read my disappointment.

I nodded. I understood—they were suspects and I wasn't, which I was grateful for. He turned on the recording device and I went over everything that I could remember since Kendall had arrived in town. I also filled Shep in on Max's valuable custom cheese and my theories about it.

After he turned off the recorder, I tried to pick his brain. "What do you think? It's somehow related to Max's will and his cheese?"

He glanced at me, silent, as he released the pen from the clipboard in front of him. He'd been a little loose-lipped in the past with his friends, but Heath's silence seemed to be rubbing off on him since earning his way into the spot of Heath's right-hand man. For all I knew, Heath had warned him about me. I'd be getting nothing out of Shep.

"If you're sure that's it, I'll just need you to sign here, then you can go." He swiveled the clipboard around so I could read the paper on it. I signed and dated it.

He took the clipboard and pen back, but his gaze stayed with me. "Would you like to speak with Marla?"

"Marla?"

"Our grief counselor. You just lost your friend in a shocking, horrible way."

It was no wonder everybody loved Shep.

"That's nice of you to offer, but I think I'm just going to go back to the shop and talk to my friends there," I told him.

"Okay. If you change your mind, she's available for you. She's really good at what she does."

I thanked him, then left the security complex. I walked

up Main Street, past Ron's Old-Fashioned Service Station and the post office. I crossed at the corner where the library was perched and walked a block down Pleasant Avenue. It wasn't until I reached my block that my stomach awoke and reminded me I hadn't eaten since this morning. I decided to pillage my shop for some cheese since I couldn't remember what food I had in my apartment. My pantry suffered greatly from all the time I spent at work.

I crossed the alley at Everett's bicycle shop to reach Curds & Whey. Even amid the shock and heavy heart of what had happened a couple of hours prior, seeing my shop always lifted my spirits. The façade was encased in wide cream-colored molding with Curds & Whey painted in teal in a sweeping font. On either side of the matching teal door, large windows displayed aged cheeses. The brightly painted milk jugs and metal sheep and cow sculptures peeking out the windows made me smile. A couple of cheese-lovers cookbooks shared the shelves.

I shuddered when I recalled Phoebe Winston's book in the window and the disastrous days that followed her event last fall. I was glad that was behind us, but now I was facing another unsolved murder, this time of a friend.

The door, kept open during business hours to invite customers to wander in, was now closed. Behind the six-paneled window was a sign that said as much. I used my key to unlock the door, but once inside, a divine salty-sweet aroma was the first sign the shop wasn't empty. It just hit me that I'd passed Mrs. Schultz's cherry red retro Huffy still locked at the rack in front of Curds & Whey. It had been hours since we'd left the park and I'd told them to close for the day. I walked to the rear of the shop, where Baz, Archie, and Mrs. Schultz were in the kitchenette.

"You're back." Mrs. Schultz left the stove and wrapped me in a hug.

"What are you still doing here?" I asked.

"We weren't going to leave you by yourself," Baz answered. "We figured you'd come here to scrounge for some food."

I chuckled. "You know me eerily well." We'd made a habit of having meals together in this kitchenette, especially when we were working through a case. The three of them were standing around a cooling tart that looked like a blossomed flower. "How pretty! What kind of tart is that?"

"Ham and blue cheese," Archie said. "It's Mrs. Schultz's recipe."

"You're okay with blue cheese, Baz?" I asked. He was a cheddar guy, through and through.

"I eat blue cheese dressing with my hot wings, so I'm good. I've never had it in a tart, though."

"Have you ever had a tart at all?"

"Good point."

"There's cream cheese in it too, so the blue isn't overpowering," Mrs. Schultz assured him. "Timing's perfect. Take a seat," she directed as she cut into it.

I wasn't comfortable being waited on by my friends, but when I'd balked in the past, it had gotten me stern looks from Mrs. Schultz. It was years since she'd been a beloved high school teacher, but she could still give a single look or a simple command like "Sit" that made you immediately heed it.

I sat on one of the farm-table benches as instructed. Baz poured lemonade while Mrs. Schultz served up generous slices of the tart. Archie placed one in front of me, and they joined me with their own.

With a flaky phyllo crust, I noted blue cheese and pine

nuts in the top layer, and ham, scallions, and spinach within.

"It's delicious, Mrs. Schultz," I said after my first bite.

"It's got an awful lot of green stuff in it, but it smells good, so I'm digging in," Baz said.

We ate for a few moments in silence.

"Do you want to talk about her?" Mrs. Schultz asked. "Kendall seemed like a very nice young woman."

I nodded. "It's funny that I worked at Max's shop about the same amount of time that I've been here and yet, I was never terribly close with any of them, even Kendall. I was closer with her than the others, but it can't compare to how I feel about you and Archie."

"What am I, a box of Halloween raisins?" Baz said.

I chuckled. "I was comparing people I've worked with."

Baz was always good for a laugh, even when the subject turned serious. Or maybe especially when the subject turned serious.

"The group from Church Cheese never broke the barriers of being anything other than work friends. This town has made me a different person," I continued. My broken engagement followed by my brother's death years ago had hit me hard. The three people in this room were the ones to finally break me out of my shell. "You guys were the catalyst. I'm talking about you too, Baz. You're definitely a Snickers bar."

He smiled, pleased. "A full-sized one, right? Not one of those minis."

Archie and I laughed, but Mrs. Schultz was dabbing at her eyes with her napkin.

"You've got me tearing up, Willa," she said.

"I'm happy about it, but it makes me sad for all the close friendships I denied along the way." I shook my head at how I'd kept myself so closed off before coming to Yarrow Glen. Pepper was right.

Mrs. Schultz patted my hand. "Don't be so hard on yourself. I spent a very brief time with them, admittedly, but their dynamic was a bit . . . off."

"Two of them seemed like best buds—Pepper and Freddie?" Archie said.

"Yeah, that kind of surprised me," I said. "Pepper always had a complaint about Kendall, Claire, or me at one time or another. Freddie came after I left, so I don't know him at all, but he must've done something to get in her good graces."

"Tell us more about them. How would you describe them?" Mrs. Schultz said.

I thought for a moment. "Well, Claire's a lot like her favorite cheese, Parmigiano Reggiano. Parm is usually a supporting player that boosts the other flavors, helping them shine. Consistent and reliable, with a sharpness you might not expect if you don't know it well."

They smiled at my description.

"Do the others. What would be their cheese?" Archie said.

I considered this for a minute. "Pepper's might be Red Witch. Raw milk, alpine style, with a paprika-rubbed rind, it's bold, creamy, and unapologetic. It's known for its vivid exterior color, but is unsung in its meltability and versatility. Pepper definitely feels she's unsung."

"And Freddie?" Baz said.

"Freddie's would be Honeybee. It's a young Gouda, light and sweet, with a touch of a bite from the acidic goat's milk it's made with. Because it has an easy flavor, it pairs well with something a bit stronger."

Archie nodded. "Like Pepper."

"That's right." I was glad for the fun diversion, but Kendall's death still weighed on me. "This is fun, but I don't think it's going to help us figure out what happened to Kendall."

"Do you think one of them did Kendall in?" Baz asked.

"Basil." Mrs. Schultz used her teacher's tone again. She was the only one who got away with calling Baz by his full name.

"It's okay, Mrs. Schultz. I've asked myself the same thing. I can't help but think Kendall's murder has to do with Max's Church Bleu," I said. I didn't want to think people I knew were responsible, but experience told me I must.

"Should we make this an official Team Cheese meeting?" Archie asked. His eyes lit up at the prospect of trying to solve Kendall's murder. The four of us comprised Team Cheese, the group name we'd given ourselves when we attempted to puzzle out a case together.

"I do have a lot of questions that I tried not to think about at the police station. It was too overwhelming then, but with all of you here, I might get somewhere," I said.

"What do we know happened?" Baz said, leaning forward on the bench and getting right to it.

"We're ninety-nine percent sure Kendall died of anaphylactic shock. She's allergic to honey, so I assume whatever was in the cup she was drinking had honey in it. Someone stole her EpiPen from her purse and threw it in a trash can in the park. They must've at some point nipped it from her purse at the park and disposed of it as quickly as possible," I said.

"Then it had to be someone at your picnic—Claire, Pepper, or Freddie," Archie said.

"Not necessarily. When I first went over to the picnic blanket, only Claire was there. She said everyone had been there, but they were coming and going. There was a pile with a grocery bag of food and Freddie's backpack. I didn't notice Kendall's purse, but I don't recall her carrying it when we walked to the picnic blanket together. Anyone at the park could've had access to it when the others were gone. I suppose they could've also switched out one of the wine bottles for mead or put some in the cups—a small amount could've been enough. If you're not paying attention, wine and mead do look alike and can have similar flavors, especially when they are mixed."

"But who would've known about her allergy and her EpiPen?" Mrs. Schultz stated.

"Kendall told us she couldn't have mead when the four of them were here at the shop," I recalled.

Mrs. Schultz had put down her fork. Her fingers were now rubbing the strings of her scarf, a habit she had to help her work out a problem. "She also said she was offered honey tea at the reading of Max's will. If she mentioned her allergy when she declined the tea, Maxine and Hugo would know too."

"They were also at the park," I said. I'd wolfed my piece of tart, hungrier than I'd realized.

"We heard your friend yelling at Roman and I saw him walk off with the police. They think it's his mead she drank?" Baz asked.

"I don't know what the bottles in the cooler will tell them. I'm sure they're doing tests on the cups. If they do know, Shep didn't tell me."

"That could be bad news for Roman," Baz said with worry in his voice for his friend.

"I know. He did nothing wrong, but as we all know, being linked to a murder is never good for business."

Mrs. Schultz let out a sigh and picked at the rest of her tart. "I hate to think one of her own friends killed her.

The outcome's the same, but it would be somehow less tragic if it was a stranger."

A stranger! I put down my lemonade. "Mrs. Schultz, you might be right. I saw that stranger at the park again," I said.

"What stranger?" Archie leaned in.

"There was a guy from the invitational who took an interest in Kendall. He was staring at her that night, and she and I even kidded about it. She said she didn't know who he was, and we laughed that maybe he was a secret admirer. He's very good-looking. But then I saw him again right after she left the shop when Hugo was here. We're getting a lot of people from the invitational in town, but part of me wondered if he was following her. Then I saw them together at the park, so I asked her about him, but she acted like she didn't know what I was talking about."

"She denied knowing him?" Baz said.

"I got the feeling she didn't want to say anything in front of the others. Maybe they would've given her a hard time, so I let it drop. It could be nothing, but I'll have to remember to tell Detective Heath about him just in case."

"So we have four suspects, if you count the stranger. Possibly six, depending on if Hugo and Maxine knew about her allergy and her EpiPen," Archie summarized.

"How well do you know Hugo?" Mrs. Schultz asked me.

"Yeah, what's his cheese personality?" Archie asked.

"I already know his favorite is Church Bleu. He never made *that* a secret. But prior to that, he lauded Rogue River Blue, even before it won its accolades and awards. He's a northwest loyalist. Come to think of it, Rogue River Blue's a bit flashy like Hugo, with its grape leaf rind and pear liqueur wash. It's bright, like his Hawaiian shirts, with a bit of a funky finish."

"Huh, it does fit Hugo!" Archie said.

Getting back to the murder, I said, "He was insistent that Kendall knew something about the Church Bleu that she wasn't telling."

"And Maxine?" Mrs. Schultz asked.

"I had a brief conversation with her at the park before Kendall was killed. Other than that, I don't know her at all. She seemed nice. Certainly nicer than she was to Hugo last night."

"That was crazy." Archie shook his head at the memory of the skirmish between the two at the invitational.

"What was?" Baz asked.

Archie filled him in on the pandemonium that erupted over the Church Bleu the evening before.

"It sounds like she really wants the cheese," Baz said.

"She insists she doesn't, but I'm not sure if I believe her." I couldn't get a read on her yet. "The others aren't making a secret of wanting it. Hugo thinks he's entitled to it, and Claire, Pepper, and Freddie see it as the golden ticket to the success of their own cheese shop. It was important to each of them."

"But which one was willing to kill for it? Or maybe they all were," Baz said.

"They'd only kill Kendall if she already had information she didn't plan to share with them, but she told me she didn't."

"Are you sure she would tell you if she did?" Mrs. Schultz asked gently.

I thought about that. "Gosh, I thought so, but maybe you're right. Maybe she didn't trust any of us."

"First we need to know whether we can eliminate Maxine and Hugo," Archie said.

"I'll ask Claire, Pepper, and Freddie if Kendall mentioned her allergy at the reading of Max's will when she declined the honey tea. I want to go check on them, anyway, and see what else they can tell me about what happened before she died."

"I'll come with you. You could be dealing with a murderer," Baz said.

"I sure hope not."

Mrs. Schultz rose with dishes in hand. She carried them to the sink.

"No doing dishes, Mrs. Schultz. Isn't it your poker night?" I said, rising from the table too. Mrs. Schultz attended a monthly girls poker night with her friends, where they played penny poker and drank chocolate martinis.

"Yes, but I don't feel right about going after what happened today," she said.

"Being with friends usually makes things better," I suggested.

"Maybe you're right."

"You should head home too, Archie. It's already been a long, weird day," I insisted.

Archie started to protest, but a yawn caught him midword. "Sorry," he said.

"Go home and get a good night's sleep. I'll fill you both in tomorrow if we learn anything important tonight."

Reluctantly, they followed my directions, and I locked the door behind them. Baz helped me wash and dry the dishes. We didn't say much, which was unusual for us.

As we were putting the last of the dishes away, Baz said, "Thinking about Kendall?"

"I feel terrible she died so young. She was our age!"

"Yeah, that's really awful."

"She had a lot of potential too—she was a great cheesemonger. It was too bad you didn't get to meet her, Baz."

"I met her."

"You did? When? At the park?"

"No, when she was leaving your apartment earlier today."

"What do you mean? She wasn't at my apartment."

"Yeah, she was. I came back after my last job to grab my carvings for the farmer's market, and I saw her coming out of your apartment. I didn't know who she was at first, so I hate to say it, but I kind of barked at her. She told me her name and I remembered you said your friends were coming by today. She said you'd asked her to feed your fish—that you had so much going on that you forgot."

"That doesn't make any sense," I said, my mind spinning with what he was telling me.

"You're crazy about Loretta, so I didn't question it. If you'd forgotten to feed her, you wouldn't want to wait until the end of the day to do it."

"No, not that part. I never told her to feed Loretta. How would she even get into my apartment?"

"She had a key. I saw her lock the door with it before she left. That's why she seemed legit."

I shook my head. I reached my hand a few inches above my head to describe Kendall. "This tall, brown hair, cute?"

"Yup, that was her. If you didn't give her the key to your apartment, how did she get it?"

I thought back. "She must've taken it when she was here in the shop. We were about to go up to my apartment and I grabbed the keys from under the counter, but then we got a bunch of people in the shop, so I put them back. She must've taken them when Mrs. Schultz and I were busy with customers."

"That's risky," Baz remarked.

I thought about the afternoon when Hugo was entertaining the group of customers. "She was gone for probably about forty minutes. She must've come back to the shop just to return the keys." *But why? Why would she sneak into my apartment?* "Did she have anything from my place with her when she left?"

Baz shook his head. "Not that I noticed."

She had her purse with her at the shop. She could've stuck something in it, but what? "What could she possibly want from my apartment? Money?"

"Maybe she thought you knew something about Max's cheese."

"But that's crazy." My disbelief shifted to hurt. If she thought I knew something about Max or the cheese, she could've just asked me. Maybe I knew Kendall even less than I thought I did. "We need to go upstairs and take a look around. I want to know why she was so desperate to sneak into my apartment."

CHAPTER 8

Baz and I followed the alley to the back of the building and climbed the stairs to our adjoining decks, separated only by a low railing. I tried the handle to my apartment door before inserting the key. Baz was right, the door was locked. I unlocked it and we stepped inside.

I rubbed the back of my neck to settle the pricks of unease that tingled there. Upon first glance, nothing seemed amiss. I could see my entire living room/kitchen combo from where I stood, cut off from the back bedrooms by a wall. The two rooms mirrored each other in one open space, the areas delineated by a butcher block island with a trio of stools tucked under two sides. My living room, with its tall ceilings and slanted hardwood floors, was filled with vintage furniture from my grandmother's farmhouse: the console I used for my TV and a wide bench I used as a coffee table. My well-worn love seat was helped by my grandmother's knitted throw blanket draped across the back. Next to the reading chair was a tall metal stool that served as Loretta Island.

I hurried over to check on her. From under the warming light in her fishbowl, she swished her long, flowy red tail hello. I breathed easier. I had no reason to think

Kendall would harm Loretta, but I also had no reason to think she'd enter my apartment without permission.

"Everything seem okay?" Baz asked, looking around. He'd been here enough times to know if anything was out of place.

"I think so."

We walked through the cozy living space to the back of the apartment. To the right, off the short hall behind the kitchen, I stuck my head into the only bathroom. All seemed as usual. I looked through the medicine cabinet. There were no medications to steal stronger than ibuprofen. I went across to my bedroom. The tall, arched windows flanking my queen-sized bed allowed the early evening light to penetrate the room. The bed was neatly made, as it was every morning thanks to my mother's edict—*A made bed is the first task of an accomplished day*—sticking with me throughout adulthood. My grandmother's handsewn quilt still lay neatly atop it.

The bedside table held a clock and a book. Nothing missing. I opened the closet door and scanned inside. I didn't have much. I wore the same thing to work virtually every day—a rolled-sleeve white blouse, khaki capris, and one of my eight pairs of Keds. My casual wardrobe wasn't much more exciting than that—usually a T-shirt and jeans. "Nothing missing here either," I called out.

"What about this room?" Baz called back.

I left my bedroom for the spare room, where I assumed Baz was. I'd set it up as a second office, as my office downstairs was little more than a closet, but I had so far only used it as storage space. Having moved so often, I'd gotten used to being a temporary resident wherever I lived. Some things just ended up staying in boxes. I found Baz sitting in my office chair.

One corner of the room was stacked with boxes, but

one misplaced box was on the floor. Its flaps weren't tucked into each other the way I always left them. I checked the others. Several of them weren't closed properly either. I opened one and saw my hodgepodge of stuff.

"Why would she be looking through these?" I wondered aloud.

"You want to go through them to see if anything's missing?" Baz suggested.

"I'm not sure if I'd remember everything that's in them. I haven't been through them since I moved in last year, except for the boxes of books for Sharice's charity sidewalk sale." A forgotten image flashed in my mind. The contents of Kendall's purse laid out on the picnic blanket. Among them, a book I recognized.

"What is it?" Baz asked, noticing by my far-off look that my mind's wheels were turning.

"They dumped Kendall's purse on the blanket to look for her EpiPen. I just remembered there was a book. I barely looked at it because I was searching for the EpiPen. Now that I think about it, I think it was *my* book."

"Why would she sneak into your apartment to steal a book?"

"Max gave it to me when I left Church Cheese Shop." I went over to the box where I'd transferred the books I was keeping. The untucked flap read BOOKS NOT DONATING in black marker. I searched the box. "The book's not here. Why would she take my *Rebecca* book?"

"Didn't you just say you donated your books to Read More Bookstore?"

"Not that one. I'm certain of it. I was looking at it again after I found out Max died. That was after I'd boxed up the others."

"Do you think she was jealous that Max gave it to you?"

"I can't imagine she would be. He only gave it to me because he knew I watched the movie all the time and he said he was appalled I'd never read the book. It was his copy, which is why it was special to me. It was marked up and he'd written a little note in it to me—it wouldn't have been a big deal to anyone else. It was something he gave me privately. Nobody even knew about it." I thought back to this morning in the shop and realized that wasn't completely true. "Oh, wait. I told Kendall all about it when we were talking about Max. When Mrs. Schultz mentioned the bookstore sale today, it must've triggered her memory about our conversation about *Rebecca*. Oh my gosh, she came up here to steal my book. But why?"

It made me sad to think Kendall had resented my relationship with Max, so much so that she snuck into my apartment and took the last thing he ever gave me. I had no idea she'd felt that way. I hated to think the only reason she came to my shop to see me was in hopes of getting her hands on that book. That wasn't the Kendall I knew. "Maybe she had a good reason to do what she did."

Baz's eyebrow shot up in skepticism. "Didn't you say she lied about talking to that guy at the park too? Add in that somebody went to the trouble of murdering her . . . I'm not saying she deserved to be killed, but maybe she's not so innocent. Maybe she was hiding something."

"Some of the others suspected her of knowing more about Max's secret cheese than she was letting on. I thought they were jealous, but maybe they were right. They knew her better than I did."

"You want to ask them about her?"

"We have to be careful about it, but I think we should. Let's go to the inn."

CHAPTER 9

I changed out of my work clothes and threw on jeans and a House of Blues shirt with a drawing of a hunk of blue cheese on it. It made me pause to think of Max. The last thing he would've wanted was for anyone to be fighting over his cheese, and certainly not for Kendall to be killed because of it. To have created such a sought-after custom cheese was the pinnacle of his life. Then to have it shrouded in mystique truly defined Max. They were the two things he loved most—cheese and mystery. To everyone else, the mysterious cheese equaled money.

Baz and I walked the two and half blocks up Pleasant Avenue toward The Inn at Yarrow Glen. Its wooden sign jutted out from the porch steps that abutted the sidewalk and led to the white boxy structure. Much like Yarrow Glen's residents, there was nothing fussy about the turn-of-the-century inn. It was charming nonetheless, with its second-story porch that wrapped around the entire building mirroring the one below it. A driveway ran along the side that led to their parking lot beyond an enclosed courtyard in the rear, and a barrier of evergreens on either side allowed privacy for each of its nine rooms.

The lobby, too, was charming—everything one would expect from an inn. There was a sitting area with matching wing chairs and a Chesterfield sofa, anchored by a dark-print rug over a highly polished wood floor. A bowl of perfectly placed green apples sat untouched in the center of an antique walnut coffee table. An arched fireplace with a simple white mantel flanked by sconces completed the cozy space.

A matching runner led past the spindle staircase to the ornate reception desk at the rear of the lobby where the chatty reception clerk, Constance Yi, noted our arrival. Constance was in her early twenties, and extremely capable at her job. She could tell guests everything about Yarrow Glen, past and present—even the gossip, which she liked to do best.

She crossed her hands over her heart and made an exaggerated sad face when she saw me. She'd obviously heard about what happened to Kendall. We walked up to the desk to say hi.

She said in a rush of words, "I heard. It's so sad. I can't believe it. She was so nice. I just saw her this morning. I'm so sorry." She finally took a beat. "The others mentioned visiting you at your shop, so I know she was your friend."

"Thanks. It's been a shock. We came by to see how my other friends are doing. Do you know if they're in their rooms?"

"They're in The Cellar having dinner. Hi, Baz," she inserted before going back to her train of thought. "I feel so bad for them. What a horrible day they've had. They were upset in the conference room with that attorney first thing this morning. By the sound of it, I don't think things went well. And now this."

"What did you hear?" I asked, knowing she'd probably been waiting for the right circumstance to share the gossip with someone.

"I couldn't hear what they were saying, even when I got closer . . ." I could imagine Constance deciding to dust the vase of flowers on the little end table near the conference room door to eavesdrop. "But there was an eruption of voices. Then when everyone came out, they looked pretty mad. Except for Maxine."

"How was she?"

"I think she seemed pleased. She had as close to a smile as I've seen on her since she arrived. Oh, not that I blame her, with her dad passing and all."

He left the cheese shop to Maxine, which might've been an unexpected boon for her. She claimed not to care about her father's cheese—this seemed to back that up. If she'd expected the secret to Church Bleu, as well, she would've been angry along with the rest of them.

"She didn't get annoyed until Hugo followed her after Kendall shut him down," Constance continued.

"What did Hugo want?" I asked.

"He insisted Kendall 'knew something.'" Constance used her fingers to make air quotes. "I don't know about what, but when Kendall said she didn't, he went after Maxine. Followed her all the way upstairs to her room."

"Maxine is staying here too?"

"They both are. Maxine and Hugo. I was surprised none of them canceled their reservations after what happened. They're all still staying through Monday. I sure hope the rest of their stay is better than it's been. Well, what else could happen?"

Baz snorted then covered it with a cough. From past experience, we knew better than to ask that question.

"I'm sure you'll do your best to make the rest of the weekend a better experience for them," I said.

"Thanks, Willa. I try," she said, her usual perky smile returning.

"We're going to head down to The Cellar. I'm sure we'll see you soon."

"Hope so," she said, her glance sliding to Baz. She wiggled her fingers in a goodbye.

We crossed the lobby again and headed to the inn's pub. The Cellar continued to be a mainstay for locals as it had been for decades, even when the inn changed hands, so there was no need for a sign at the door. The inn's guests were simply directed to "the red door down the short hallway off the lobby." We descended the steps, and the tranquility of the lobby vanished entirely.

Even without the acoustic band playing yet, the former wine cellar turned pub was lively. "Margaritaville" wafted through the speakers.

"That's right, they're doing Jimmy Buffet Weekend. Their special is Cheeseburger in Paradise. Now I'm *really* glad we came," Baz said. Baz never met a burger he didn't like.

"Didn't we just have dinner?"

"A tart's not dinner, it's . . . a tart."

"This might go better if I'm on my own, anyway, since they just met you today."

"Cool. I'll be at the bar if you need me. Should I order you one?"

"No, I'm good."

"Are you sure? 'Cause I like mine with lettuce and tomato. Heinz fifty-seven and—"

I pushed him toward the bar, still speaking in Buffett lyrics as I scanned the room for the Church Cheese crew.

The room seemed to hold as many tables and chairs as could fit, leaving narrow pathways to get to and from the bar. Wrought-iron ring chandeliers hung from the ceiling, the candle-like bulbs playing off the stone walls and floor. Several oak-lined arched nooks broke up the long wall, each with just enough space for a U-shaped booth to be tucked into. The booths were my favorite place to sit, as the cozy nook muffled the noise. In one of them sat Claire, Pepper, and Freddie. To my surprise, Hugo was with them.

I approached the table, we exchanged hellos, and they made room in the six-person booth for me to join them. The remains of a mostly eaten plate of nachos sat in the center of the table.

"I wanted to check on you to see how you're doing," I said to the group.

Freddie lifted his margarita. "I'm on my third, if that's any indication." They each had a margarita in front of them—it must've been the drink special. "It's the first time I've ever been interrogated."

"I didn't like that room they put me in and the way the detective questioned me. It felt like he thought one of us had something to do with it," Claire said. She sucked on the straw of her rather large margarita, already three-quarters empty.

"He has to question everyone who was with Kendall at the time of her death. I'm sure it was just routine," I told them. Technically that was true, but I doubted it was just routine. "Were you questioned, Hugo?"

"No. Why would I be?" Hugo said a little indignantly.

"You were there too. I saw you standing over us when it all went down," Pepper said.

I missed seeing Hugo there.

He began to stutter. "Th-that was after, when Claire started screaming. *Everybody* ran over. The police would have to question everyone at the park, in that case."

"Detective Heath is pretty thorough," I said, which seemed to make Hugo even more nervous.

"I wonder if they know yet what killed her," Claire said.

"Her honey allergy. Duh," Pepper said. She took a healthy sip from her glass. It must've been a spicy margarita, as I noticed a slice of jalapeno clinging to an ice cube.

"I figured that much, Pepper. You don't always have to be so harsh, you know. That's why you were never Max's favorite. He didn't like the way you treated people," Claire said.

I'd never heard Claire stand up to Pepper like that before.

Pepper didn't back down. "Customers want to know about cheese. I know cheese. I wasn't his favorite because Kendall had to have that spot all to herself. Remember how happy she was when Willa left?"

"Pepper! She wasn't happy, Willa," Claire assured me.

We hadn't been super close, but I didn't think she would've been happy about my leaving. Then again, if she'd resented my relationship with Max, maybe she *was* happy about it. Either way, Claire was right—Pepper was harsh. But that didn't mean she wasn't telling the truth. Kendall stole my keys and snuck into my apartment. What did I really know about her?

"I just meant she was happy to be Queen Bee. She was the one who convinced Max to hire Freddie instead of another experienced cheesemonger more like Willa," Pepper stated.

"And that's exactly why you're so close with Freddie, because he's not certified and doesn't know as much as you," Claire said. That margarita seemed to be giving her some liquid courage.

"Hey!" Freddie said. "I'm right here."

Hugo leaned across the table and said to Freddie, "If you want to switch rooms and leave those two, I'm right down the hall." He winked as he took another sip of his drink.

Freddie gave Hugo a once-over with raised eyebrows as if assessing the offer before rejecting it. "I have a boyfriend."

Hugo shrugged, unbothered, and drank again.

"I didn't mean to offend you, Freddie. I would just like it if Pepper showed a little compassion. I just lost my friend," Claire said. She tore at the remains of her napkin, continuing the trail of napkin bits from where she'd been sitting before I'd arrived.

"We all lost Kendall," Pepper said. "Don't you think I'm gutted about it too?"

Claire didn't seem to believe her and ignored Pepper's uncommon display of vulnerability.

"Do you all feel like you knew Kendall well?" I asked.

"She and I were very close," Claire said.

I expected that, so I pushed on. "She didn't keep anything . . . secret?"

"What are you getting at, Willa?" Pepper didn't sound irritated by the question, rather, interested.

Hugo spoke up before I had to answer Pepper. "Sure she did. Kendall had secrets."

I jumped on Hugo's response. "About what?" Maybe that margarita and the Jimmy Buffett music would loosen him up enough to say something he knew about Kendall that he wouldn't normally let slip.

"About where Max's cheese is," he responded.

"She said she didn't know anything, Hugo. Let it go," Claire said.

"I hate to agree with Hugo, but I'm sure she knew more about that clue in Max's will than the rest of us," Freddie said.

He and Hugo clinked glasses in solidarity.

"What clue?" I asked.

A thump under the table preceded Freddie stifling a

yelp. I thought someone may have kicked him under the table. He backtracked poorly. "She has more of a clue as to who Max left his cheese to, is what I meant. It came out wrong."

I had a hunch he was lying, but it seemed everyone but me was in on it, so I let it go.

"It doesn't make sense. Kendall was loyal," Claire said. She quickly wiped away a tear with what was left of her paper napkin. "Look at how good she was to her mom, dropping everything whenever her MS flared up."

I'd witnessed this myself, although Kendall never liked to talk about her mother's multiple sclerosis. "I can't even imagine how she's coping," I said. Thinking about her family made me feel bad for having to question Kendall's honesty and motives.

Claire threw the rest of the napkin onto the table. It obviously wasn't helping to stem her anxiety over the situation. "How does an accident like that happen? When we bought the wine, the meadery guy swore there'd be no traces of honey in it."

"If they thought it was an accident, you all wouldn't have been interrogated," Hugo pointed out.

"Didn't you say it was just routine, Willa?" Claire asked with a hopeful voice.

"Yes, it's routine for them to question the people there to assess what really happened. What I'd like to know is, where was her EpiPen?" I knew it was thrown in the trash, but I wanted to hear *their* theories.

They looked at one another, saying nothing and suddenly all terribly thirsty.

"Do you think she accidentally dropped it somewhere in the park?" I asked, studying each of them, trying to see who might reveal their guilty conscience.

"She *happened* to drop it and then *happened* to drink

wine spiked with honey? Come on, Willa," Pepper scoffed.

"There's another possible explanation," I ventured. "What if it was taken from her bag?"

"You think this was done to her? On purpose?" Claire stared at me, aghast.

"Claire's the one who shared a room with her," Freddie offered hastily. "Pepper and I have our own."

"So you're accusing *me* of taking her EpiPen?" Claire cried.

"No one's accusing you, Claire. Calm down," Pepper said.

I needed to keep a lid on this pot of personalities before it boiled over. "Tell us what happened when you got to the park."

Claire returned to tearing at her napkin. "We found our spot, put our stuff down . . . and then I think it was *Freddie* who opened the wine." She looked smugly at Freddie in revenge.

The others stared at Freddie too.

His gaze darted around the group. "I didn't put any honey in the wine," he declared nervously.

"We know you didn't, Freddie. We were all there together," Pepper said. She shot Claire a dirty look.

"You all weren't *always* there at the picnic blanket, though," I reminded them.

"We left to check out the farmer's market a couple of times. We might've lost track of each other," Pepper said. She shrugged one shoulder in nonchalance.

"You and Claire left our stuff there when you came looking for us. Anyone could've messed with the wine," Freddie said more confidently.

"Even Hugo." Pepper's gaze landed on him.

"Me? Freddie just said it could've been anyone," Hugo

countered. He licked the salt off the rim of his glass before taking another swig. I wondered if the flush in his cheeks was from the drink or the accusation.

"If someone tampered with it on purpose, they had to have known Kendall was allergic to honey," I said, waiting for the answer I'd been looking for.

"That's right. How would I have known that?" Hugo sat back, more relaxed, sporting a satisfied expression.

"Kendall said so at the reading of Max's will. Constance even asked her about it and complimented her on her purple glittery EpiPen case Kendall took out," Claire said.

Hugo acted unaffected. "I wasn't paying attention to that."

"You were too busy chomping at the bit to get the will read," Pepper said to him.

"Don't act like it was just me. We were all there for the same reason."

I broke into their argument. "Even Maxine?"

Hugo's air of indifference vanished. "She pretends she doesn't care, but she cares, just like the rest of us. You saw her last night at the invitational." Hugo shook his head in judgment, as if his behavior hadn't been even worse.

"Nobody really knows. She hasn't been friendly," Freddie said.

"She hasn't been *un*friendly," Claire said in Maxine's defense. "She just keeps to herself."

She'd been open with me, but I decided not to share that with the group.

"I think she was gearing up for a battle with us over the cheese, because everyone was saying Max would leave it to Kendall. Then none of us got it," Pepper said.

"You think she would've contested the will if Kendall or one of you had inherited it? She got the shop, and she's been pretty insistent that she doesn't care about the Church Bleu," I said.

Hugo rolled his eyes. Freddie and Pepper looked at each other with smirks like I was naïve.

Freddie said, "How could she not care? The shop is chump change. That cheese is worth a fortune."

The booth was quiet after Freddie's pronouncement. They'd all been quick to point the finger at one another for Kendall's death. Maybe I had to consider whether any of them were right—one of them could be Kendall's killer.

CHAPTER 10

I didn't sleep well and woke up with the sun. In the living room, I said good morning to Loretta, who seemed barely awake herself. I fed her, then made a latte with my fancy coffee maker, my only splurge that wasn't related to Curds & Whey. I took my latte outside to the narrow deck to inhale the spring air.

In the distance, rolling hills lined with vineyards sat behind a light haze of fog. My first-generation CRV and Baz's pickup truck were the only two vehicles in the narrow lot behind our building. The brilliant sun shone gold on the trees beyond the lot where Jackrabbits Run trail looped through the mature oaks and evergreens that eventually opened onto the park behind the town hall.

I thought of Kendall taking her last breath in the park. Heath had said this was his business, not mine, but how could I believe Kendall's death was none of my business? She was a former co-worker and friend. Okay, she did some things that made the friendship part questionable, but she still didn't deserve to die. It didn't seem right to push thoughts of her aside and not try to find out who did this to her.

I continued to wrestle with my conscience about Heath

and this case as I went back inside my apartment to shower and change into my work clothes. The closer I became to Heath, the more I wanted to respect his wishes. He could take care of this; I knew he could. I just wasn't the kind of person to take a back seat. As my father used to say, *If you're going to sit in the back seat, don't expect to always get where you want to go.*

When I'd gotten ready for the day, I checked my phone for the time. It was still too early to open the shop, especially on a Sunday when we opened an hour later. Although there was always something to do there, I wasn't feeling myself this morning, demonstrated by the fact that I was hankering for something sweet for breakfast. One of Hope's cinnamon rolls would satiate my craving. Rise and Shine Bakery opened for customers at seven. I rarely went down there since Archie brought the breads of the day from the bakery to our shop for our sampling menus. Today, I'd take advantage of waking extra early.

I left my apartment and walked through the alley to the front of the building and past the windows of Curds & Whey. Pudge, a large tabby cat, was lying in front of the door of Carl's Hardware, patiently awaiting his first meal of the day from Carl. He had a clipped ear, a sign that he'd been a stray who was captured, neutered, and released again. He'd hung out in Carl's alley enough that Carl had begun feeding him, giving him the name Pudge and the physique to fit his new name. The cat had taken to Carl so much that Pudge now spent a good deal of his days inside the hardware store, often taking naps on the shelves. If you went into the store for something he happened to be lying on, you were out of luck—you'd have to return another time. I bent down and slowly extended my hand. He tolerated a few strokes between his ears, and I knew not to push it beyond that.

"Sorry I didn't think to bring food down for you, Pudge," I said to him.

He stretched his neck to sniff my fingers to make sure I was telling the truth, then stared at me with his chartreuse eyes, asking why I was still here then.

"Okay, I get the hint. Have a good morning."

I crossed the alley after the hardware store, passed Lou's Market and Read More Bookstore and Café and continued down the street to the end of the block.

The shops along Pleasant Avenue were in a hodgepodge of mostly older flat-roofed buildings, which were renovated into shops and cafés with second-story offices or cozy apartments. They were uniformly connected in pairs with alleys in between the buildings, some narrow, some big enough to drive through to the back lots. Rise and Shine was the exception. It was located in a single-story cottage of faded clapboard. The bright blue awning shaded the door as well as the two oversized six-over-six paned windows to the right of the entrance.

I walked across the Bake Someone Happy welcome mat to enter the snug shop, where I was enfolded in the aroma of fresh breads just out of the oven and ribbons of sugar scenting the air. Customers were clustered in front of the narrow space between the entrance and the counter.

I hung back and watched Jasmine, her arm tattoos visible under her T-shirt and bright blue apron, deftly packing paper bags with bagels and serving up fruit-topped pastries and fat muffins coated with sparkling sugar from the glass display cases flanking the register. Hope's manager, Claude—a bald guy in his forties with a goatee, who used to own his own bread bakery—was behind the register ringing up their purchases and serving to-go cups of coffee. Hope must've been doing the baking this morning, as I didn't see her. I peeked between customers to look at one of the display cases and was happy to see they wouldn't run out of cinnamon rolls by the time it was my turn.

As I approached the counter, Claude said to Jasmine, "Can you get this customer? I need to check on the breads."

Jasmine nodded as Claude walked through the swinging door to the kitchen.

"Hi, Willa," she said. "Claude's bringing out more bread if you don't see what you want."

"Thanks, Jasmine. I do have to decide on bread for the shop, but I know for sure I want one of your famous cinnamon rolls."

She went to the glass case to get one. I perused the baskets of breads on the upper shelves behind the counter. Archie usually knew which cheeses we'd planned to highlight, so I trusted him to choose the breads that would work best with them. I'd have to text him and let him know I'd be picking them up today.

Claude stepped halfway out of the kitchen, holding the swinging door open. "Jas, we're out of the sesame bagels."

"Already?" she replied.

"Ran out of sesame seeds. I guess I need to start double-checking Hope's inventory lists too." He rolled his eyes and retreated to the kitchen.

As he did so, I glimpsed someone familiar behind the swinging door. As it closed, I tried to get a better look through its small round window.

Jasmine was back at the register with my cinnamon roll. "Have you decided on the bread?"

I returned my focus to Jasmine. "Oh, the bread. Uh, no. Was that Archie I saw in the kitchen?"

"Yeah. He's been so great. He picked everything up so quickly. And he gets along with Claude better than Hope does. It's the only reason Claude doesn't complain about Hope sleeping in until nine most days." She leaned in and said more quietly, "Well, he still complains, but I don't blame him."

Archie was working at the bakery? Why wouldn't he have told me?

"So . . . bread?" Jasmine said, pulling me away from my internal questions.

"Sorry. I'll just let Archie get it like always." I finished the transaction and left with my cinnamon roll in a bag.

I walked up the sidewalk back toward my shop. That must be why Archie had been so tired lately. He'd been waking at the crack of dawn to work in the bakery. Was he doing it for extra money, or just to help Hope because she didn't want to get up early? Either way, why wouldn't he tell us? Was he thinking of leaving Curds & Whey? My heart dropped at the thought. I'd have to find some way to broach the subject with him, but it would be an uncomfortable conversation.

"Willaaaa!" The sound of my name flew past me.

It was Everett in a colorful helmet and plenty of Lycra, zooming past on his ten-speed, with his hand in the air in a wave. I threw my arm up and waved back, even though he'd already passed. Another cyclist, their torso low to the bike, pedaled next to him.

As I watched them zoom up the street, I noticed Heath rounding the corner of the Golden Glen Meadery into the alley. He must be going to talk to Roman. My mind started spinning as fast as the wheels on Everett's bike. Was Heath just getting an early start or did this mean bad news for Roman?

CHAPTER 11

"Heath!" I called from several yards away.

He stopped and looked my way.

I trotted up the sidewalk to meet him. "Are you going to see Roman?"

"Good morning to you too," he replied.

"Oh, sorry. Good morning. I've been up a while."

"Didn't sleep well?"

"How did you know?"

"You had a rough day yesterday."

The understanding and sympathy I read in his face brought out an overwhelming desire to lean into him for a long, strong hug. But that wasn't happening. "So *are* you going to see Roman?"

"I am."

"Don't tell me he's a suspect." I hated to think of Roman in the hot seat again. He'd been through the wringer a few months ago when a guy he'd been fighting with ended up dead and he didn't have an alibi.

"You don't have to worry about Roman. I just want to talk to him," Heath assured me.

My head dipped back in relief. "About the wine and the mead? It was his mead that killed her, wasn't it?"

Heath looked at me and said nothing, which only gave me the opportunity to ask more questions. "Did someone switch out the wine bottle for a mead bottle or was it just in her cup or did they spike the bottle—?"

"Willa. I know it was your friend who was killed, but let me handle this, okay?"

"No, I am. I am. I just . . . have questions."

Heath chuckled. "You always have questions. But so do I, and it's my job to ask them. Okay?"

"Okay, fine." I couldn't fault him. It wasn't like I expected him to tell me, but it sure would make it easier on me if he would. "If there are any big developments, you'll let me know?"

"If there's anything I can tell you, I will," he promised.

Relief again. "Thanks."

Neither of us made a move to leave.

"There is one other thing," he said.

"What is it?" I asked.

"Do you want to get a drink at The Cellar tonight?"

My eyebrows shot up in surprise. "You actually want to meet with me to talk about the case?" In the past, anything I'd gotten from him was given piecemeal and reluctantly.

His hand went in his trouser pocket and the other scratched his smooth, well-defined jaw. "Not to talk about the case. Just to . . . talk."

I froze, all except my heart which was beating as fast as a hummingbird's wings in my chest. Was Heath asking me on a date? He stared at me, waiting for an answer. I snapped out of my shocked stupor.

"Yes!" I said, *wayyy* to eagerly. *Gosh, Willa. Calm down! Play it cool!* I cleared my throat and started again, this time trying to not sound like a teenager being asked to the prom. "Yeah. Sure. I'd love to."

The smile that broke out on his face made me temporarily forget my embarrassment.

"Is eight o'clock okay?"

"Perfect!" *Willaaaa.* "Sounds fine," I said with restraint. "Great."

There was that smile again—the one that took me by surprise the first time I saw it, the one that made me consider Heath as someone other than just a detective. The one he rarely shows, but when he does . . .

I sighed. Then realized I sighed and stopped breathing altogether, hoping he hadn't noticed.

"Roman's expecting me, so . . ." He nodded toward the alley where he'd been headed before I stopped him.

"Right. Have a good day then, Detective. I mean, Heath. I mean . . ."

"Jay. Call me Jay."

"I'll see you tonight at The Cellar, Jay."

"See you tonight," he replied. He started down the alley. I couldn't help but watch him. That assured gait, that suit that skimmed his broad shoulders . . . I was in mid-sigh (again) when his head turned my way. I spun around so he wouldn't catch me staring, but I knew it was too late. I bolted across the street with my face flushed red and warm.

It wasn't until I was unlocking the door to Curds & Whey that I looked back one last time at the meadery. Heath had disappeared down the alley.

I stepped into my shop, feeling a sense of comfort just being inside it. My awkwardness immediately vanished. I giggled, thinking about going on a date with Heath. Scratch that. Jay. Could I get used to calling him Jay? I'd always thought of him as Heath. I looked at the bag I'd forgotten was in my hand and remembered why I'd gone out this morning in the first place.

I left the cinnamon roll in the bag for now and prepped the blue cheese spread I'd decided on making for today's sampling. I took out a block of cream cheese and freshly cut into a wheel of Stilton. While they were coming to room temperature, I dug into the bakery bag. I pulled apart the yeasty cinnamon roll, my fingers sticky with its thick coating of icing before popping a piece in my mouth. It practically dissolved on my tongue, the buttery cinnamon flavors melding together.

Heath asking me out wasn't the only thing that had surprised me this morning. I wasn't sure how to talk to Archie about the bakery. It was entirely his business what he did with his time away from the cheese shop, but if he wasn't happy here, I wanted to know about it and try to remedy it. Or maybe the idea of working side by side with Hope at her bakery appealed to him more. I couldn't compete with young love.

With every last crumb of the cinnamon roll eaten, I washed my hands and started on the spread. It was a simple recipe, highlighting the blue cheese. I stirred the cream cheese in a bowl until it was softened, mixed in some chopped walnuts, then crumbled the Stilton and gently folded it in. I spread it on thin crackers and brought it to the front sampling counter.

Through the window, I saw Mrs. Schultz arrive by bike, the skirt of her floral dress tucked between her and the bicycle seat. I walked outside and wished her good morning as she secured the vintage Huffy on the bike rack. She smoothed out her dress, which fell above her ankles, and adjusted her bright yellow scarf.

"Good morning," she replied in her usual chipper manner. She looked over at the meadery. "Something going on over there?"

I hadn't realized I'd been staring at the meadery again. Not much got past Mrs. Schultz. I decided to keep my date to myself for now. Who knows if a drink with Heath would turn into anything more? "Heath went over there to talk with Roman. It's killing me that I don't know if he's done yet."

"There's only one way to find out," Mrs. Schultz said, leaving me on the sidewalk still staring across the street as she entered Curds & Whey.

I followed her in. "I can't chance that Heath is still there. I told him I'd leave the questioning to him."

"What did you and Baz find out last night?"

I filled Mrs. Schultz in on the stolen *Rebecca* book Max had given me, when it dawned on me that I had forgotten to tell Heath about it. "I can't believe I just saw him and forgot to tell him that Kendall snuck into my apartment."

"It might be a good reason to go over there." Mrs. Schultz's eyebrows raised. "Or are you still nervous about talking to Roman?"

I wasn't feeling any trepidation about it this morning, but that was because Roman might be in trouble. Archie walked into the shop before I got a chance to answer Mrs. Schultz.

"Morning," he said. He padded over to the checkout counter with his bakery bag of fresh breads and took a clean apron from underneath. "So what did I miss from last night?"

For Kendall's sake, I'd have to face my discomfort of being in the same room with Heath and Roman together. I decided to kill two birds, maybe three, with one stone— talk to Heath about the book, talk to Roman about the case, and avoid talking to Archie about the bakery. Win, win, win.

"Mrs. Schultz can tell you about it. I've got to go across the street. I'll be back in a jiffy," I said.

I waited for a car to pass to cross the road. There was more activity now that the shops were getting ready to open. Lou, whose market opened earlier than the other shops, was out front sweeping his sidewalk. I caught a glimpse of Sharice replenishing the tables in front of her bookstore with shallow boxes of used books for her sidewalk sale. As I crossed the street, I waved to Everett, who was setting up some bicycles out front of his shop. I received a wave and a "Hey, neighbor!" in return.

At the Golden Glen Meadery, I pushed on the glass door, but it didn't budge. It was still a few minutes before Roman would open. A light from the rear of his shop caught my attention. He and Heath must be in his tasting room. I went around back through the alley and buzzed at his back door. I waited but he didn't answer. I buzzed again.

Roman opened it up, and his face cleared when he saw it was me.

"Hi. I hope it's okay that I came by," I said.

"Of course. Come on in."

I'd been here plenty of times to deliver cheese platters to pair with Roman's mead for scheduled customer tastings. Unlike the cool industrial feel of his shop, the tasting room was masculine in a cozy way. The transom windows along the outer wall added natural light to the room, which was separated from the retail part of the shop by a sliding barn door. A horseshoe of round, high-top cocktail tables hugged the walls, partially framing a grouping of comfortable-looking worn-leather chairs and a sofa in the center. The focal point of the room was the striking handcrafted black walnut bar lined with stools for eight. On the olive wall behind the bar hung a large painting of Roman's Golden Glen label. His mead was simply showcased on a single glass shelf beneath it. Behind a closed door was a basement-like space where his mead was made and stored.

I glanced around the room, but it was just the two of us. "Heath left?"

Roman slumped down on the couch. "A little while ago."

A sigh of relief escaped me. Talking to Heath could wait until we were alone. I sat next to Roman. It was physically closer than I'd been to him in months, but I sensed he could use a friend.

"Was it the mead?" I asked, addressing the elephant in the room. He didn't need me to clarify. He knew I was talking about the cause of Kendall's death.

He nodded, staring at the floor.

"You know this isn't your fault, right?" I said gently.

"I know. At least there wasn't any trace of honey in the wine bottle. Heath said it was just in the cups."

"So there's no doubt someone purposely killed her."

"Using my mead." His head dropped even lower.

I put my hand on his knee. "Roman."

He looked up at me.

"Someone intentionally did this awful thing. There's nothing for you to feel guilty about," I assured him.

"It's hard to think that something I love and spend my life on could kill someone."

"I know. I'm sorry."

"Thanks, Willa." He put his hand on top of mine and squeezed.

"Are we opening or what?" Gia appeared at the sliding

barn door with meadery keys in her hand and an attitude the moment she saw me. Her lips pressed together
tightly, matching the severity of her hairstyle, pulled back
into a ponytail, not a strand escaping. She was still going
through her workdays in sky-high heels and tight skirts
above the knee, as she'd done when she'd worked at Apricot Grille. She continued to hold a grudge against me
for suspecting her former restaurant manager boyfriend of
murder. It made it easier for her to have a new reason to
also dislike me—Roman.

I brought my hand back to my own lap.

"You can open. I'll be up front shortly," Roman said
to her.

She didn't try to hide her displeasure at seeing us
together. I smiled at her but got nothing in return. She
turned and stomped away, her heels clacking on the
poured concrete floor.

After she'd walked off, he said, "I want to help you find
who did this."

"How do you know I'm going to get involved?"

He looked at me the way Heath did when I'm being
predictable. "I figured you'd want to know who murdered your friend. And if it was one of your other Church
Cheese Shop friends who did it."

Of course, he was right. "What did Heath ask you?"

"He wanted to know what happened when they came
to the meadery yesterday."

"They were at my shop first. It was Freddie who
seemed adamant about buying mead."

"All three of them were excited about it. I did a little
impromptu tasting, seeing as they said they were old
friends of yours."

"Not friends, exactly. Former colleagues, more like it."

"Well, your old colleagues enjoyed it and bought a

bottle to have right away and the guy, Freddie, got a case to bring home."

"A case?"

"Yeah, I delivered it to the inn myself," he said.

"So they had plenty of mead, enough that one bottle gone missing wouldn't be noticed?" I considered.

He stood from the couch, frustration kicking in, causing him to pace. "I sold to a lot of new customers in the last couple of days. Most of them seemed to be from that cheese event. It could've been anyone who put mead in their cups."

"Only those who knew she had a honey allergy. Do you remember any strange or suspicious customers?"

"Strange? Probably. Suspicious? No."

"How about Maxine or Hugo? Did they buy any?"

"I don't know who they are."

"Of course, you wouldn't." I shook my head at my blunder. "They weren't hanging out with Freddie, Pepper, and Claire, but they know them."

Roman stopped pacing. "Now that you mention it, there *was* a woman who came in that they knew. She was really fit, short hair, around forty maybe?"

"That's Maxine! What was the vibe between her and the others like?"

Roman thought for a moment. "They said hi to one another, but it was more like a polite hello. But then they asked her if she was sticking around because they wanted to talk to her about something later."

I nodded in understanding. "Her father, Max, owned the cheese shop where they work and where I used to work. My former colleagues had plans for it, but they just found out that Maxine inherited it."

"What happened to Max?"

"He had a terminal illness, but he died in a car accident.

He'd apparently implied that he was leaving the secret of his cheese to Kendall, who was going to share it with Claire, Pepper, and Freddie."

"What do you mean, the secret?" He returned to his seat next to me on the couch.

"Where it's made and aged, and its recipe. Max was a bit eccentric, and the secrecy surrounding his cheese made it all the more talked about and valuable."

"So one of them killed Kendall after she shared the secret with them?"

"Well, they had the reading of Max's will yesterday morning and none of them inherited the secret. At least that's what they say. Kendall may have."

"You mean she may have inherited the secret secretly?" His lips tweaked upward, showing off the dimple in his left cheek that wasn't hidden by his close-shaven beard.

"Okay, make fun, but I think that's exactly what happened. Max liked to play games. He might've given her the information ahead of time, knowing he was dying. She hadn't been as honest with me as I'd thought she was."

"What about?"

"She snuck into my apartment and stole a book Max had given me when I left his shop, and I don't know why." I was still so perplexed and disappointed by it. "But if Kendall did know Max's secret, Claire, Pepper, and Freddie aren't the only ones who had motive to find out what it was and then kill her, so they'd be the only one with the information. Hugo hasn't tried to hide how much he wants the secret to the cheese."

"Who's Hugo?"

"The president of the board of the NWCS—the cheese society that runs the event they're having at the conference center. If he owned the premiere cheese, it would elevate his status within the cheese community and lock him in as president of the board for the fore-seeable future."

"I'm trying to keep this all straight, but I don't get why Max's daughter—what's her name? Maxine?—wouldn't have inherited her father's cheese. Why does everyone think Kendall has it?"

"Max and Maxine had been estranged for practically her whole adult life. And you have to understand how Max felt about this cheese. He would never leave it in someone's care who didn't appreciate what went into making it. Maxine knows nothing about cheese. She says she doesn't even care about it, but that's unlikely. The Church Bleu is worth a lot of money. Nobody's taken off to claim it, so if one of them killed Kendall to find out where the cheese is made and aged, they didn't get their answer." Another thought occurred to me. "Unless the one who did get it is pretending not to know, so there's no suspicion on them."

"Wow. They all have motive."

"Looks like it. And opportunity. They were all at the park." I thought about the farmer's market. "And so was a guy who'd been keeping his eye on Kendall. It makes me wonder if *he* had something to do with it."

"What can I do to help us figure this out?" Roman said.

"Let me think about it and let you know. Right now, I've got to get back to the shop, and it sounds like you've got customers." Voices emanated from the other room of the meadery.

We took ourselves off the couch, and he accompanied me through the tasting room to the front door. I could al-most feel Gia's stare burning through me like a laser.

Roman opened the door for me and leaned in close. "I mean it, Willa. I want in on this."

I nodded. "I'll be in touch."

I walked back to my shop with another reason to solve this murder.

CHAPTER 12

The street and sidewalks bustled with people now that all the shops were open. The first customers were already in Curds & Whey. I put on my apron, and we worked in an easy rhythm as customers streamed in and out. It was a couple of hours before we had a lull, but as soon as we did, Archie and Mrs. Schultz asked about Roman.

"Heath confirmed there was mead in the cups, so Roman's pretty upset about it. He wants to help us investigate. I don't blame him for wanting to be involved in helping solve this. Are you two okay with that?"

"Sure. Why not?" Archie said.

"We're fine with it, but will you be okay working closely with him on this?" Mrs. Schultz asked me. She had witnessed my freak-out about even calling him just yesterday.

I hadn't thought about how it might affect me. Even though I knew that Roman and I weren't right for each other, I still missed him. Keeping my distance made that hurt lessen. We'd been flirty friends before we started dating—there had always been a possibility of more between us. I wasn't quite sure how to get back to the friendship without the flirty chemistry.

"Maybe this is a good way to see if we can be friends," I decided.

Everett walked into Curds & Whey. "Hey, neighbors!"

We all said hello. Everett was out of this morning's cycling attire and wore shorts and a T-shirt with The Kick Stand logo on it. I noticed his dog, George, sat dutifully outside the open door of Curds & Whey, sniffing Guernsey. Archie went outside to pet him.

"What brings you by? Did you get a hankering for blue cheese?" I offered up a cracker with the spread.

He accepted it. "I won't refuse, but that's not why I'm here. I came by to see if we could talk sometime about partnering up." He popped the blue-cheese-smothered cracker in his mouth and nodded in satisfaction.

"Partnering up?" I asked.

"Our businesses. Ginger's been baking some healthy treats for me to sell to my customers, and we sell out every day. People renting and riding bikes like to have nourishment. So I'd like to propose that I start selling a small box of snacks that include cheeses. Of course, that's where you'd come in. I've floated the idea to my bike rental customers, and they said they'd be interested in something like that."

"That's a great idea. Sure. When should we meet to talk about it?" We both took out our phones and chose a time tomorrow, the day our shops were closed.

"That was awful what happened at the park yesterday, wasn't it?" Everett said after we'd put the meeting into our respective calendars. "And now I hear they're saying it was murder?"

"Yeah," I replied.

"The young woman who died was an old friend of Willa's," Mrs. Schultz told Everett.

"Oh, gosh. I didn't know that. I'm sorry. Anything I can do?" he offered.

"Did you happen to see anything suspicious while you were there yesterday?" I asked.

"Can't say I did. I only knew something was going on when the paramedics pulled into the parking lot. Sorry I'm not any help."

"That's okay. Did you have a fun ride this morning?"

He smiled. "Ah, you heard me say hello when I zoomed by! I was getting an early morning ride in. It was a little more than I'd bargained for. My biking partner was going full throttle."

"Was that Ginger with you?" I recalled thinking it might've been a woman on the bike next to his.

"No, it was a woman here for the cheese invitational. Maybe you know her? Maxine Dumas."

"I do," I said, leaving out that she was one of the murder suspects.

"I should know better than to bike with a professional cyclist."

"I didn't know that about her. I just met her yesterday. I used to work for her father up in Ashland, Oregon, before I moved here."

"She mentioned that her dad was being honored at the invitational. I didn't realize you knew him. Small world."

"I only got a chance to speak with her briefly. I would've liked to have gotten to know her better."

"We mostly talked about biking. She said she had to stick around for a couple of days, so she wanted to ride while she was here. I gave her a discount on her rental so she can ride whenever she wants this weekend."

"A professional cyclist. That's interesting. She's probably traveled the world." It must be why she said she "bounced all over" and didn't live near her father.

"Yeah, I'm totally jealous about it—getting to spend your life biking. Although I'm sure it's a lot harder than it sounds. I don't know if I'd have the discipline for it."

"Your bicycle shop's the next best thing," Mrs. Schultz said.

"*Your* bike's very pretty, Mrs. Schultz." Everett looked through the window at her pristine cherry red retro cruiser with a white flower-appliqued basket attached to the long handlebars. "My customers always comment on it when you're parked there."

"My pride and joy. She might need a tune-up soon," Mrs. Schultz replied.

"Bring her by any time." Everett turned to Archie, who was sitting with George by the doorway. "What about you, Archie? Are you still thinking of getting a bike?"

When Archie knew he wanted to move out on his own, he'd considered a bike for transportation. He rubbed the dirt off his shorts as he stood and joined us in the shop. "Not since I've been living at Hope's. I kinda miss the excuse to skateboard, though."

"I take George out for a run every day after work. You want to come by on your skateboard later and join us?"

"That'd be awesome!" Archie said.

"I better get back. See you later, Archie." Everett walked out with a wave, and a happy George followed him back to his shop.

"You want to take lunch first today? I'm not hungry yet," Mrs. Schultz said. I could see she was still pampering me after yesterday.

"Are you hungry, Archie?" I asked.

"Nah, I'm good. I had two bagels and a cinnamon roll this morning before I left Hope's," Archie said, patting his stomach. His beanpole physique made it hard to believe he could put down that much food at once.

"That might explain why you've been crashing in the afternoon," Mrs. Schultz said. "Sugar and carbs will do it every time."

And getting up at the crack of dawn. I kept the thought to myself. Not surprisingly, it seemed Hope was a little in over her head at the bakery. It was understandable. She hadn't been very interested in learning the ropes until she was the bakery's legal owner at twenty-one, which hadn't served her well. And now with her focus on learning to make fancy cakes, it seemed she was relying on others to keep the long-standing bakery afloat. I admired all Hope was trying to accomplish, but I hoped she wasn't taking advantage of Archie. I didn't want his own dreams of being a cheesemonger thwarted by this new relationship.

I removed my apron. "I forgot to check my post office box yesterday with all that went on, so I'll do that now and then grab some lunch. Text me if anything comes up here."

"Will mooo," Archie said.

Mrs. Schultz and I threw him a weary look.

"It doesn't work so well without the costume, huh?" he said.

I chuckled. "I'll be back shortly."

"No worries," Archie called after me.

No worries—if only I could be more like Archie.

CHAPTER 13

The post office was between the library on the corner and Ron's Old-Fashioned Service Station, where my CRV went in for its needed oil changes and tune-ups and I could count on Ron's guys not to try to sell me on any unnecessary repairs. Plus, I could get one of those curvy glass bottles of Coca Cola for a dollar from their machine. That sounded like it would hit the spot right about now—the day was heating up. After crossing Main Street, I ran into Claire, Pepper, and Freddie on the corner.

"Hey guys. How are you doing?" I asked.

"Ask us in an hour. We're off to be interrogated again by Detective Heath," Freddie said.

"Really?"

"We heard they think Kendall was murdered." Claire's eyes looked red, as if she'd been crying.

"I heard. I know, it's awful," I said.

"Who would do that to her?" Claire implored.

"The police must think *we* would," Pepper said, ever the realist.

"I don't like this." Without napkins to shred, Claire wrung her hands.

"Don't be nervous. The police may have discovered some more information the detective wants to ask you about. I bet you'll be a big help in solving this case," I said, trying to reassure them they were witnesses, not suspects.

"Why isn't Hugo being questioned? And what about Maxine?" The pitch of Claire's voice heightened to near hysteria.

"Maybe that's what this is about. They've got dirt on Maxine they want us to confirm," Pepper said.

They looked a lot brighter at the theory, even Claire.

"Let's go see the hot detective then," Freddie said, slicking his hair back with his hands.

"Let me know how it goes," I said to them.

I watched them walk off to the security complex. If they were going to be tied up at the station, maybe it was a good time to go to the inn and ask about the case of mead that was delivered there yesterday. I hoped Constance would be working since we had the best rapport. Plus, she had a good eye for what was going on around the inn.

I decided to forego the post office for now and instead crossed the street and walked up Pleasant Avenue to the inn, where I was relieved to see Constance at the reception desk.

"Willa, hi!" Constance always had a bright welcome.

"Hi Constance. I'm glad you're here. I'm hoping you can help me with something."

Her eyes lit up. With others, I usually had to conceal my investigatory questions, but with Constance, it was the opposite. She loved being in the middle of the action and spilling the tea.

"Roman told me he delivered a case of mead here yesterday," I told her.

"That's right. I had to wait for Del to come take it to Freddie and Pepper's room," she said. I was familiar with Del, The Cellar's bartender.

"Where was it kept before then?" I asked.

"On the floor right here next to the reception desk."

"So other people could've seen it?" I wondered if seeing the case of mead had given Maxine or Hugo a deadly idea.

"Sure. I'd have been tripping over it if he'd put it behind the desk with me." She leaned in and whispered, "Is the case of mead involved in the *murder*?" Her lips pulled back in a *yikes* expression.

"No, I don't think so." I shrugged off my recent questions, as if the mead meant nothing. The police never publicly said it was Roman's mead that caused Kendall's death, since they didn't have anything to prove it. Although there was already talk of it, thanks to the Church Cheese Shop group, I didn't want to be the one giving more life to it. It did make me wonder if a bottle could've been stolen before it made it to Freddie's room. It would eliminate the paper trail of buying a bottle from the meadery, but it would also be riskier.

"It's creeping me out to think one of our cheese guests might be a murderer." Constance mouthed *murderer* even though she was already speaking in a whisper.

"Let me know if you hear any chatter about it, but try not to say too much to anyone." I knew that was a tall order to ask of Constance.

"Ears open, mouth closed. Got it." She closed an imaginary zipper on her lips and threw away the key.

I said goodbye to Constance, glad to have the assistance of her eyes and ears.

I began walking out of the inn, still thinking about the mead, when I noticed Hugo hunkered in a wing chair with his laptop. What was he up to? He was so focused he didn't even notice me come up behind him. I glanced at his computer screen to see what was keeping his attention. He was scrolling through a list of names and phone numbers.

He suddenly noticed me and snapped the laptop shut before I could get a good look.

"What are you doing?" he barked.

"I came over to say hi. You were pretty immersed in what *you're* doing."

"Oh, sorry."

"I thought you'd be at the invitational."

He waved the idea away. "I don't have the stomach for it after yesterday."

I nodded, my stomach churning every time I thought about yesterday at the park. "What happened to Kendall was horrible."

"Yeah, that too."

"*Too*? What else?"

"The will reading! Not inheriting Max's cheese has got me all spun around. I'm spending almost every minute trying to figure out who he left it to."

I crossed my arms and stared at him. "You're really broken up about her death, I see," I said sarcastically.

He sighed and splayed his hands in front of me as a mea culpa. "I feel bad for her. She was a nice girl, as far as I knew. But there's nothing I can do about it and if I don't start trying to figure out what Kendall knew, the others will beat me to it. Don't let their tears fool you. They're thinking about Max's cheese as much as I am."

I sat on the sofa across from him. "Why do you think Kendall knew something even if Max didn't bequeath the cheese to her in his will?"

"Because he liked to play games like that. What did she tell you?"

"Nothing."

"Come on, Willa. You owe me. If it wasn't for you, I

would've followed her out of your shop yesterday and gotten some answers. You must know something. Were you and Kendall conspiring together?"

"I have no desire to have the secrets of the Church Bleu," I said honestly.

"I'm not sure I believe that. That cheese put Max and his shop on the map."

"And I was happy for Max, but I saw all the hassles that came with that when I worked for him. I'm not Max."

"So then help me out. I'll give you a cut if I find it. It's not about the money, Willa. Do you know what kind of notoriety this would earn me, to be the conservator of the Church Bleu? NWCS would be the premiere cheese society in the country, and it would be all because of me." He leaned over his laptop and lowered his voice. "I'm in hot water after the fiasco with Maxine on Friday. The board wants to call a special meeting when the invitational wraps up tomorrow. They were itching to replace me before then and now they've got their excuse. So what if I've had the longest tenure? That just means I'm best at what I do. If I can find out where Max's cheese was made and aged before they hold their meeting, I can prove to them I still deserve to be president. Tell me what Kendall told you."

"I'd like to help you out, Hugo." *Not.* "But she didn't tell me anything."

He growled his dissatisfaction with my response. "Maxine's not giving up any information either. She's the one who got me into this bind." Hugo's face turned redder the more frustrated he became. "Darn Max and his games. He teased us with that will."

I thought back to what Freddie had let slip at The Cellar last night. "You mean the clue he left in it?"

"So Kendall *did* tell you."

"Not Kendall. You heard what was said at The Cellar last night. It was bound to get out."

"So Freddie and the gang spilled it all, did they? Great! Now they're telling everybody. So do they have any idea who Rebecca is?"

Rebecca? I went along with it. "Uh, no, they don't know."

"*Rebecca holds the answer* isn't any kind of clue unless you know who Rebecca is. She's the one Max left his secret to. If I can find her, I can convince her that I'm the one who should have it." He placed his laptop on the coffee table and stood. He stared into the cold fireplace. "Someone else has to know who Rebecca is."

Rebecca. An idea sparked to life, but my thoughts were interrupted by A. J. Stringer, the thirtyish editor of our free local newspaper, the *Glen Gazette*. His hand rested on the strap of the worn canvas messenger bag he wore across his torso over his ever-present green Salvation Army jacket, T-shirt, and faded jeans. As usual, his curly black hair was untamed.

A. J. had helped me gain some information about cases in the past, as long as he got information from me in return. Running a small-town paper like the *Glen Gazette*, he couldn't chance printing sensational headlines about Yarrow Glen's citizens being possible murder suspects during a case. However, the *Case Closed* feature articles he ran after a culprit was caught, detailing all aspects of the case, were popular among the residents and fed his appetite for investigative journalism. Now he was shooting for more and had started a weekly podcast documenting true crime cases in the northwest.

He nodded my way then said to Hugo, "I hoped I'd find you here. I'm dropping my latest podcast this afternoon and I thought you might want in on it."

"I told you I'm not doing it," Hugo said. He sat back down in his chair to prove his point.

"The people who worked for Max Dumas's cheese shop have already done it. That secret cheese has to be the reason that woman was killed. Don't you want to help solve Kendall's murder by telling us what you know about the Church Bleu?"

"I'm not giving up anything I know about that cheese. You think I want even more people after it?" Hugo's attention turned to Maxine descending the stairs.

"Maxine!" He sprung out of the chair to meet her.

Her whole face visibly tightened when she saw him, and she hustled past him out of the inn. He raced back, grabbed his laptop, and went after her.

I picked up the thoughts that had scattered when A. J. had walked in.

Rebecca holds the answer.

A. J. sat in Hugo's chair and leaned in. "What do you know, Willa? You weren't here with Hugo by accident."

"He inadvertently told me the clue left in Max's will," I said.

"There's a clue? The group on my podcast said how Max liked secrets and puzzles, but they didn't tell me about a clue in his will. So what's the clue?"

"Rebecca holds the answer," I said as I continued to work it out in my mind.

"Who's Rebecca?"

"She's not a woman. It's a book—*Rebecca*. I'm sure of it. You know, the classic novel by Daphne du Maurier? Max was clever putting a clue in a used book. Why would anyone think anything of it?"

"You gotta explain further. I'm a little lost," he said.

I thought back, putting the pieces together aloud. "I was telling Kendall about the book and then about

Read More Bookstore's sidewalk sale . . . That's how she must've made the connection that the name in Max's clue referred to the book. I bet it's got a riddle inside that would've made sense had I known what I was looking for."

"Wait a sec." He dug into his bag and brought out a small recording device. He turned it on, and the tiny red dot of light brightened. "Okay, start from the beginning."

I snapped myself out of my extrapolations. "Put it away, A. J. I have to figure out what this means for the case." Now I knew why Kendall stole my book. The police had a clue in their possession they weren't even aware of.

"We can do it together. As long as we do it quick. I gotta finish editing my podcast. I scrapped this week's planned episode so I could do this one. It'll be the talk of the town. I'm calling it 'Case of the Bleus.' Whaddya think?" He smiled at me, nodding, obviously very impressed with himself and wanting me to be impressed too.

"We'll talk later. I have to go." I had to talk to Heath.

A. J. was still calling after me as I left the inn.

CHAPTER 14

I left a disappointed A. J. at the inn as I headed for the police station. On the way, I called Mrs. Schultz to tell her I'd be delayed and to take turns with Archie for their lunch breaks. I hastened to the security complex and went straight to the police partition. I always managed to catch the same security guard at the desk. I thought of him as Bruce because of his bald pate and *Die Hard* demeanor. I asked him to call Detective Heath.

"He's in interviews right now," he said.

"I know, but this is important," I replied.

"I can give him a message."

"How about Officer Shepherd. Is he in?"

He called Shep, then buzzed me in through the locked door.

He walked me to the common area where officers were working at desks or taking complaint statements. I recognized Shep's buzz cut peeking over the back of a computer screen. Bruce left me and I approached the desk.

Shep greeted me. "Take a seat." He gestured to the chair at the side of his desk. "What can I do for you?"

I sat down. "There's something I remembered about Kendall's death that I think is very important."

Shep gave me his full attention. "What is it?"

"There's a book that was in Kendall's purse when she died that I believe she stole from me that day."

"The contents of her purse is in evidence. I could make a report, but you wouldn't get it back until the case has been resolved, and maybe not even then if it's deemed material to the case."

"I'm not here to file a complaint. I think she stole the book because it might hold the secret to Max's cheese. If I'm right, it might be the reason she was murdered."

He shifted in his chair to fully face me. "When did you see this book?"

"It was with her pile of stuff that was dumped from her purse. It didn't really register at the time because I was searching for her EpiPen. But thinking back, I'm almost certain it was my book in that pile."

Shep still looked confused about how it might relate to her death, so I explained from the beginning, including how she'd snuck into my apartment. "It could mean she *did* know the secret to the cheese, and she may have told someone who wanted it all for themselves," I finished.

He turned to his computer and hit some keys. "I have the list of potential evidence here."

I swung around to look at it and he put his hand up. "Not for your eyes."

I sat back and tried to be patient while he looked it over.

He slowly shook his head. "There's no book listed here."

"Are you sure?" I pushed forward and was denied again.

I saw him scanning the screen again. "Sorry, no book."

"I know it was there. I bet someone took it in the commotion. The only people who might've suspected it was important are the ones who were at the will reading and heard Max's clue—*Rebecca holds the answer.*"

"You're certain it was your book?"

I thought about it again. "Yes. I'm certain it was *Rebecca*. Kendall must've put two and two together after I told her Max had given me the book, so she took it. She might've confided in someone that there was a clue in it, and then they killed her to get the book."

"Or someone saw the book on the picnic blanket and made the connection on the spot—just like you did—that *Rebecca* wasn't a person, but a book," Shep said.

"I didn't think of that. So whoever took it might not even have known Kendall had it before that moment. If they just saw the opportunity and took it, it means they might not be the killer."

Shep was quiet for a moment. "If that book has the answer everyone's looking for, then whoever has it could either be the killer or the next to be killed."

I rubbed my arms to chase away the goose bumps.

Shep had me add the book to my formal statement and promised he'd tell Heath about it.

I left the police station wondering who had *Rebecca*. I'd read it a year ago, after Max had given it to me, and opened it again when I came across it just a couple of weeks ago. There was a short note that didn't strike me as odd, but I wasn't trying to read anything into it at the time. Thinking about it now, I couldn't remember the exact wording, but it still seemed innocuous. Maybe there was more to it.

I was so preoccupied thinking about the book that I passed the post office and had to backtrack to check my mailbox. The post office boxes were in the first room just beyond the entrance to the small flat-roofed building, accessible even when the post office was closed for business. My growling stomach reminded me I still needed to grab lunch. I turned my attention to what kind of tacos I'd get at the Let's Talk Tacos truck when I pulled out the mail tucked between a folded eight-by-ten mailer envelope that was stuffed into my box.

"Interesting mail today, Willa?" Beatrice, who ran the consignment thrift store, was suddenly at my shoulder. She was in her late sixties, by my estimation, and had a fantastic wardrobe of vintage pieces. Today she wore a tank top under baggy, soft-denim overalls, embroidered with flowers on the wide legs. She paired it with red high-tops. Her ever-present blue-framed spectacles hung on a bejeweled chain around her neck.

"Hi, Beatrice. I doubt it's anything interesting." I shuffled through the mail, most of them junk-mail flyers that I'd deposit in the blue recycle bin on my way out.

"No return address on that big one. That's curious," she said, craning her neck forward. I noticed that she'd put her glasses on and was looking down her nose through them to get a better look at my mail.

"It's probably something from a vendor. Have a good day." She'd have to get her curiosity satiated by someone else's mail today.

She offered a strained smile of defeat and turned the key into her own mailbox. "Ta-ta."

I had to admit, Beatrice was right—it was a bit curious, so I opened it as soon as I left the post office. Inside the larger envelope was a business-sized envelope with the name and address of an Oregon attorney's office. Now I was even more intrigued. I ripped it open.

I pulled out a handwritten letter on a single page that began:

Willa,

This is for your eyes only. Don't tell anyone about this letter.

I skipped to the bottom of the page to see who it was

from. It was signed by Max. *Max!* I pressed the letter to my chest and looked around me. Liz, a server at The Cellar, said hi as she and a friend walked by. I returned the greeting, hoping there was no indication that my heart was beating out of my chest. As soon as they passed, I folded up the letter and stuffed it back into the envelope. I couldn't read this on the sidewalk in public. I needed to get back to Curds & Whey.

CHAPTER 15

I forgot about lunch and power walked the block and a half down to Curds & Whey. Archie was behind the counter describing the lingering bitter notes that kept you coming back for more of Curát de búfala, a hard buffalo-milk cheese we'd recently gotten from Barcelona. Mrs. Schultz was wiping down the sampling counter. I slipped the letter behind the counter and stuck my apron on.

"Are you okay?" Mrs. Schultz whispered to me. "You look a little red in the face."

"I was in a hurry to get back," I answered nonchalantly. I didn't want to get into it with a customer in the shop.

The older gentleman was sold on the Curát de búfala. Archie cut and weighed it and rang up the purchase. The man thanked Archie on the way out, leaving the shop empty of customers.

"You two have to take a look at this." I retrieved the envelope. "It's a letter from Max."

"From the great beyond?" Archie's eyes widened.

"From his attorney. Max must've written it and told him to send it to me upon his death. I only started to read it. He said not to show it to anyone, but I'm sure that doesn't mean you two."

They stood on either side of me as I unfolded it and we read it together.

Dear Willa,

This is for your eyes only. Please don't show this letter to anyone.

I didn't invite you to the reading of the will because I didn't want the others to know that you are the recipient of my Church Bleu secrets. I love all my employees equally, but I know that you're the only one who truly understands what this cheese means to me. Just in case this letter gets into the wrong hands, I have left you clues. If you can figure them out, you'll know the location of my Church Bleu and my final wishes. I instructed everyone to be together in Yarrow Glen for the reading of my will in hopes that you discover from them the first clue, which my attorney communicated to the others. However, only you will understand its meaning, since I gave you possession of the answer the day you left my Church Cheese Shop. Start there.

Max

"I knew it," I said under my breath.

"You knew what?" Archie asked.

"It all clicked into place after Hugo told me the clue in Max's will when I saw him at the inn. *Rebecca has the answer.* One of the things I saw when Kendall's purse was dumped out on the picnic blanket was a book. I didn't pay any attention to it until Baz told me Kendall had been in my apartment and I realized my copy of *Rebecca* that Max had given me was missing. It was then I realized the book I'd seen from her purse must've been mine, but

I couldn't understand why she would take it. Now that I know the clue they all got from Max's will—*Rebecca has the answer*—it all makes sense. Kendall had figured it out first. *Rebecca* is the book Max gave me, not a person. There must be a clue to where the Church Bleu is inside of it."

Archie pointed to the bottom of the paper where Max had carefully written a list of numbers. "Do you think these are the page numbers where he put the clues?"

"They must be. If only I still had that book." I sighed in frustration.

"Where is it now? Who picked up everything from her purse?" Mrs. Schultz asked.

"The police took everything, but I talked to Shep and it's not in evidence with her other things."

"What does that mean?" Archie asked.

"Someone must've taken it in the commotion before the police came," I said.

Mrs. Schultz began to rub her scarf again. "That means someone else knew the book was important."

"And someone else has the clues we need," Archie added.

"It doesn't seem like they'd be able to do anything with the book without these numbers, but I can't be sure they couldn't figure it out on their own until I see what's in the book," I said. I gnawed on my lower lip while I tried to figure out a way to get the book back.

"Who do you think took it?" Mrs. Schultz asked.

"I'm fairly sure Hugo didn't. He was still trying to find a woman named Rebecca when I saw him at the inn and he hounded me relentlessly for any information I might have. The book was taken from the picnic blanket, so someone had to have known from Kendall that there was a clue in it, or they figured it out on the spot." My hands balled into fists in frustration. "We can't do anything without the book!"

"Does it have to be *your* book? Maybe we could figure it out just by looking at any paperback *Rebecca* if the page numbers match up," Archie said.

"That's a great idea," I said, feeling hopeful.

"Ask Sharice. She might have a copy," Mrs. Schultz suggested.

"What would I do without you two?"

"That's what Team Cheese is all about. You should go check with Sharice right now," Archie said.

He was right. Getting a copy of *Rebecca* was the key to solving Max's clues and possibly Kendall's murder.

CHAPTER 16

I dispensed with my apron once again and took a right outside the shop on my way to Read More Bookstore and Café. Past Carl's Hardware, under the green awning of Lou's Market, I saw a strapping man with dark hair wearing a collared shirt and sea blue shorts—comparably preppy to yesterday's outfit. It was the Henry Cavill lookalike! He entered the market. I needed that book, but this was my chance to see who this guy was and if he could have anything to do with Kendall's murder. I hurried my pace and took a detour into Lou's.

I didn't see him when I entered. I hurriedly scanned the produce section, which was closest to the door. The narrow aisle of fruits and vegetables was made more crowded by a sale display of oranges in the center. Lou's teenage protégé, Trace, in his green market apron, came through the swinging door in the back, wheeling a produce-stocking cart of more oranges. He navigated the cart around crates of avocados and tomatoes to get to the sale display.

"Hi Willa. Can I help you find something?" he asked when I approached him.

"Hi Trace. Did you see a guy just come in here—dark-haired, cleft chin, looks like Superman?"

"You mean with a cape?"

"No, a white button-down shirt and blue shorts. A tall, good-looking dude who's not from around here."

"I don't think so. Did he do something wrong?"

"Maybe. He hasn't stuck around long enough to find out—he keeps eluding me. I'm going to look down the aisles. If you see a guy who fits that description, try to keep him here until I come back around."

"Okay. I'll keep a lookout."

"Thanks."

I stopped at each of the five aisles but didn't see him. I quickly walked to the back of the store near the refrigerated cases. He wasn't there either. It was like he'd vanished.

I had to get to the bookstore, so I gave up and decided to let Trace know I was leaving, when there Superman was, in the produce aisle, choosing an apple.

"There you are," I said, not meaning to say it aloud.

He looked at me, then immediately put down the apple and hurried away from me toward the exit.

"Wait! I need to talk to you!" I yelled.

Suddenly, Trace crossed in front of him with his cart of oranges and blocked his path. The man tried to deftly juke around the cart, but instead, ran into the pyramid of oranges on the lone display, sending the fruit toppling down and rolling across the floor.

"Are you okay, sir?" Trace said to him, keeping his cart firmly in place.

I caught up to them. "Why are you running from me?" I asked the stranger.

He straightened and stepped away from the display, almost tripping over an orange. "Why are you running *after* me?"

"Because you've been stalking my friend and now

she's dead." *Oof. Maybe I could've handled that more delicately.*

Lou came over from the register. "Trace! What's going on?"

"It was my fault, Lou," I said, as Trace began picking up the oranges.

"How is this your fault?" he grumbled.

"I'll explain later. Right now, I think *this* guy's got some explaining to do."

"I just came in to buy a snack. Listen, I'm very sorry to hear about your friend's death but I have no involvement in that. I certainly haven't been stalking anybody," the man said.

What did I expect him to say? I really should've thought through how I would handle this when I eventually caught up to him.

"Was she the one who died in the park yesterday?" Trace asked.

"Yes." I turned back to the man. "And I saw you talking to her before it happened. Who are you, and what are you doing in Yarrow Glen?"

He seemed to assess the situation—Lou, Trace, and I all staring at him. We'd caught the attention of several shoppers too. There was no sneaking away this time.

"Do you mind if we step outside and talk privately?" he asked me.

"Not at all," I answered.

Trace pulled the cart away, allowing us to pass. I smiled my thanks to Trace as I followed the man out the door. We walked to the corner of the sidewalk by the alley where we wouldn't be in anyone's way. He looked around and seemed to be stalling.

"So?" I said, staring up at him. My gosh, he was even better looking up close. That cleft in his chin was virtually a crevasse. But good-looking people could be murderers too.

"If I'm going to tell you who I am, you should tell me who you are," he said.

"I'm Willa Bauer. I live here in Yarrow Glen. Your turn."

He glanced at his boat shoes with a slight grin, seeming to take my response in stride. "My name is Nathan Parker. I'm a freelance feature writer for magazines."

"So you're here to write about Max Dumas's Church Bleu?" If he was writing about Max's cheese, that meant he'd done his research and knew how valuable the cheese was. That could be a motive for him to go after Kendall.

"The cheese? That's an interesting story, but everybody's on that one. No, I'm here for *All Things Sonoma* magazine to write a feature on Yarrow Glen from a tourist's perspective. I was trying to keep on the down-low so business owners wouldn't know I'm writing a story on them, and I could portray a more realistic viewpoint."

"Oh." *Uh-oh.*

"If I was talking to your friend, which I don't recall, it was only for the magazine piece."

I swallowed, the bad taste in my mouth lingering from jumping to such a bad conclusion. "I'm really sorry. Please don't hold this against the town. It's a very welcoming place . . . usually. I thought you'd been stalking her."

"You'd know a thing or two about stalking," he quipped.

"Touché."

He softened. "Your friend died. I can see why you might not be yourself."

"That's very understanding of you. Is there anything you need while you're in town? I'm happy to help."

"If you could keep this to yourself, I'd appreciate it. I'd like to continue to be incognito."

"My lips are sealed. Promise." I pretended to close a zipper on my lips, as Constance had done earlier.

"Thanks. Have a good day, Willa Bauer."

"You too."

He nodded and crossed the street, probably just to get away from me.

Ugh. I continued to strike out with the people who worked for that magazine. First it was Guy Lippinger, the critic who'd wanted to give me a terrible review for no reason and ended up dead outside my shop. Then it was Marcos, their photographer, who I'd butted heads with during the last investigation, and now Nathan Parker. I wish I hadn't told him my name. At least I didn't tell him I owned Curds & Whey. This was the first time I hoped somebody *wouldn't* visit my shop.

I couldn't jump to conclusions anymore. I had to follow this case methodically, piece by piece, just like Max's puzzle.

CHAPTER 17

After returning to Lou's to help Trace with the oranges, I went next door to Read More Bookstore, where several tables lined the length of the storefront, pushed up against the picture windows. Donated boxes of used books, spines out, covered the tabletops. I looked over the shoulders of the people browsing the books. I scanned the spines myself, but soon realized it would take quite a bit of time to look through all the boxes. I'd already been gone long enough from the shop. Maybe Sharice would know if the store had a copy.

I entered the bookstore, anxious to find Sharice and *Rebecca*. Sharice was an illustration artist who had opened Read More to supplement her income and used the apartment above it as her studio space. It explained why the store exuded a fantastical quality, from the painted checkerboard floor to the ceiling light fixtures with drum shades made to look like classic book covers.

I recognized Sharice from the back, her neat cornrows leading to a terrific explosion of hair and her colorful geometric leggings under a long T-shirt giving her away. She was bent over the end of one of the narrow aisles creating a knee-high stack of hardbacks, a necessity since the shelves were overfilled with books.

"Hi, Sharice," I said.

Sharice turned her attention from the books, her brown eyes indicating concern behind cat-eye glasses when she saw me. She straightened and put her free hand on my arm. "Willa. How are you doing? I heard the woman who died at the park was an old friend of yours. I'm so sorry."

"Thanks. Yeah, we worked together before I moved here."

"What a horrible thing to happen. She was in yesterday not long before she died. I recognized her afterward from the photos in the paper this morning."

"What a difference a day makes. I can still hardly believe it." I sighed.

"What can I do for you?" she asked.

"I'm wondering if you could point me in the right direction of a certain book. A paperback of *Rebecca* by Daphne du Maurier."

She switched the load of books to her other arm. "That was the one your friend was asking about too. Were you two in a book club together? She was pretty intense about it, so I was glad to be able to find one."

"She bought one from here?" *Then why did she take the one from my apartment?*

"Yeah. I spent quite some time looking for it when I should've just asked Dante. When we were talking about her this morning, he said he'd put a copy of *Rebecca* on our Lending Shelf in the café just the morning before. It was too marked up to sell."

"Did it have a note on the first page?" I attempted to contain my excitement.

"I'm not sure. I haven't looked at it."

"So she bought a different copy than the one that was marked up?"

"Mm-hmm." Sharice nodded.

"Do you still have the one on the Lending Shelf?"

She shrugged. "It might still be there."

"Thanks, Sharice. Talk to you later."

I hurried over to the café, which was cleverly hidden behind a chest-high hinged bookshelf that was propped open during café hours. I went straight to the Lending Shelf, which consisted of two rows of used books café goers could read for free. If they wanted to finish it at home, they could take it, with the agreement that they'd eventually return it or swap it out for another book.

The book's purple spine immediately stuck out from the rows of paperbacks. *Rebecca!* My fingers fumbled to get it off the shelf and into my hot little hands. I opened it to find Max's note to me scrawled across the title page. Relief coursed through me. I'd mentioned my donation of books to Kendall, so she must've come here to look after coming up empty at my apartment. Maybe she was banking on the fact that we'd donated it to Sharice. The book I saw that had fallen out of her purse at the park must've not been my book after all. It was another copy of *Rebecca*. I had no idea how my copy had gotten mixed up with the donation books, and it felt like a miracle I'd gotten it back.

Gemma and Daisy Melon waved me over from one of the comfy seating arrangements. In their mid-eighties and widowed three times over between the two of them, the Melon sisters were always seen together. Daisy's stories tended to wander, but both were much sharper than they let on, and were instrumental in helping to solve two police cases last winter. With their cotton candy–like hair and fashionable matching track suits in different colors, it would be hard to tell them apart if not for Daisy's ever-present flower somewhere on her person. This time she wore a daisy pin on the collar of her peach-colored zip sweatshirt. Two hot teas sat on the low table between them.

"Hello, ladies. How are you today?" I asked after heeding their summons.

"Lots of activity lately with all the people from the cheese show and Sharice's sidewalk sale," Daisy said.

"Not to mention what happened at the park yesterday," Gemma added.

"Why do people say 'not to mention' and then mention it?" Daisy asked. She pointed to an unoccupied wooden chair nearby and indicated for me to bring it over. I did and sat down with them.

"Poor girl. What do you know about it, Willa? You're our resident sleuth," Daisy said.

"Me? I think I have some competition in you two," I replied.

"We heard the girl was murdered." Daisy's eyes widened.

"Have you heard anything else?" I asked.

The elderly sisters also had good listening skills. As Mrs. Schultz had once pointed out, when you're a woman of a certain age, you become invisible to the public, which is only a plus for listening in on conversations.

Gemma reached for her tea. "We heard Roman's mead killed her."

"Her honey allergy killed her. There was nothing wrong with Roman's mead," I said emphatically. Roman didn't need *that* going around. No wonder he was itching to help me solve this case.

"We haven't heard much else, unfortunately," Daisy said with a sigh for the lack of gossip. She went back to sipping her tea.

"There *are* lots of strangers in town. We told Mayor Trumbull we didn't need that big convention center, didn't we, Daisy? Next thing you know, they'll build one of those huge hotels and put the inn right out of business," Gemma said.

"I don't think our mayor would ever approve such a thing. She knew the conference center would attract more out-of-towners to our shops," I explained.

"Are those the kind of customers you want?" Gemma peered at me from over her tea cup.

"Exactly! Customers who aren't aware that these are our seats for afternoon tea?" Daisy put in.

"I'm talking about possible murderers, Daisy. We'll be listening to A. J.'s crime podcast this afternoon. I bet *he'll* have some information." Gemma looked at her delicate silver watch. "It's coming up in a few minutes. We'd better get to the library. We listen on the library headphones," she said to me.

"Do you need a ride up there?" The library was at the corner, two blocks up. The Melon sisters were remarkably spry, but it would still be quite a walk for them, especially if they were in a hurry.

"No thank you, Willa. Lou said he'll take us," Daisy replied.

"Really?" *Grumpy Lou?*

"Well, Cyrus volunteered—the sweet man that he is— but he's not cleared to drive because of his heart condition, so he volunteered Lou."

Cyrus was Lou's father, who actually owned the market named after his son. Lou now ran the market after a heart attack slowed Cyrus down several years ago. He still made Lou drive him from his independent living community to work every day, and Daisy had a mad crush on him.

"We'd better get over there. Lou's been grumpier than usual lately," Gemma said.

"Any reason?" I had a feeling it might be because Mrs. Schultz hadn't been very receptive to his overtures.

"Does there have to be a reason when it comes to Lou?"

I agreed with a shrug.

I helped the sisters out of their comfortable chairs, and they left through the café door.

Ginger, Baz's former crush, was behind the counter whipping up coffee drinks and energy smoothies. I waved to her as I was hurrying out, colliding with someone in the process and dropping the paperback from my hands. It was Nathan Parker. His stunned expression followed by a panicked look matched my feelings—neither of us were happy to see each other. I swiftly picked up the book off the floor. "Sorry," I mumbled, avoiding his gaze further, and continued out of the store with my head down. I had hoped he'd forget me, and literally running into him sure didn't help.

I strode up the sidewalk gripping *Rebecca* to my chest. This book might keep us one step ahead of whoever wanted the clue it held enough to kill Kendall for it.

CHAPTER 18

Curds & Whey was busy when I walked in. Archie and Mrs. Schultz peeked at the book in my hands and flashed me excited smiles. I carefully hid it under the counter until we could look at it together.

My stomach rang the lunch bell again. It had been hours since I'd planned on eating, but the flow of customers didn't let up. Archie and Mrs. Schultz had taken turns to get in their lunch breaks and insisted I get something to eat. What could I whip up for sampling and steal some for myself?

The recipe I'd given to a customer yesterday for my easy Dolce Dip sounded like a good idea. In the kitchenette, I mixed sour cream, mayonnaise, and some leftover scallions from the tart Mrs. Schultz had made. I crumbled in some of the buttery-textured Gorgonzola Dolce, squeezed in a bit of lemon juice, and grinded fresh pepper into it. In lieu of hot wings, I chose some sturdy crackers and sliced into a loaf of crusty French bread that Archie had chosen from Rise and Shine bakery this morning. I set out the dip and accompaniments for customers, setting aside some for myself.

I hurriedly snacked on my tasty Dolce Dip, my thoughts still tumbling over the fact that Max sent me a letter. He said in the letter that he didn't have favorites, and yet the others insisted he was leaving it to his "favorite cheesemonger." Was that just a part of his game? It both warmed my heart to think he trusted me so much and gave me another pang of guilt in equal measure. I should've stayed in touch.

The shop was too busy to ruminate further, so I returned to the front until it emptied of customers, which wasn't until nearly closing time. Archie and Mrs. Schultz immediately huddled behind the counter with me as I took out the book.

"You found a *Rebecca* book," Archie said, eager to look inside.

"It turns out that this is the book Max gave me. It was accidentally donated with the others, which means Kendall didn't take mine after all."

"Sorry, Willa. That must be my fault," Archie said. "I remember there was a paperback sitting on top of the box of books I was bringing down to Read More, so I threw it in with the others without even looking at it."

"That's okay. It was my fault for being so careless with it in the first place. It meant a lot to me even before I knew it held this clue. I shouldn't have left it lying right on the box of books to be donated. Besides, if you hadn't accidentally donated it, Kendall would've found it in my apartment and we wouldn't know where it is," I said. I thought about that morning. "Kendall heard you talk about the book donations, so when she came up empty looking for *Rebecca* in my apartment, she must've gone right to Read More to see if it had been donated. Lucky for us, she bought another copy of *Rebecca* by mistake, probably thinking it was mine."

"And we've got your copy back now," Mrs. Schultz said, pleased at the outcome.

I unfolded the letter so we could see Max's list of numbers and opened the book. Although I didn't notice any clues in it at the time, the note Max had written on the title page held a new meaning now:

This book holds special significance to me, as do you, Willa. Keep it close to you.

Max

"Wow, he had this whole thing planned for over a year," Archie marveled.

"The opening gambit," I said, feeling Max's absence acutely.

"So do the page numbers correspond to something?" Archie had started to bounce on the balls of his feet again, demonstrating his excitement.

"Let's take a look."

We went to the first number on the list, page forty-two. The letter *E* was circled.

Archie scrambled to get a pen and wrote the letter down. We continued like this for all seventeen of the listed numbers.

EEHRISLEHETCEERST

"It doesn't spell anything," Archie's mouth screwed up in disappointment.

Mrs. Schultz squinted at the letters. "It must be a word scramble."

I looked at the wall clock. I was glad it was Sunday, when we closed an hour early. "It's time to close the shop. I'm locking up so we can figure this out." I took the keys and locked the front door, turning the sign to read CLOSED.

"This is going to be impossible if we don't know how

many words we're unscrambling," Archie said as I returned to the sampling counter.

Mrs. Schultz retrieved her reading glasses from her purse. "I always told my students to take a second look at the problem." She looked at the letters we'd written and then Max's list of numbers again. "It seems to me these numbers are grouped."

I looked at the list of numbers again. There was an extra space between some of them.

"You might be right! Maybe each group spells a word," I said.

We divided the letters on the page into the four groups the way Max had divided the corresponding page numbers.

EEHR ISLE HET CEERST

"The first word is *here*," Archie called out. "Here isle . . ."

"No, it's not *isle*. It's *lies*." I wrote them down.

"*The*," Archie offered for the third word. He tried to work out the longer word. "Trees . . . Street . . ."

"Secret," Mrs. Schultz said, solving it.

I filled in the sentence. "Here lies the secret," I read.

We high-fived and called out "Woo-hoo," but our excitement at solving the word scramble dissipated almost immediately.

"What does that mean? I thought the answer to the word scramble *was* the secret," Archie said.

"*Here lies the secret*. There must be more." I flipped through the book. "There are more letters circled."

Mrs. Schultz turned Max's letter over to see if we'd missed another clue. "There's nothing else on the paper."

A knock on the door startled us. I saw Baz's face

through the door's paned window. I unlocked it and let him in, locking it again behind him.

"I'm so glad you're here. We've got a lot to tell you," I said.

"I've got something to tell you too, and you're not gonna like it," he replied.

"Uh-oh. What?"

"I was just listening to A. J.'s podcast on my way home from a job. He had everybody from Church Cheese Shop on it."

"He told me he had them on today. What did they say?"

Baz took out his phone, which was already queued up to the podcast. "It's not what *they* said, it's what *he* said." He tapped play and A. J.'s voice sounded from the phone.

"I have an important addendum to today's topic," A. J. began. "I received information from a *very* reliable source that we have one hint where the secrets of the sought-after Church Bleu may be hidden: *Rebecca has the answer.* That was the only clue Max Church left his inner circle. *Rebecca has the answer.* This same very reliable source points to the possibility that Rebecca is not a *who* but a *what*. Here's another hint: it may be the kind of *what* that can be found in a place where you might *read more*." He emphasized the last two words.

I felt sucker punched. "That lowlife!"

"Stay tuned to next week's podcast for more true crime reports and interviews until we have a *Case Closed*," A. J. finished.

Baz turned off the podcast.

"How could he? He never divulges information until a case is over with." I was fuming.

"That was when he wrote the *Case Closed* articles. I think he's feeling a little bolder on the podcast, especially since the people involved aren't locals," Baz said.

"Sharice is a local and he might've put her in danger if the murderer figures out his stupid clue means Read More Bookstore. He's ruined everything! I've got to talk to him right now."

"We'll stay here and finish the closing duties," Mrs. Schultz offered.

I'd completely forgotten about our closing routine for the shop. "You don't have to do it on your own."

"We'll be sticking around anyway. We have to finish solving the clue," Archie said.

"The clue?" Baz looked to us for answers.

"The game is afoot," Mrs. Schultz said to Baz with dramatic flair.

"Fill Baz in while you close the shop. I'll be back shortly to make us some dinner," I said.

"I hope it's not A. J.'s head on a plate," Baz quipped.

"It just might be," I replied.

I stormed out of Curds & Whey and stomped all the way to the Gazette building on the west side of Main Street. The walk didn't do anything to dissipate my anger. If anything, the longer I thought about it, the angrier I became.

Except for the receptionist, the others at the *Gazette* didn't keep regular hours, so even though it was after five o'clock, I was fairly positive A. J. would still be in the building. I swung open the door and beat a path to the back stairwell.

My mind briefly registered Deandra's voice calling, "Hi, Willa," from her cubicle. I climbed the stairs and entered the second-story closed loft where A. J.'s office was. He was at his desk, feet up, with a satisfied grin on his face, which disappeared as soon as he saw me. I slammed the door closed behind me.

"How dare you!" I yelled.

He threw his legs to the floor and sat up. "What's the matter?"

"What's the matter? I just listened to your podcast!"

"Don't be mad that I didn't share some of that information with you first. You left me high and dry at the inn. It was good, wasn't it?" His wide grin returned.

"I'm talking about the information you got from me. The *confidential* information you got from me about the clue and the book."

"Was that confidential? You didn't specify."

"Are you kidding me? Everything we say to each other about a case is confidential. I thought we had an understanding. I didn't even mean to tell you any of that. I was just working it out in my head."

"Oh. Sorry then." He shrugged as if that made it all right.

"It's too late to be sorry. You could be putting Sharice in danger if anyone thinks she has the book. Why did you bring up her bookstore?"

"Max's employees kept talking about how he loved puzzles and riddles. I thought turning it into a riddle would be on brand with the episode."

"You shouldn't have mentioned the book at all!"

"Is it important? What did you find?" He left his chair.

"Like I'm going to tell you. You are the last person I'll be sharing any information with about Kendall's murder from now on."

"Excuse me." Deandra, the *Gazette*'s longtime reporter on community events, interrupted my rant from the now-open stairwell doorway. "Sorry, I knocked but you didn't answer. There are some people downstairs asking to see you, A. J."

"No problem, Deandra." A. J. swept by me, happy to leave his berating.

"We're not done here, A. J.!" I stormed down the stairs after him.

I knocked into him when he stopped short as we rounded the landing. I was about to yell at him some more when I saw why he'd stopped. Pepper, Freddie, Claire, Hugo, and Maxine all stood at the bottom of the stairwell, staring up at me and A. J. All the possible suspects may have heard everything.

CHAPTER 19

Maybe they didn't hear anything. Maybe our voices didn't carry. Maybe them being here had nothing to do with A. J.'s *reliable source*. I could always hope.

A. J. acted nonchalant, like we hadn't just been yelling. "Did you listen to the podcast? You guys were great, weren't you?" he said to them, a grin on his face.

"Are *you* his reliable source?" Pepper glared at me.

And there went my hope, out the window.

"She was snooping around me at the inn," Hugo said. "I should've known something was up."

"What do you know about this, Willa?" Claire asked. "Why do you think Max was referring to a book and not a person?"

They were all staring at me, even Maxine, who was hanging back and keeping silent.

"I don't know any more than you do," I finally said. I knew it was weak, but it's all I had.

"You know enough to tell *him*." Pepper pointed to A. J.

"I only shared the clue that Hugo told me about. And I apologize for that. I didn't mean for A. J. to put that information on the air."

"*You* told her?" Freddie turned on Hugo, all eyes now on him.

"Sh-she said you guys already told her," Hugo sputtered.

Claire sighed. "We had a leg up. Now everybody's going to know how to look for the Church Bleu."

Pepper appeared calmer. "So we're looking for the book *Rebecca*? There has to be more clues than just that. What else do you know, Willa? Did Max tell you something?"

"I haven't been in touch with Max in almost a year," I said truthfully.

"She wasn't even invited to the will reading," Freddie reminded them. "This is all Hugo's fault."

"I'm the one who didn't want to do the podcast, and for exactly this reason," Hugo insisted. "But now that it's out there, tell us the rest of it, Willa."

"There is no *rest of it*. That's all I know," I insisted.

"A. J.?" Claire said.

A. J. threw his hands up, demonstrating he had nothing further.

"I'm not wasting anymore time here." Hugo stomped out of the building.

The rest of them stared at us a few moments more, but when it was obvious we were staying quiet, Pepper pulled Freddie with her, and Claire followed them out. That left Maxine.

"I'm glad you're here. Have you changed your mind about being on my podcast?" A. J. said to her. "I promise you, I don't know anything else about Max's clues and secrets."

Maxine spoke for the first time. "I don't care whether Rebecca's a person or a book. I want to hear more about my father's car crash. Do you really think he was murdered?"

Murdered? I stared at A. J., my mouth agape. What other bombshells were in that podcast?

CHAPTER 20

Maxine asked to speak with A. J. privately, so I had no choice but to leave. Of course, I only pretended to leave. I stood at the bottom of the stairs and tried to listen in on their conversation. I couldn't hear anything.

"Is there anything you need?" Deandra asked from behind me, which was her polite way of telling me I shouldn't be eavesdropping.

I turned from the stairwell. "Could you hear what A. J. and I were yelling about from down here?" I asked her.

"I could hear raised voices, but not words until I was almost at the door."

That made me feel a little better. Still, they'd all figured out I was his source, which meant I couldn't pretend I was an outsider anymore. I said goodbye to Deandra and left. If I ever decided to speak to A. J. again, I'd find out what was said between him and Maxine.

I left the Gazette building and walked across the street to the taco truck for dinner for the crew. Cooking something cheesy usually calmed me, but tonight my head was so filled with questions, I couldn't even think of something to make. Dinner from Let's Talk Tacos was an excellent substitute. Their street tacos had been on my mind since lunch.

I walked back to Curds & Whey carrying two paper bags of tacos, replaying what I'd said to A. J. Did the others believe me when I said I knew nothing? Without more context, how damning was it?

I hadn't even wrapped my head around the possibility that Max's car crash might not have been an accident when I reached the Golden Glen Meadery. It was closed, as expected. I didn't see Roman inside. I thought I should call him when I got back to the shop and catch him up. I knew he wanted in on this, and we could use another head to figure out what this latest clue meant. *Here lies the secret.*

I crossed the street to Curds & Whey. When I entered, I heard voices coming from the kitchenette. One sounded unmistakably like Pepper. My nerves buzzed to life again. Did they come here looking for the book?

I hurried to the back of the shop, but only Archie, Mrs. Schultz, Baz, and Roman sat around the farm table. Baz's phone was in the center, playing A. J.'s podcast. *Oh, thank goodness!* Baz turned it off when they saw me.

"Hi, Willa. Baz called me. I hope you don't mind," Roman said.

"He saved me a phone call. But now he might have to eat six tacos instead of ten." I set the bags on the table.

"That's okay. Baz and I have dinner plans," Roman said.

"Sorry, Wil, I didn't know you were getting dinner." Baz stuck his hand in and pulled out a taco for himself, anyway. "It'd be rude not to have one since you got 'em."

"Carnitas in this bag, chicken in this one," I told them.

Archie pulled one out for himself and Mrs. Schultz did the same, along with some napkins.

"How'd it go?" Roman asked me.

"I only made things worse." I plopped down on the bench next to Mrs. Schultz and stuck my elbows on the table. My chin rested in my hands in a pout. Even the savory aroma of tacos couldn't lift my spirits.

Mrs. Schultz patted my back in consolation. "What happened?"

"I told him off all right, and I was kind of loud about it," I admitted.

"You? Loud?" Baz exaggerated his shock.

I ignored his sarcasm. "Anyway, when we went back downstairs, guess who was there listening in? Everyone from Church Cheese Shop, plus Maxine and Hugo."

"Why were they there?" Roman asked.

"They'd all been listening to the podcast. They wanted to know how he found out about Max's clue, since none of them told him."

"Uh-oh," Archie said through a mouthful of taco.

"You got that right. With me standing right next to him, it didn't take much to figure out I was his 'reliable source.' They badgered me for information, but I stuck to my guns that I didn't know anything."

"Did they buy it?" Baz asked.

"Hard to tell. They gave up and blamed Hugo."

"That's something at least. We were just listening to the podcast," Mrs. Schultz said.

My mind jumped to the other shock of the evening. "Did A. J. say something about Max's car crash not being an accident?"

"Yeah." Archie put down his taco and extended his fingers on either side of his head in a *mind blown* gesture.

"Did you talk to A. J. about it?" Roman asked.

"No. I had no idea. Maxine brought it up. That's why she was there. She wanted to know more about it. What did A. J. say?"

"He looked at the records of the crash site. They ruled it an accident, but seeing as how Kendall may have been killed for the Church Bleu, A. J. hypothesized that Max might've been run off the road on purpose," Baz said.

I put my head in my hands, feeling like I needed the help to keep all this overwhelming information inside it. "I'll have to listen to the podcast later and see what evidence A. J. has to back up his theory. It horrifies me to think Max might've been killed too."

"It could just be A. J. dramatizing the situation for his podcast. Most of the time, a car crash is just an accident," Roman said.

"He thinks someone surprised him and ran him off the road because there weren't any skid marks," Archie told me.

"I was told he had some kind of medical emergency while he was driving, which would explain that," I said.

"His car could've been tampered with," Baz suggested.

The hairs on my neck stood up and I scratched them away. I'd been in an out-of-control car last fall. Luckily, we all made it out safely, but it had been a scary few minutes.

I thought it through in my head, not ready to believe it was anything but an accident. "If someone followed Max to find out the location of the cheese, why kill him?"

"Greed? They didn't want to wait for him to die?" Archie guessed.

"So why kill Kendall too?"

"They must've thought she was onto something. They could want to be the only person who knows about the Church Bleu," Baz said.

This didn't bode well for me. Every suspect we had now believed I knew something.

CHAPTER 21

I forced myself to eat a taco, which awoke my appetite. I could tell Baz was using all his willpower not to go in for another.

"So what about that clue that's not really a clue—*Here lies the secret*?" Archie said. The book had been sitting next to him on the table. "I wrote down all the letters that were circled that weren't in the clue, but there's a lot of them. If they're supposed to tell us something, I can't figure it out."

"I'll look through the book and the letter again and see if he's left us anything else to help us figure it out," I said.

We all rose from the table.

Archie's phone dinged and he checked it. "It's Hope. She wants me to pick up dinner. Uh-oh. I was just going to go back to get my skateboard and head over to Everett's."

"Here, take the rest of the tacos for her." I handed him the bag and followed him to the front door.

"Cool. Thanks, Willa."

Before unlocking the door, I said, "Can I talk to you for a minute?" This wasn't the best time, but I had a feeling there'd be no *best time*.

"Sure. What is it?"

I hesitated. I hated asking a question that might result in an answer I didn't want to hear. I also didn't want Archie to feel I'd been spying on him.

He noted my nervousness. "Is this about my being tired? I'm sorry, I'll try to do better."

"You're doing fine. I'm just wondering if there's a reason?"

Archie shrugged. "Staying up too late, I guess."

"I see." He didn't want to tell me he was working at the bakery.

"I wanted to talk to you too, but not now with everyone here . . ." He looked over at the others who were leaving the table in the kitchenette.

"Okay. Maybe tomorrow since we're closed?"

"Sure. Tomorrow. After I sleep in."

I smiled at him. "Okay. Have a good night." I let him out the door and sighed. I couldn't even think about losing him at Curds & Whey.

"Look at the time. We better get going," Roman said to Baz.

"Meet you in thirty?" Baz replied.

They fist-bumped, and Roman left out the front door with Mrs. Schultz, who was clipping on her bike helmet.

I locked up. I had to get on the move too. Now that I had a moment to think of something else besides the case, I felt myself getting excited about my date with Heath.

"Bros night out?" I asked Baz.

"Something like that." He didn't look at me when he said it.

"I know things have been a little awkward with me and Roman these past few months, but you don't have to feel weird about still being good friends with him."

"No, I know."

I grabbed the book and Max's letter, the leftover crusty

French bread, and the Stilton from this morning's sampling. We left by the stockroom door that opened into the side alley, then took my stairs up to our apartments.

"It's not exactly a guys' night out," Baz said out of nowhere, as he straddled the low railing between our decks.

"You got a hot date?"

"Well . . ."

I would've clapped my hands in excitement, but as it was, I clapped the book and bread together. "You have a hot date, and you didn't tell me? Is it Ginger? Is that why you didn't tell me? Spill it."

"No, it's not Ginger. I don't know who it is. It's a blind date." He paused. "Roman set it up. We're double-dating."

Now I knew why he didn't tell me. "Double-dating. Ohhh."

"I feel kind of weird about it since you guys were together," he said. He scrunched up his face, afraid I'd be hurt.

"No, it's okay. I mean, who's going to know more single women than Roman?"

"Meow."

I laughed. "Okay, I know that was catty of me. You gotta give me one once in a while."

"You had your chance. Oh wait, that's what you said to me about Ginger."

"Touché. This breaking-up stuff isn't easy, even when you're the one who does the breaking up."

"I know. Maybe you should get back out there too."

I laughed. "That's a great idea. Let's triple-date!"

"Give Heath a call," Baz fired back.

"I don't have to."

"Why? Because you think you already *know* it's not going to work out, negative Nelly?" Baz pursed his lips, obviously tired of hearing my list of excuses to remain on hiatus from dating.

"No, because I'm going on a date with him tonight," I replied, feeling satisfied to prove him wrong.

"Get out. Are you just saying that?" Baz peered at me, trying to decipher if I was lying.

"Would I ever just say that?"

His skeptical expression broke. "Get out!" he said again, playfully pushing my shoulder.

I laughed. "We're just going for drinks."

"That's awesome, Wil! When did he ask you? How did it happen?"

I didn't want to talk too much about it and jinx the date before it happened. "Don't you have a date to get ready for?"

He glanced at the time on his phone and threw his other leg over the railing to stand on his side of the deck. "I want all the details after. Well, maybe not *all*."

I chuckled. "Ditto. Or at least your portion of the double date."

He unlocked his door as I did the same to mine. "Look at us. On the prowl again," he said.

I entered my apartment and closed the door on our laughter.

I dropped everything on the kitchen counter and went over to feed Loretta, then brought her over to my bench turned coffee table. "Did you hear that, Loretta? I'm going on a date with the hot detective. Can you believe it?" My stunning betta fish swished from side to side, seeming to appraise me. "Don't worry. I'm going to shower and change. Oh gosh, what am I going to wear? It's super casual, though, just drinks at The Cellar." A thought popped in my head that momentarily squashed my happy anticipation. "Oh no. I never asked Baz where they were going on their double date. What if they're going to The Cellar too?" I went over to my cell phone on the counter to text Baz, but didn't pick it up. Maybe it was best if I didn't know.

I wondered what kind of date Roman would choose for Baz. Then I wondered if Roman's date would be Gia or if he'd found someone new. Well, it had been three months since we'd stopped seeing each other. It wasn't any of my business who he was seeing. Why was I still feeling these occasional pangs of jealousy? I shouldn't be worried about running into them tonight. We were bound to end up in the same places when we started dating other people, so I'd have to get used to it. I just didn't think it might happen so soon.

I went into the bathroom and started the shower, remembering that I wanted to listen to A. J.'s podcast for myself. Maybe I could learn a little more about Claire, Pepper, and Freddie, and that car crash.

I thought I knew Claire and Pepper fairly well. Claire had been Kendall's shadow at work. I didn't agree with Pepper's assessment that Claire idolized Kendall. Pepper's jealousy got in the way of her understanding what a real friendship was. Except with Freddie. I knew virtually nothing about him except that he and Pepper seemed to be attached at the hip and it obviously wasn't romantic. Now Claire didn't have an ally. Without Kendall as their connection, would the three still be able to run a shop together? Did any of them really want to or was one of them trying to discover the cheese's secrets for themself?

The post-shower fresh feeling dissipated by the time I was done blow-drying my hair. The apartment retained the heat from the day and was still feeling uncomfortably warm. I went around making sure all my tall windows were opened as much as possible to get a breeze through the house. I threw on shorts and a T-shirt that read *Cheese is my love language*. I definitely wouldn't be wearing this tonight, but until I cooled off again and had some dinner, I didn't have the mental bandwidth to figure out what I'd be wearing on my date.

I went to the kitchen in search of food, regretting giving up my tacos for Hope. I could use some comfort food to combat these pre-date jitters. I opened the fridge and saw nothing but vegetables. Ah, yes—I'd been feeling like I needed to eat healthier, so I bought produce the last time I was at Lou's. What was I thinking? At least I had the Stilton to dress up a salad. I added butter lettuce, pecans, dried cranberries, and mushrooms mixed with some balsamic vinaigrette. A generous helping of the blue cheese crumbled on top balanced the sweet salad. I queued up A. J.'s podcast after a couple of bites. Delicious, but not exactly comfort food. My gaze latched onto the French bread.

I tapped the arrow on my phone to start the podcast and turned on the oven broiler. I minced a couple cloves of garlic, then creamed butter with what I had left of the creamy blue cheese while I listened.

They talked about Max and their plans for Church Cheese Shop. They must've spoken with Maxine about buying the shop, because they seemed quite confident it would be theirs. I paid closer attention to Freddie's background. Claire had alluded to his lack of cheesemonger experience, but I was surprised to learn Church was his first cheese shop. No wonder Pepper buddied up with him—he wasn't a threat to her.

I added the minced garlic to the butter-cheese spread and sliced what was left of the crusty French loaf lengthwise, then slathered the spread on each half. I grated some fresh Parmesan over the top and stuck it under the broiler until the cheese was bubbly. Luckily, it was done in mere minutes, so I didn't add to the heat of the kitchen. I took the cheesy garlic bread to the butcher block island to eat with my salad. The hardest part about making it was waiting for it to cool enough to take my first bite. The crisp outer layer gave way to the soft cheesy middle, erupting into bold flavors on my tongue. *Mmm.* Now *that* was comfort food.

I listened intently when A. J. brought up the information he'd uncovered about Max's car crash. He quoted parts of the report, mentioning the lack of skid marks, as Mrs. Schultz had said.

"The police tell us the autopsy reports indicate the cause of death wasn't the accident itself but an acute coronary event—a heart attack. Did the heart attack cause the crash or did the crash cause the heart attack? It doesn't dismiss the possibility that he could've veered down that embankment because he was trying to lose a car that was following him or that he was run off the road," A. J. said.

The others were quiet on the subject. Claire was the only one who spoke up.

> Claire: *"I don't see how that kind of speculation helps anybody. No one would want to hurt Max."*
> A. J.: *"What about the anonymous nine-one-one call reporting the accident?"*
> Pepper: *"There was an anonymous call?"*
> A. J.: *"It's public information."*
> Claire: *"They must've been calling for help."*
> A. J.: *"So then why didn't they give their name or stay with Max until help arrived?"*

I paused the podcast. I hadn't heard about the anonymous 911 call. It sounded like the others didn't know about it either. I wondered if Heath had looked into this since Kendall's murder. I hated to think it could be true, but A. J.'s questions were valid. I restarted the podcast. Pepper, Freddie, and Claire had nothing to add to A. J.'s theory. It seemed no one had answers to his questions about Max's car crash.

> A. J.: "Max never told any of you where he was going? You never tried to follow him?"
> Pepper: "We never knew when he'd go."
> Claire: "And we knew he didn't want us to. We loved Max."
> A. J.: "What about you, Freddie? You were the newest member of the team."
> Freddie: "I was just along for the ride. Pepper and I will stick together no matter what."

My assessment of their friendship was right. They were very close.

> A. J.: "Was there a fracture in your group? Was Kendall going to take the valuable blue cheese for herself?"
> Pepper: "That's a moot point. She didn't inherit the Church Bleu."
> Freddie: "The secret died with Kendall."

I paused the podcast. Freddie sounded like he thought Kendall knew something. I tapped play.

> A.J.: "I thought you said Kendall didn't know the secret."

Freddie: "Somebody knows."

A. J.: "What about his daughter, Maxine? She's the obvious person to inherit from her father. He left her the business. Wouldn't his shop and his Church Bleu go hand in hand?"

Pepper: "I think the shop was her consolation prize."

A. J.: "And Hugo Potts? There was an incident at the cheese invitational where over three hundred people heard him say the cheese should be his."

Pepper: "Hugo's delusional. Max would've never left it to him. We'll find where it is. I'm sure he wants us to have it."

A. J.: "Then why wouldn't he have just given it to you?"

Pepper: "Max was a prankster. In hindsight, handing it over wouldn't have been his style. He wants everyone to play along, but I'm certain he wants us to have it in the end."

Freddie: "I agree."

A. J.: "And you, Claire?"

Claire: "I think so too."

A. J.: "Max Dumas wanted everyone to play along, but some people might be playing a deadly game. It's possible Kendall's death is directly related to acquiring the secrets of the Church Bleu—that someone wanted what she knew about the cheese and killed her when they got it."

Claire: "That's what doesn't make sense. She didn't have any information about the cheese. If she did, she would've told us."

A.J.: "Are you sure you knew everything about your friend? The secrets of the victim often reveal the murderer."

Silence.

A. J.: "Thank you to Pepper, Claire, and Freddie for your insights into this intriguing investigation I'm calling *Case of the Bleus*."

No thanks were given in return. I wondered how much of the interview's final moments were edited out.

A. J. returned for his addendum where he outed the information I'd given him. I turned off the podcast. I didn't need to get angry all over again. Thank goodness for comfort food.

I continued with the rest of my salad, holding out one piece of the garlic bread for my last bite. But I didn't concentrate on my food for long. Everything I'd heard was like a sliding puzzle in my brain. I kept moving around the pieces, but the correct solution wouldn't appear.

According to Pepper, Freddie, and Claire, they were still planning to purchase and run Church Cheese Shop together. It wouldn't make sense for one of them to kill Kendall if she really did know something—without her and the Church Bleu, it only made their endeavor more difficult. But Kendall hadn't sounded as certain as the others about running the shop as a team. Maybe *Rebecca* wasn't the only thing she kept from them. If she confided her doubts to any of them, they could've suspected her of running off with the Bleu. Could the three of them have orchestrated her death together?

CHAPTER 22

I cleaned up the kitchen while Loretta looked on. I kept thinking about the possibility that the three were working together. But I also had to consider Hugo as a suspect. Hugo was unapologetically still on the trail of the cheese and believed Kendall knew its secrets. He didn't seem to know anything when I saw him at the inn, so if he *did* kill Kendall, he didn't discover anything.

"Sometimes desperate people do impulsive things, don't you think, Loretta? Maybe he got fed up with Kendall not sharing what he thought she knew." I continued to work out my suspect list with my fish as I washed the dishes and basked in the nice breeze blowing from the window over my sink. "We have to think about Maxine too. She claims to have no interest in cheese. She's a cyclist who's admittedly never shown an interest in working at her father's shop, so that could be true. But she might feel it should've been hers to inherit, not Kendall's. If Maxine saw Kendall with the book, she might've figured out what the *Rebecca* clue really meant and assumed Kendall had the answers. But Kendall couldn't have had them because she had the wrong book. She had a second copy that didn't have the letters circled. Did Maxine kill her, take the book at the park amid the commotion, and then discover it wouldn't help her?" I didn't have the answer. "Who do you think it is, Loretta?"

Loretta made a lap around her bowl.

"You're not the only one going in circles." The dishes done, I dried my hands and went over to the book on the counter and fanned through its pages. Archie was right—there were more letters circled, but how would we ever unscramble them? I picked up Max's letter with the clue. I looked it over again but it yielded nothing new.

I folded the letter and brought it into the bedroom with me along with Loretta to finish getting ready. I placed Loretta on my bedside table and flopped on the bed, tossing the letter aside. I was ready to give up, but my mind steered me back to the possibility that Max had been purposely run off the road.

"Why kill him?" I watched Loretta's red tail swishing back and forth in a slow, easy rhythm that propelled my thoughts. "Everyone knew he was dying, including Max himself. For some reason, he'd told everyone he'd left the cheese to his favorite cheesemonger, so they knew he had a will." Then it hit me. "You might kill someone who was already dying to make sure he didn't change it." I smiled at my fish. "Thank you, Loretta." Pepper and Freddie didn't like that he and Maxine had been getting closer these past months. Were they nervous that he would give his daughter the Church Bleu?

An alarm blared and shot me out of my thoughts. It was coming from outside my bedroom window at the front of the building. "My shop!"

I popped off the bed and ran out of the bedroom, stuck my Keds on as fast as I could, and bolted out the door, slamming it shut behind me. I flew down the stairs and down the alley. I rounded the corner and came to my shop, which was safe and sound under the glow of a streetlamp. From here I could tell the alarm wasn't sounding from Curds & Whey. My rapidly beating heart slowed immediately, but my body remained on high alert, wondering why someone's alarm had gone off.

The insistent noise had to be coming from only a few doors away. It sounded farther down the street toward the market. I hustled toward the noise, covering my ears as the shrill sound only got louder. I landed in front of the bookstore at the same time as Archie, who'd run across the street from Hope's with his shoelaces untied. The glass door of Read More Bookstore had a spider crack in it as if someone had thrown a large rock or a brick at it.

With our hands over our ears, we backed off the sidewalk to get away from the deafening sound. Now everyone who lived above their shops had emerged from their apartments to see what had happened. The lights flicked on from Lou's Market next door. I looked around for Sharice but didn't see her.

A siren added to the blaring noise. Red lights cut through the darkness. Archie and I hopped back onto the sidewalk as a squad car quickly pulled in front of us. Shep and Officer Melman bolted out of it. Melman took off down the alley to the back of the building. Over the din, Shep directed everyone to step back.

Another car barreled down the road and swerved haphazardly across the diagonal parking spaces in front of Lou's. Sharice got out of the car, tapping at her phone. The alarm went silent. My ears, however, kept ringing.

"What happened?" she said, concern blanketing her face.

"We just got here," I told her.

The door to Lou's Market opened, causing Shep to put a quick hand on his taser. Lou emerged, holding a baseball bat.

Shep released the taser. "Geez, Lou, what are you doing?"

"I heard the alarm from my apartment and thought it was the market, so I went in through the back door to catch him," Lou said.

"That's dangerous."

"For the intruder, it is." He tapped the barrel of the bat to his palm in a threatening manner.

Melman's voice sounded over Shep's radio. "All clear back here."

"Come up front," Shep instructed into his mic. He noticed the crowd had only retreated a few paces. "Everyone, please go across the street for your own safety."

Sharice noticed the crack in her door and winced.

"Who did this?" she cried. I went over to her and placed a hand on her shoulder for moral support.

"We just arrived, Sharice. We hope to have some answers for you soon," Shep told her. "Lou, did you see anyone in the back of the building when you left your apartment?"

"No one," Lou responded, still tapping the bat to his palm.

"You're not using the bat, Lou. Please, put it down."

Melman arrived from the alley, and Shep once again placed his attention on us. "Please, everyone, across the street. That includes you two." He was talking to me and Lou.

Another squad car and an unmarked vehicle pulled in. I recognized Heath's Dodge Charger. Officer Ferguson got out of the squad car and Heath immediately directed him to take care of those of us near the bookstore. I hung back as long as I could.

I watched as Heath and Shep fit their hands into blue

latex gloves and tried opening the door, but it was still locked. From what I could see, it looked like Sharice offered up her keys, then stood against a patrol car to wait while the rest of us were shuffled to the sidewalk across the street.

I found Archie again. Hope was with him, her hands stuffed in the pockets of her hoodie.

"I don't know why you're all always chomping at the bit to attract tourists. This is what happens when a bunch of strangers are in town," Lou growled.

Archie looked at me. I could tell he was as skeptical about the stranger theory as I was. If it was just some random burglar, I didn't think they'd choose a used bookstore to loot.

The red lights attracted more onlookers from the busier end of the street up by Apricot Grille and the inn. Baz and Roman must've still been somewhere on their double date—I didn't see them, nor Everett.

Murmurs went around the crowd with questions about what people saw or heard and where they were when it happened, but there seemed to be no witnesses to the event. I had no idea what happened, but only a few hours before, I'd warned A. J. that he might've put Sharice in danger. I was betting this had to do with his podcast and his big mouth.

"I was just about to do my nails," Hope said, adding her account of where she was. "We went to the window when we heard the alarm, then Archie took off to see if it was Curds and Whey."

"Thanks, Archie." I gave him a quick, one-armed squeeze.

Freddie came into the fold. "What's going on?"

Lou assessed the stranger critically and stepped away.

"What are you doing down here?" I asked Freddie.

"I was taking a walk. It's a beautiful night. Did something happen at the bookstore?"

"Maybe a break-in. Did *you* see anything?"

"Nothing suspicious. I heard police cars, so I came over to see what it was about."

Behind Freddie, I recognized A. J. approaching the scene with his camera at his eye, snapping photos. He had some nerve. Officer Ferguson stepped in front of him, blocking his view. They had a brief encounter, followed by A. J. putting his camera in his messenger bag and retreating. He tried to approach Sharice, who was leaning against the squad car, but he was denied, as well. It didn't deter him, however. He took out his notepad and pen and found several people in the crowd anxious to be quoted in the paper.

A. J. glanced my way. There was no guilt on his face, just that journalist's hunger I recognized from previous big stories he'd wanted to break. He nodded like he was about to come over, but my eyes bore through him. He immediately discerned that I was still plenty ticked off at him and looked away.

I felt horrible for Sharice, waiting for them to search her store. And I'd feel plenty guilty if this had something to do with the book and A. J.'s podcast. I approached the intimidating Officer Ferguson. "Would it be okay if I go to Sharice? For moral support?"

He stared at me impassively for a few long seconds, so that I thought he wasn't even going to respond. Then he surprised me by giving a single nod. I took that as a yes, and went over to her. He didn't stop me.

"Sharice, are you okay?" I could fully imagine the heartache of seeing the front door to your pride and joy smashed like that.

"I don't know who would do this. It doesn't look like

they got in. They're making sure no one's inside. I'm keeping my fingers crossed." She nervously shifted her cat-eye glasses as she spoke, as if a better focus would produce something she wanted to see.

Her barista Ginger, in a T-shirt, denim cut-offs, and running shoes, trotted over to us. "Sharice!" They hugged. "I'm so glad you called me. What happened?"

It didn't take Sharice long to bring Ginger up to speed, since we didn't know anything yet. We kept our eyes focused on the front door where Heath and Shep had gone in. As soon as they came out, Sharice sprang toward Shep. Somehow A. J. had dodged Lurch and beat her to him.

"Did you find anything?" A. J. asked Shep.

"Come on, A. J., give me a break. I have to talk to Sharice." Shep sidestepped him to get to Sharice, but A. J. lingered behind him.

"How bad is it?" she asked Shep.

"It looks untouched," he replied.

She closed her eyes and exhaled in relief. Ginger put an arm around her.

"It could've just been a vandal or a burglar who was deterred by the alarm. But can the two of you go in with us and tell us if you notice anything missing or damaged, just to be sure?"

"Of course," Sharice said.

Ginger's auburn ponytail bounced as she nodded her head.

Shep escorted them to the bookstore, and A. J. walked over to me.

"Untouched. What do you make of it?"

"What do you think, A. J.?" I stuck my face in his. "You put her bookstore on blast as a possible connection to the cheese everyone's after, and tonight someone tried to break in."

"You're blaming me?" He looked incredulous. "Why would someone break into a place for a book when they could walk into the store and buy one? It doesn't make sense."

I hated when logic got in the way of a good tirade. Maybe A. J. was right, but it was too much of a coincidence. There must be a connection.

Heath walked over to the crowd. A. J. left me in a hurry to get a quote. I made my way to stand near Archie and Hope again.

Heath ignored A. J. and addressed the crowd. "If anyone thinks they saw something, please stay behind so we can speak to you. If not, please go back to your homes. We're keeping two officers on the street to patrol. Everyone will be safe tonight."

"I hope Sharice is all right," Hope said to me and Archie.

"Me too. I'm glad Ginger's with her. We should check in on her this week to see if she needs anything," I said.

Hope pulled Archie in closer. "I'm glad I have you, so I don't have to be scared tonight."

Archie wrapped both his arms around her. "I'm glad I won't have to worry about you being okay." He turned to me. "Are you going to be all right by yourself tonight, Willa?"

"I'll be fine. Don't worry about me. You two go home and have a good night," I said.

Hope released Archie. "Oh, I see my friend over there. I'll meet you at the house in like two minutes, okay?" she said to Archie.

He shrugged. "Sure."

We parted as the crowd began to disperse. I was surprised to see Nathan Parker among the onlookers. *Oh great.* I wondered if this would be in his article on Yarrow Glen. What a week for him to be doing a feature on our cozy little town.

I felt a tap on my shoulder and turned. To my surprise, it was Hope again.

"Hi, Willa. There never seems to be a time to catch you without Archie, so that's why I sent him to the house without me. I need to talk to you. He's always saying how you and Mrs. Schultz give good advice and I need some. I don't really have anyone older to ask."

Ouch.

"Sure. What's up?"

Hope glanced over her shoulder to make sure he was really gone, before leaning in to say, "It's about Archie. But you can't tell him I talked to you about this."

"That depends on what it is you're about to say. He and I *are* good friends."

"You'll be helping him out. Helping us both out." She barreled ahead without an assurance from me. "What would you do if you've made a commitment to someone that you don't think you can keep? But you really care about that person and don't want to ruin the relationship you've built just because you want a change?"

My heart sank. It sounded to me like Hope was speaking on Archie's behalf. I was afraid this was the reason he was keeping his job at the bakery secret from me—because he didn't know how to tell me he wanted to leave Curds & Whey. I hated the thought of losing Archie and I hated that he was obviously wrestling with how to tell me. I had to make it easier on him.

"I don't always do it myself—in fact, I hardly ever do it myself—but in hindsight, I've found it's usually best to be straightforward with someone. As long as you're honest and speak from your heart and know that it's what you really want, everything will turn out the way it's supposed to."

"You really think so?" She squinted her eyes, skeptical.

I didn't blame her, but I trudged on with my optimistic advice. "Yes. What's the alternative, really? It's going to have to be said, eventually. I mean, whatever it is, right?" I added. I wasn't supposed to know what specifically she was talking about.

"You're right. It can't be put off forever. You won't tell Archie I asked you, will you?"

I didn't see the point in it. "No, I won't."

"Thanks, Willa!" She smiled and trotted home.

I couldn't believe I was losing Archie. Was it really what he wanted to do or had Hope convinced him? I'd have to wait until he was ready to talk to me about it. Hopefully, that would be tomorrow like we'd planned.

A few clusters of onlookers continued to hang out on the sidewalk, relaying the breaking news to the folks who'd just arrived to check out the commotion. Heath caught my eye as A. J. was still hounding him for a statement.

"Later, Stringer," Heath said, leaving the journalist to come over to me. "How are you? Shep said you were the first one here."

"I was in my apartment and came as soon as I heard the alarm. I thought it was Curds and Whey. Archie came over too. We didn't see anybody running away."

"Sometimes it's easier to get away if you just blend in instead of running," he said, glancing into the crowd.

"I didn't think about that. In that case, Freddie was here."

"What would Freddie's motive be for vandalizing the bookstore?"

"I have a theory. There are a few things I need to tell

you." It was time to tell him that I had the copy of *Rebecca* with Max's clue.

A. J. sidled up next to us, probably hoping to hear some inside scoop, which I wasn't about to give him, not after today.

"Can you come by the station tomorrow?" Heath asked me, knowing better than to speak in front of A. J. too.

"Sure."

Heath's gaze stayed on me. "I'm going to have to work later than anticipated because of this, so . . ."

"I figured." I tried not to sound as disappointed as I felt. We had to talk in code with A. J. right there, but it wasn't a surprise that Heath had to break our date. It heartened me a little to see that he looked disappointed too.

"Do you have someone to walk you back to your apartment?" he asked.

"I'll go with her," A. J. offered.

"Not necessary," I said firmly.

"Indulge me?" Heath said, his eyebrows arched in a plea. He wasn't aware of what he was asking of me.

I'd been making an effort not to fight Heath at every step, but, ultimately, it was his hint of a smile that caused me to give in. I reluctantly said goodbye to Heath as he returned to the crime scene.

I shook off my warm, gooey feelings for Heath, and walked briskly toward my apartment with A. J., keeping my eyes looking straight ahead.

"You're still mad at me, huh?" he said.

I looked behind me to make sure we were alone. The two yellow circles of light on the alley pavement didn't make me feel secure that we were. In fact, the creepy shadows made me glad Heath had forced A. J. on me.

"I don't want to talk out here," I said.

"We'll talk in your apartment then." He followed me up the stairs.

I dug into my pocket for my keys and realized they weren't there. "That's right. I ran out so fast, I didn't lock up." The door handle turned in my grasp. At least I didn't lock myself out.

Once inside, he said, "Listen, Willa, I'm sorry I said anything on the podcast, but you don't really think what happened to Sharice's store was because of that, do you?"

I put my anger aside so I could work this out in my head. Maybe A. J. could help me and be good for something. "I don't know how, but it's too much of a coincidence. The bookstore was closed after your podcast and it's closed tomorrow, so maybe they were anxious to get their hands on it. Or maybe they thought I'd get to it first. I know there must be a connection. They all know about the book now and they know that *I* know something about it."

"If you'd explained everything to me, I would've known not to say anything about it."

"So now it's *my* fault?"

He took his messenger bag off and plopped it on the floor so it leaned against the living room chair. "I think we work better together than apart, is all I'm saying. What's up with the book, anyway?"

A. J. had a point. He was more dangerous with only partial information. "Let me show you."

I turned to the counter to get the book, but it wasn't there. I could've sworn I put it there when I got home. My keys were still in the bowl. I did a quick scan of the living room. My heart picked up speed in my panic.

"What's the matter?"

"The book. *Rebecca*. I brought it upstairs with me when I left the shop, but it's not here."

"Are you sure you brought it home?" A. J. asked.

"I'm certain of it. I was flipping through it and then I took the clue . . . It must be in the bedroom." A stream of hope trickled into my panic. A. J. followed me into the bedroom. Loretta's bowl was still on the bedside table. A folded piece of paper was on the bed. There was no book. I snatched the paper from atop the quilt. The spelled-out clue was still there—*Here lies the secret.* "This is the clue, but the book is gone."

"What clue?"

"I'll explain later, just help me find the book."

I walked in and out of the bedrooms, the bathroom, and through the whole kitchen and living room. I described the book to A. J., and he helped me look, to no avail. "It's gone. Someone was in my apartment and now they have the book."

CHAPTER 23

A. J. went outside to get the police. Within minutes, I heard Heath's heavy footsteps taking the stairs two at a time. A. J. wasn't far behind.

I explained to both of them about Max's letter and the clue we deciphered in the book.

"Shep said you came in to report that Kendall stole that book yesterday," Heath said, confused.

"Let me back up." Before I explained further, I said to A. J., "You're not to tell a soul about any of this."

I saw him muster his strength not to reach for the recorder in his messenger bag. He agreed, but I could see it pained him.

I explained about the mix-up with the two *Rebecca* books—how Kendall's copy was one she'd bought from Read More Bookstore, thinking it was the one Max had given me with the clues inside, but it wasn't. She was right in thinking it had been donated to the store, but the copy she'd bought wasn't mine. I didn't realize it until after I'd gone to the station and spoken with Shep.

Heath asked for Max's letter, and I reluctantly handed it over.

"Nothing else seems out of place?" Heath asked.

I scanned the room again. "No. The book is the only

thing missing as far as I can tell. It was on the counter. I made it easy for them."

"Who knew you had it?"

I explained to him about A. J.'s podcast and my argument with him that had possibly been overheard by the Church Cheese contingent. "After they saw us together, all of them suspected I had the book with possible clues inside, but they didn't know about the letter from Max that would be needed to solve it."

"So the copy that was taken from Kendall after the picnic doesn't have anything useful in it?" Heath asked, trying to make sense of the dual books.

"Except for a great story, no. It's just a random copy. But Kendall must've thought it would lead her to an answer, and whoever took it probably thought so too, at least until tonight when they must've realized, thanks to A. J., that I knew more about the book than I'd let on."

"And your copy that was stolen tonight *does* have clues in it, but they're useless without Max's letter," Heath reiterated.

"Right. I mean, at least I think they are. He had tons of letters circled, but I can't imagine being able to figure it out without the correct page numbers telling you which letters are important."

"What was the big clue you deciphered before it was stolen?" A. J. asked, practically salivating.

"That's just it. It didn't seem like much of a clue. All it said was *Here lies the secret*. There must be more to it. I thought I'd have time to study it later." I crossed my arms in frustration. It was such luck that Sharice still had my copy in her store, and I was able to get it back. Now it was gone again.

"Let's forget about the clues for now. How did someone get in here?" Heath asked, inspecting the door.

I cringed. "I didn't think to lock up. I just ran down-stairs as fast as I could when I heard the alarm. I'm sorry, I know it was stupid."

"Don't be so hard on yourself. That may have been the plan," he said.

"What do you mean?"

"They didn't get into Sharice's store. We figured that when the alarm sounded, the burglar ran, but given this . . ." He stopped. "A. J., I don't want a whisper of any of this hitting the paper or your podcast. Under-stand?"

"I got it, you two, I got it. Nothing leaves this room. Scout's honor." A. J. lifted his hand in a three-fingered Boy Scout sign.

I trusted A. J. not to cross Heath. A newspaper edi-tor making an enemy of the police wouldn't be a smart move. A. J. may have been slick, but he wasn't stupid.

Heath continued, "It's also possible throwing some-thing at Sharice's door was a diversion to get you and everybody else to the bookstore so they'd be sure no one would be in or near your apartment or Baz's. They must've counted on you running out without locking up. Although it's a warm night, and they could've broken the screen and climbed in that way if you had locked the door." He pointed to the opened kitchen window.

The living room window was over the stairs and not reachable, but if you weren't worried about Baz next door hearing you, you could climb into the window over my sink. That explained why they set off the alarm—Baz would be sure to be out of his apartment too. I immedi-ately went over and tugged on the kitchen window to close and lock it.

"Was this what you wanted to talk to me about tomor-row?" Heath asked.

"Yes. You do believe it's all connected, right? Kendall's murder and Max's cheese?" I said.

"They seem to be intersecting," he agreed.

A. J. scratched his head in thought. "If the murderer took your book to figure out the clue and they somehow do figure out more than you did, we can just wait to see who ends up claiming the Church Bleu and we'll know who the culprit is."

I wasn't willing to play a game of chance. "But how would we prove it? Now that there's this dark shadow over the cheese, someone may not even claim it as the Church Bleu. They could take its secrets and pretend it's their own creation."

"I guess you're right. No one would ever be able to prove otherwise," A. J. conceded.

"We can't even be sure it was the murderer who was in my apartment tonight. Kendall snuck in here too, and she was no killer." Max's car crash flashed into my mind. *Or was she?* Everyone thought she was inheriting the Church Bleu. Was Kendall the one who wanted to ensure Max wouldn't change his mind and leave his cheese secrets to Maxine?

"Heath, what do you know about Max's car crash and the anonymous nine-one-one call?" I asked.

"Let's concentrate on one thing at a time, Willa. I'm putting an officer outside your door," he said.

"You don't have to do that. They got what they came for," I replied.

Heath sighed but didn't protest, giving in to my stubbornness. "Melman and Shep are on patrol. I'll make sure they keep watch. I have to check alibis for tonight. That could narrow it down." He came closer. I could smell a hint of his cologne, intoxicating notes of citrus and wood. "Will you be okay here?"

If I said no, would he stay with me? I hesitated a moment too long.

"I'll add Ferguson to the patrol and keep my phone on. Call me if you need anything," he said.

Why was I fighting it? I didn't mind him making sure I was safe. "I will. Thanks."

"Lock the door behind me." He gave A. J. a warning look to keep his mouth shut and to look out for me, all in one stern glance.

A. J. ran his hand through his curly black hair, obviously a little nervous about the unspoken dictums.

Heath left and I locked the door behind him as I was directed.

"I fell right into their trap running out like that," I said, mentally kicking myself.

A. J. plopped into a chair. "Boy, Willa, I'm sorry. I got caught up. I thought by making it a riddle, it would cause some interest. I honestly didn't think anyone would be in danger, especially not you. I really am sorry. From now on, my lips are sealed. At least with anything you tell me."

I could tell his apology was heartfelt. I took a seat in the living room. "Thank you, A. J. I appreciate that. And I know you didn't do anything on purpose. I'm responsible too. It was because I came to your office that they suspected I was your source and that I had the book."

"It was from my big mouth they heard about what you and Kendall figured out—that *Rebecca* was a book and not a person."

"One of them already knew—the one who killed Kendall and took the other book from her at the park."

A. J. leaned forward. "Right. There are two *Rebecca* books missing now."

"Yup, but I don't know if it's the same person who took

both. Since all five of them realized I was involved, any of them could've planned tonight's diversion."

"What someone did tonight was risky. The good news is, if the ones not involved were seen somewhere else at the time the alarm went off, it could really narrow down who snuck in here. This could turn out to be a break in the case."

"I suppose you're right."

A. J.'s brows furrowed. I could almost see him trying to work it out. "We saw Freddie. Was that his alibi or was he trying to blend into the crowd after setting off the bookstore's alarm and sneaking into your apartment?"

"You know who else was there? Nathan Parker."

"Who's he?"

"He's a magazine guy. He says he's doing a story on Yarrow Glen for *All Things Sonoma*, but coincidentally he's always around when something happens."

"It's a small town."

"I saw him talking to Kendall at the park, but neither one would fess up to it. Wouldn't you remember talking to a person who died less than an hour later? And why would *she* pretend she hadn't talked to him either? Lou thinks whoever threw a rock at the bookstore is one of the strangers in town. Maybe Nathan Parker is our stranger."

"I could ask Marcos about him," A. J. offered.

I snapped my fingers. "Marcos!" Marcos was a photographer at *All Things Sonoma* and an old colleague of A. J.'s in their L.A. days. I'd met him last winter when the wealthy Harrington family bought the magazine and then became embroiled in a murder case. "Will you contact him for me?"

"You bet. I owe you."

A. J. took his phone from his messenger bag. After a

few quick texts, he informed me that Marcos was having a drink at The Cellar. "He said we can join him."

"Great. Let's go."

This time I made sure to bring my keys and lock the apartment. I wasn't going to make it easy for anyone to get in from now on.

CHAPTER 24

Just a few steps away from the Inn at Yarrow Glen, A. J.'s phone buzzed. He checked his texts. "It's from the police station. They've got their statement ready."

"You go ahead. I've got this," I said.

"Okay. Hey, Willa, I want to continue this story on next Sunday's podcast. Are you going to be okay with that?"

"If I don't have this figured out by the time they leave on Tuesday, I'm going to have a lot more problems than your podcast."

"If I find out anything before then, I'll run it by you."

"I appreciate that."

A. J. backtracked and left for the police station while I continued to the inn.

I entered the lobby and went down to The Cellar where Marcos said he'd be. It would probably be easier just to scan the place for groups of women—if he came alone, he wouldn't be for long. Marcos Navarro was exceedingly handsome, and with his stylish clothes you could easily confuse him with one of the celebrities he used to photograph at premieres in L.A. before working for *All Things Sonoma*. For our little town, he was definitely upscale.

But it was a slow Sunday night, and I easily spotted him at the bar.

"Hi, Marcos."

He turned and gave me his hundred-watt smile. I didn't delude myself into thinking it was special for me—he just had an everyday swoon-worthy smile.

"Hi." He shifted to look past me, presumably for A. J.

"A. J. had to bail. I hope it's okay I came by myself?" I wanted to tread lightly with Marcos, something I hadn't done the previous times we'd encountered each other, which made our short-lived acquaintanceship rather combative. In fact, I was a bit surprised he'd agreed to see me, but I knew it was due to his longstanding friendship with A. J.

"Sure. Let's get a table. You want a drink? They're pushing the margaritas tonight."

I heard Jimmy Buffett's "It's Five O'Clock Somewhere" playing from the speakers. I declined the special and ordered a Pinot Noir from Del, the bartender, and Marcos got another beer. We argued over who would pick up the round until he finally acquiesced to letting me get it. He carried our drinks to a nearby table. I wasn't the only one being more polite this time around.

As we sat at the table for two, I noticed Baz at a booth with Roman and Gia and a cute blonde I didn't recognize. *Great.* They *did* come here on their double date. Baz noticed me and raised his hand in a hello. I looked away immediately. I didn't want Roman to think I'd come here to spy on them. I was supposed to be here with my own date. Baz must be wondering why I was here with Marcos and not Heath.

I took a hefty swig of my wine.

Marcos peered over his shoulder. "You still have a thing for Massey?"

Was I that obvious? I kept my attention firmly on Marcos. "No. We're . . . incompatible." I quickly changed the subject. "How are things with you? I was a little surprised when A. J. said you were still working for the magazine."

"It's in transition right now, but as long as I've still got a job, I'll do it. They actually want to make a go of it, and they want me around to help."

"Good for you!" I had heard something similar from Ginger, who was friends with one of the Harringtons.

Marcos changed the subject to the reason I was here. "So A. J. said you wanted to know about someone? Or was that just a ruse to get me to have a drink with you?"

I almost sprained my eyes rolling them so hard. I guess he hadn't changed that much—his large ego was still intact. As good-looking as he was, he had no idea how much I'd rather be having this drink with Heath. Jay. I halted those thoughts before they derailed me. "Marcos, I'm not trying to trick you into a date."

"You trying to make a certain guy jealous?" He looked over again at Roman. "I *am* the guy to do it."

My gosh, it was like sitting at a table with *Beauty and the Beast*'s Gaston. I took another sip of wine and focused on why I'd come. "A. J. said you might know Nathan Parker. Do you? Is he a real writer?"

"Very real. Well-respected," Marcos said.

"So then he *is* here to write a feature on Yarrow Glen for *All Things Sonoma*?"

"It's possible, but it didn't come up in the meetings we've had about the next couple of issues. I'm not in on all of them, though."

This didn't rule him out as a suspect. He could be using it as an excuse to stick close to the others and see what they know about the cheese.

"I'd heard he retired," Marcos added, drinking from his pilsner glass.

"Retired? To do what?" *Concentrate on cheese, perhaps?*

"To . . . retire, I suppose. I don't know. The guy's gotta be pushing seventy. It's about time."

"Wait a second. I'm talking about Nathan Parker."

"Me too."

"You're sure you don't have him mixed up with someone else?"

Marcos took out his phone tapped at it, then turned the screen to face me. "There you go."

I looked at his name and a picture of a much older man than the one who claimed to be Nathan Parker. That was definitely not the man I met. "Maybe there are two writers with the same name?"

Marcos shrugged. "I don't think we'd be doing a feature on Yarrow Glen, no matter who's writing it. They want to steer clear of the town for a while so as not to remind people what happened here last time." Instead of a wedding shower at the Harrington mansion, there was a murder—not exactly great publicity for them or their magazine.

I felt so stupid. "Then he gave me a false name." Maybe some part of what he told me was the truth. "Has there been any writer at the magazine who's new?"

"Just about everybody. I'm the only one who stuck around who's not a Harrington."

"He's in his thirties, dark hair, very good-looking . . ."

"You're describing me," Marcos said with a wink.

I plowed on, pushing Marcos's healthy ego aside. "He looks like Superman—the guy who played Superman, anyway."

Marcos answered when he finished a gulp of beer. "Doesn't sound familiar."

"This means I've been bamboozled." I should've listened to my instincts.

"He probably just wanted to impress you. Don't take it so hard. It's not the first time someone's lied about who they are for a hook-up."

"A hook-up? That's not what this was about!" My face reddened.

"Whatever you say. This is a no-judgment zone." He put his beer to his smiling lips.

"Thanks for the information, Marcos."

I took a last hefty sip of wine and stood from the table. Against my will, my gaze steered toward Roman's table. Marcos stood up and gave me a hug. He saw my surprise.

"It'll give him something to think about," he whispered.

I appreciated that he was trying to do me a solid, but I was fine with Roman dating, as long as I didn't have to see it.

"Take care, Marcos. I'll see you around," I said.

"Stay out of trouble," he said as I left.

I made a beeline for the stairs, being sure not to look at Roman and Baz's table as the chorus to "Why Don't We Get Drunk" followed me up the stairs.

When I reached the lobby, Constance flagged me down. I went over to the reception desk to see what was up.

"I heard about Read More Bookstore. Have you seen Sharice? How is she?" she asked, full of concern.

"She's shaken up, of course. Nothing was taken, as far as I know. Just some damage to the front door."

"Vandalism, you think? My gosh, I thought the kids stealing those parade floats last year was bad enough."

"I'm not sure what the reason was, but I'm sure the police will figure it out."

"Is hot Heath on the case?" Constance gave me a mischievous grin. She found him far too old for herself, since he was close to forty, but always gave me a thumbs-up when she saw the two of us together.

I chuckled. "He is."

"He's got his hands full between that and Kendall's murder." She leaned in, even though the few people coming and going through the lobby weren't close enough to hear. "I wonder if that big event the mayor's brought in attracted some riffraff."

"Are you thinking of anyone in particular?" I asked, knowing Constance pays attention to people.

"No. Anyone like that wouldn't be staying *here*. But you never know the kinds of people huge events like that bring in. Oh, no offense, Willa. I don't mean cheese people are bad. Your friends staying here have been nice guests."

"No offense taken. Did you see any of them earlier tonight?" Maybe Constance could provide alibis for some of them.

She looked over at the lobby's cozy sitting area. "They were listening to A. J.'s crime podcast together over there when they all stampeded out."

"And after that? Did they come back?" I wondered where they'd gone off to after they left the Gazette building.

"Most of them came back, then went out again a little bit later. I gave them some restaurant recommendations for dinner. Except for Maxine. She's been in her room ever since she returned. I brought her up some ice for her knee."

"Did she hurt it?"

"She said it's an old injury, acting up from a bike ride this morning. Did you know she's a professional cyclist?"

"Everett mentioned it. What time did she come back?" I wondered if she'd hurt it racing up to my apartment after hurling a rock at the bookstore's door.

Constance looked off for a second, thinking about it. "It was only a little while after the others returned the first time. Before dinner time."

Drats. I wouldn't have minded being able to narrow it down to her. Unless she was faking it so she'd have an alibi and she snuck out instead. Or she was telling the truth, which would mean I'd have to cross her off the list. I was getting nowhere. My mind returned to the stranger impersonating Nathan Parker.

"I met someone else briefly at the cheese event, but I didn't get his name. I wonder if he's staying here." I described him to Constance.

"Oh, you mean the preppy Superman." Her tone said she wasn't a fan.

"Is he staying here?"

"No, but I saw him at the farmer's market yesterday. He was very rude."

"Really? How so?"

"I was there with my sister, Lonnie. She noticed him right away, you know, because of that dark and dreamy look he's got going on. Anyway, he was just standing by himself by a tree near the picnic area, so Lonnie wanted to chat him up. I figured, why not? So we walked over to him and said hi, and he looked straight at us and walked off! Can you believe that?"

"That *was* rude. Where did he go?"

"Nowhere! He just went to another tree and stood around. I mean, sure Lonnie was smiling at him like the Joker, but still, he could've been polite and said hi. I told her he was too old for her anyway. We left him alone after that. We can take a hint. I wouldn't lose sleep hoping to meet him, Willa."

That made up my mind. No journalist would shy away from talking to the very people they're supposed to be writing a story about. He didn't want to be bothered, because he didn't just happen to be at the park—he was waiting for Kendall.

I smiled at Constance as if her assumption was right. "Can't blame a girl for trying. I guess it's a good thing I haven't seen him again then. I'd better get going. Nice to chat with you."

"Same here," Constance said, her greeter's smile making a natural appearance on her face again.

As I was walking out of the lobby, Claire entered. She said hello and took me aside by the arm. "I'm glad you're here. I'm sorry about how we all jumped down your throat earlier today at the newspaper office."

"Don't worry about it. I understand. Emotions have been running high." The only way to find out anything was to try to remain friendly with all of them. If she really didn't have anything to do with this, I'd feel terrible for her. "Did you have a nice evening?"

"It was okay."

"Where'd you go?" What I really wanted to ask was, where were you when Read More Bookstore was vandalized?

"We went to dinner at that nice place on the corner. Apricot Grille?"

"All three of you?"

"Hugo tagged along too. Oh, I'm sorry, Willa, we should've asked you."

"That might've been an uncomfortable dinner after what was said at the *Gazette*."

"That's true. With Hugo there, it was already awkward."

"So where is everybody now?"

She shrugged. "I stayed behind for a drink. Or three. This weekend has been a disaster from start to finish. Tomorrow can't come soon enough. I'd have left already but Freddie and Pepper insist on going to the invitational's closing ceremonies, and we all drove together. I loved Max, but I've had enough. Now I got a message that Detective Heath wants to talk to us again in the morning."

"Oh? What about?" I bluffed. I knew he wanted to question their whereabouts at the time Read More Bookstore's alarm went off.

"We have no idea. In order to do both, we've got to go at nine thirty a.m., right before we leave for the invitational. I hope this means he's got news for us about Kendall's murder."

"I hope so too."

"I'm going up." Claire indicated the stairs.

"Before you go, I wonder if I could ask you about someone?" I'd struck out twice tonight trying to find out who this Nathan Parker impersonator really was. Third time's a charm? I described the mysterious preppy Superman, as Constance had dubbed him.

"I'm sure I'd remember if I saw a guy who looked like that. Maybe he's turned back into Clark Kent. Why are you asking about him?"

"I saw him talking to Kendall at the park on Saturday."

"Really?" This caught her attention. "Do you think he has something to do with her death?"

"I have no idea. It's just a . . . loose end." I didn't want to say any more than that.

"It sure is." She shook her head, her eyes becoming

glassy with fresh tears. "I wish I had stuck closer to Kendall."

"You can't blame yourself, Claire."

"I'm going up to bed. I'm tired."

"Get a good night's sleep."

As I watched Claire ascend the staircase, feeling bad for her, I noted the purse she carried was big enough to fit my paperback of *Rebecca* inside.

CHAPTER 25

We were closed on Mondays, but my internal clock woke me up at the same early hour. It was certainly later than the dawn wake-up call I'd been used to when I was growing up working on my family's dairy farm, so I wasn't complaining. I made a latte and took it out to the deck and listened to the birds sing wake-up songs from the woods.

Baz came out on his deck with his own mug of coffee. "Morning, Wil." He sipped from it and grimaced. "How do people drink this stuff?"

"Think of the thirty-seven grams of sugar you're saving not having your daily whipped mocha choca frilly, or whatever it was you used to get."

He looked forlornly at his coffee. "I've been trying for months, but half-and-half and sugar don't quite do it for me. I guess I can always have my hot chocolate." He didn't sound too pumped about it.

"You still won't go back to the bookstore café because of Ginger? I thought things were okay between you."

"They're fine, but I'm afraid if I go back, she'll think I want her vegan sludge smoothies that I pretended to like when I wanted to date her. How am I supposed to tell her I want the stuff I used to drink without hurting her feelings?"

"I guess you'll have to get used to drinking regular coffee. I wonder if they'll be open tomorrow. Have you heard what happened?"

"Yeah. Word made its way around last night. It explained why you weren't on your date with Heath. How is Sharice?"

"I don't know. She was shaken up, of course. That's not all that happened last night." I told him about the book being stolen.

"Holy huckleberry, Wil! Why didn't you come over and tell me when you came to The Cellar?" Baz's mom forbid cursing from her five children, so *huckleberry* was the worst I'd ever heard out of Baz's mouth.

"I didn't want to interrupt your date," I told him.

"You would've done me a favor."

"Uh-oh. It didn't go well?"

"She wasn't into me."

"How do you know that?"

"Let's just say she spent a lot of time getting a drink at the bar as soon as Marcos showed up."

"Ah."

"What were *you* doing with him? You two looked pretty chummy."

"That's what I was going to tell you about next." I told him about Nathan Parker who wasn't really Nathan Parker.

"That's another person to add to our suspect list?"

"I know. We're not exactly narrowing down—" I stopped when I heard a car engine in the alley. I didn't want to be overheard. Baz heard it too.

A man in a white uniform came around the corner. From the bottom of my stairs, he called up, "Twenty-three A Pleasant Ave?"

"Yup. That's me," I called down.

He waved a large cardboard mailer envelope over his head to show me why he was asking and took the steps two at a time. He handed it to me with a smile. I tried to keep my voice steady as I took it and thanked him.

"Have a good day," he called back as he pounded down the steps.

Baz and I stared at the stiff mailer with no return address until we heard the *beep, beep, beep* of his truck backing out of the alley.

"This was sent to me in a different way, but it looks very much like the last one," I told him. I put my latte on the railing, and with shaky hands ripped open the top. Sure enough, the business-sized envelope inside had the same attorney's return address and my name scrawled in Max's handwriting.

"Another clue?"

"We'd better get Team Cheese together."

Roman was the first to meet us at Curds & Whey, followed by Mrs. Schultz with a bowl of berries in case we hadn't gotten breakfast. Without whipped cream, Baz wasn't as interested as he might've been. I felt bad having woken Archie on the one day he'd planned to sleep in. He scrambled in last with an entire day-old sourdough loaf from the bakery, tearing off a piece to munch on.

I locked the door behind him and joined the others at the kitchenette's large marble island where everyone stood staring at the envelope in the middle of it.

"So that's the next clue, huh?" Roman said.

"It came this morning. It's just like Max to try to be stealth by sending them to me at different locations."

"Let's see what it says," Archie said.

I tore open the envelope and unfolded the paper inside.

"These look like riddles," Mrs. Schultz said at first glance.

I read the first one.

My thunder comes before the lightning.
My lightning comes before the clouds.
My rain dries all the land it touches.
What am I?

"I can see why they call them riddles. I have no idea," Roman said. "What about the next one?"

You'll see this
once in a minute,
twice in eleven seconds,
but never in a day.

"Why eleven seconds? That seems oddly specific," Baz said.

"Kind of ironic that these are clues, because I'm feeling pretty clueless," Archie said, rubbing his temples.

"How about this one?" I said.

You'll find this at the end of a rainbow.

"Is he referring to his cheese as a pot of gold?" Baz guessed.

"I don't think that's it. Max never saw his Church Bleu in terms of money," I said.

"If it's leading us to the location of where the cheese is made and aged, then maybe he's talking about one of the Gold Rush towns," Roman suggested.

"That's a good guess," Baz said.

"It's worth consideration. Let's hope the other clues narrow it down even more," I said.

I read the closing of the letter.

Finally, Willa, return to Rebecca.

I looked at both sides of the paper. That was all there was.

"That doesn't help us with the rest of the circled letters," Mrs. Schultz said, puzzled.

"Let's look again," Archie suggested.

"We can't. Someone stole the book from my apartment last night," I told them.

"What? Are you all right?" Roman asked, stepping around the island to be next to me.

"I'm fine. I wasn't there at the time. Detective Heath thinks what happened to Sharice's bookstore might've been a diversion to get me quickly out of the apartment, and it worked. I didn't even stop to lock up. Plus, they didn't have to worry about Baz being home, either."

"So now someone has your book and the first clue?" Mrs. Schultz, today in a maxi skirt and a cotton blouse, began to pace and rub her light scarf in worry.

"I took the clue out before then, luckily, so they didn't get that. But I had to give it to Heath, so now we don't have the numbers anymore, either."

Archie pulled a folded piece of paper from his pocket. "I copied the numbers yesterday along with the extra letters when you were at the *Gazette*, just in case they meant something more."

Baz patted him on the back.

"Genius cheesemonger-in-training," Mrs. Schultz said, halting her pacing.

"I wish I'd been thinking as clearly as you, Archie. But

it doesn't change the fact that one of the others now has my book," I said.

"That could be *good* news," Archie declared.

"How could this be good?" I asked him.

"We had no way of knowing who killed Kendall, but now all we have to do is find which one of them has your book and it'll lead us to the killer." Archie smiled in satisfaction.

"He has a point," Roman said.

"*All* we have to do? How are we supposed to do that?" I wished I could feel as optimistic as the others.

Mrs. Schultz snapped her fingers. "Two can play at the diversion game. Let's use it to get them out of their rooms at the inn."

"Like pulling the fire alarm!" Archie called out. He ignored the rest of the sourdough loaf in his excitement over formulating a plan.

I shook my head. "That won't work. They won't let us in to search the rooms. Besides, if they think there's a fire, they're sure to take the book with them."

"I guess you're right."

"But you're on the right track, Archie. They're meeting Detective Heath before they go to the invitational. Nobody would dare bring stolen property to the police station." I was warming up to this diversion idea. I looked at the clock. We only had an hour until they left for the station.

"That solves one part of the problem. They'll all be out of their rooms. But how do we get in?" Baz said.

"You could ask Constance," Archie said. "She *has* been your *inn-formant*."

We chuckled at Archie's pun.

"Gossiping about guests and going into their rooms for us are two different things. I highly doubt Constance would do that and I wouldn't feel comfortable asking her to," I said.

Mrs. Schultz's fingers had been working overtime on her scarf and now she had an idea. "Let's take a page from the best heist movies."

"Like *Ocean's Eleven*?" Archie bounced in excitement.

"*Ocean's Five*, in our case," Baz said.

"*Bauer's Five*," Archie corrected, putting my surname at the helm of this scheme.

I got back to Mrs. Schultz's plan. "How so, Mrs. Schultz?"

"Diversion through chaos. We can manage some chaos, can't we?" she said, a gleam in her eye.

Being a former drama teacher, Mrs. Schultz's love of directing kicked in. Her excitement spilled over to the rest of us. Soon, we were brainstorming ideas until it turned into a cohesive plan. We began to think maybe we could really pull this off.

Roman was silent for a few moments. "I hate to be a wet blanket, but what happens if it works, and you find the book? It can't be used as evidence unless the *police* find it in the room, but they won't have probable cause to search one of their rooms."

Roman was right and it tempered our excitement.

"Maybe we should hand these riddles over to Detective Heath instead," Baz said.

I wasn't giving up that easily. "I plan to, but as long as Kendall's murderer is determined to find the clues Max left, I'll still be targeted. Whoever took the book is going to figure out soon enough that the circled letters inside need a clue to help decipher them. They're going to know it's out there, and guess where they're going to come looking? Max didn't know how serious this would become, but he's put me in the center of it. The only way out of this is to find the book, solve the riddles, and use them to set a trap for the killer."

This wasn't something the police would help me with. I'd have to be the one to do it.

CHAPTER 26

The entire plan hinged on everything going perfectly. Mrs. Schultz helped everyone rehearse their parts until we felt as prepared as we were ever going to be. Timing would be key.

"Everyone needs to go get their props. I'll run home to get into wardrobe and apply my stage makeup," Mrs. Schultz announced.

I unlocked the shop door so everyone could leave to ready themselves. Roman was going to his meadery to put together a fake case of mead—most of it packing material so it wouldn't be too heavy. Baz was heading upstairs to get his toolbox. Archie was going to be my wingman, so he would be staying behind with me.

As Baz, Roman, and Mrs. Schultz herded out the door, Everett appeared, with George in tow.

Everett! I'd forgotten all about our meeting today to discuss making cheese snack boxes for his bicycle customers.

George greeted everyone enthusiastically as hellos were exchanged before Roman, Baz, and Mrs. Schultz took off. He remained by Archie's side, as Archie crouched down to give the dog proper ear rubs.

"I'm so sorry, Everett, I forgot all about our meeting

today. I hate to admit, I've been so preoccupied with what's happened with Kendall, I haven't given it the thought I should," I said.

"That's understandable. Next Monday then?" he replied.

"Is that okay? I'm so sorry. I should've contacted you."

"Don't worry about it. Come on, George. It's your lucky day. You get an extra walk. You want to come with us, Archie?"

Archie stood. "Sorry, I can't. I've got some stuff to do."

"Have you given any more thought to what we talked about yesterday?" Everett asked him.

Archie's eyes darted to me and then back to Everett. "I haven't told her yet," he said under his breath.

I realized I was overhearing a conversation Archie apparently didn't want me to. "I'll let you guys talk."

I walked back into the shop and closed the door between us. My stomach was in knots. If he'd confided in Everett about leaving the shop, he must be serious about it.

It was only another minute before Archie returned. I shut the door behind him so we wouldn't be disturbed.

The fact that we had to go to the inn as soon as the others returned strengthened my resolve to finally come right out and ask him. We walked to the kitchenette.

"Archie, I need to ask you something, and I want you to know that anything you say won't affect our friendship."

"Okayyy," he said, apparently wary of what I'd say next.

My mouth had a couple of false starts before I finally spit out the words. "Do you want to leave Curds and Whey to work at Rise and Shine with Hope?"

His eyebrows shot up in surprise. "What? No way! Why would you think that?"

I wanted to feel relieved, but was he still trying to keep

it from me? "I stopped by the bakery yesterday morning and saw you working."

"You did? Oh man. I guess I should've told you."

"From what you just said to Everett, it sounded like you were afraid to tell me."

"I wasn't afraid, I just didn't know how to tell you." He plopped on the bench. "It's not working out, me living at Hope's. You and Mrs. Schultz were right—it was too fast. I want to move out, but *she's* the one I've been too afraid to tell."

This time I let the billow of relief in, but it was soon mixed with disappointment for Archie.

"I'm sorry. I know that'll be a difficult conversation for you. It's never easy." I thought about when I broke it off with Roman. Even when it's the right decision, it's never easy.

"I'm sorry I didn't tell you about working at Rise and Shine. I haven't been *officially* working there, just helping out Hope," he said.

"You mean she hasn't been paying you?"

"She has so much going on with the bakery and culinary school, and she doesn't get along with her manager. She can't fire him because he's really good at running the bakery for her. And she hates getting up so early. So one morning I offered to help her out. Then it turned into two mornings, then a week, then she kind of started expecting me to do it every morning."

"It's really nice of you to want to help your girlfriend, but it's okay to speak up for yourself so you don't get taken advantage of."

"I feel bad that she's doing everything on her own. Living with her makes me feel like I have to take it on too. Am I a bad person for not wanting to?"

"Oh, Archie." I sat down next to him and gave him a hug. "You are the furthest thing from a bad person. It's natural for you to want to help out someone you love, but it's also natural—and healthy—for you to stay your own course."

"Now you know why I want to move out. And also why I'm scared to tell her. I don't want her to feel like I'm abandoning her since I want to leave the bakery too. I don't want to break up with her, I just want it to go back to the way it was before we lived together."

"That's a tough one. The best thing to do is to be honest with her, as scary as that is."

"That's what Everett said too."

"Listen, she's going to be fine. She's been doing a great job, considering. After you two get this all hashed out, I'll get some of the other shop owners together and see if we can meet with her and offer our help. Maybe she just needs some sound business advice."

"You'd do that for her?"

"I should have thought to do it sooner."

"Thanks, Willa." We hugged again. "You really thought I'd leave Curds and Whey to be a *baker*?"

I chuckled. "The pull of love makes people do strange things."

"I suppose it does. But leaving cheese?" He shook his head slowly. "I don't think I could do it."

The shop door opened, and Baz and Roman, pulling a case of fake mead with a hand truck, walked in. Archie popped off the bench to meet them. I smiled as he retreated—a cheesemonger in the making.

Mrs. Schultz joined us shortly after, wearing jeans, which I'd only seen her in a handful of times since I'd known her.

"Mrs. Schultz!" Archie exclaimed, as surprised as I was.

"It's for the role, Archie," she said.

I looked at the clock. "Claire said they were leaving at nine thirty. We still have some time."

"Do you think they'll go to the station early?" Baz asked, obviously antsy to put our plan in motion.

"How are we going to know for sure that all of them went?" Roman asked.

"Good point. Maybe you two could go up there and watch for them to leave," I said.

"They can't go to the inn. That'll ruin the plan," Archie said.

"We don't have to wait at the inn. There's a bench in the front garden of the library. It's right on the corner. They'd have to pass by to get from the inn to the security complex," Roman suggested.

"Sounds good," I agreed.

I anxiously watched as Roman and Baz left the shop and walked up the street to the library.

Archie stood in the doorway. "What should we do while we're waiting?"

I walked back inside the shop with him where Mrs. Schultz awaited us. "While we've got the time, let's try to figure out these riddles," I said. "But first, we need cheese. It helps me think. Mind if we use your bread, Archie?"

"There's plenty."

"There are still lots of berries too," Mrs. Schultz said.

"Perfect!"

I tasked Archie with slicing and toasting the chewy sourdough while Mrs. Schultz sliced her strawberries and blackberries. I took out Humboldt Fog, a mold-ripened goat cheese distinguished by a thin gray line running through the white cheese and around the outside under the rind. The gray layer is an edible vegetable ash that changes the goat cheese's acidity level, encouraging mold growth. Besides being pretty, Humboldt Fog is velvety, lemony, and herbaceous, and great to eat any time of day.

Atop the sturdy slices of buttered toast, I added the tangy Humboldt Fog and juicy sliced berries. *Now* we could think properly.

"Let's take a look at these riddles again," Mrs. Schultz said as we sat around the farm table munching on our light and flavorful breakfast toast.

> *My thunder comes before the lightning.*
> *My lightning comes before the clouds.*
> *My rain dries all the land it touches.*
> *What am I?*

We were still stumped.

"What's the rainbow one again?" Archie asked.

I read it aloud.

> *You'll find this at the end of a rainbow.*

"What do you think of Roman's Gold Rush theory?" Archie asked.

"We'll keep it in the pool of possibilities. Can you think of anything else it might be?"

"A cloud? The sky? A leprechaun?" He shrugged and folded the toast like a sandwich to take a hefty bite, berry juice dripping onto his plate. I handed him an extra napkin. He finished his bite. "Nothing makes sense."

"That's why it's a riddle. We can't think about it the way we first perceive it," Mrs. Schultz said, using a fork and knife for her toast.

We all read it to ourselves again.

"A rainbow just ends. There's literally nothing at the end of it," Archie said.

"*Literally.* I think you're onto something, Archie," Mrs. Schultz said, her face clearing of tension. She looked over the riddle again. "If we're thinking literally, then it must be a *W.*"

Archie's eyebrows knit in confusion and then relaxed. "Ohh, I get it. The letter *W.* If that's it, you're a genius."

"I second that. Let's look at the other riddles and see if reading them in a literal sense works for them too," I said.

You'll see this
once in a minute,
twice in eleven seconds,
but never in a day.

We focused on the words and letters themselves as we worked it out.

"The letter *N* is found once in the word *minute*, twice in the words *eleven seconds*, and there's no *N* in *a day*," Archie said excitedly.

"Look at that!" I checked it over. He was right. "So the answers to those two riddles are *W* and *N*." I wrote them down. "Maybe this is going to spell something too?"

"I don't think the thunder-and-lightning riddle is going to be solved the same way," Mrs. Schultz said as she concentrated on the page.

"Do you think the answer starts with a *W*?" I asked.

"The *N* riddle was first, we skipped over it. If it's in order, it's *NW*," Archie said. "Maybe it's the start of another word scramble."

Mrs. Schultz had another idea. "Aren't *NW* the first two letters of the acronym for the cheese invitational?"

"The NWCS," I replied.

"Do you think Max left another riddle at the invitational?" Archie asked.

I had to think hard about that. "It's a possibility. His attorney may have hidden a final letter somewhere in the building, maybe even the directions to where the cheese was made and aged." I felt a seed of excitement.

Archie brightened. "We're getting somewhere!" He finished his cheesy berry toast in one final big bite.

"It makes sense that the answer to these riddles would be the secret location. There's only one more riddle left. The answer to it must be *C* and *S*?"

We silently read the riddle again, looking for a way for the answer to fit.

"What's that acronym stand for again?" Archie asked, as we silently read the riddle again.

"The Northwest Cheese Society."

We pulled out words and counted letters, but nothing held together.

Mrs. Schultz sighed. "I think I may have steered us on the wrong path."

"It was a promising theory, anyway," I said, giving up.

Archie's prior optimism wasn't going to be squashed so easily. "How do we know it's not right? Maybe we just can't figure it out. We could go to the invitational and poke around."

"I'd hate to spend the time if we're wrong. We don't have a lot of it to waste. Everyone's leaving tomorrow."

"It just seems to make the most sense. We've got the *north* and the *west* parts."

That gave me another thought. "You're right about that,

Archie. Maybe we *do* have the *NW* solved correctly. It could be referring to a location northwest of here. He'd crossed the border to California from Oregon when he had his accident, so it must be somewhere in California.

Their eyes lit up with fresh possibility.

"Let's try the first riddle again," Archie said.

We nodded, the seed of optimism growing.

My thunder comes before the lightning.
My lightning comes before the clouds.
My rain dries all the land it touches.
What am I?

We kept the paper in the middle of the table as we read it over silently to ourselves, trying to make a connection with any location.

"It's got to be a clue to the location. What kind of place would there be thunder and lightning and dry rain?" I wondered.

A knock caught our attention. I hurried to the door to unlock it and let Baz and Roman in.

"Did they all pass by?" I asked, as we joined Archie and Mrs. Schultz at the farm table.

"Yup. The three of them that were at the mead tasting. They were with a guy with spiky yellow hair," Roman said.

"Hugo," Baz said.

"And the woman we'd talked about—Maxine. She wasn't far behind."

My stomach twisted in nervous excitement. "Okay, good."

"She was carrying a cooler bag," Roman said.

"That would be the Church Bleu she was bringing to the invitational afterward," I said.

"Do you think she would've stuck the book in there too?" Baz asked.

"I doubt it. They'd do a bag check at the police station. She could count on the security officer not knowing about the book, but that's awfully risky."

"What are we waiting for? Let's go!" Archie said, standing.

"We should wait just a bit longer, so Constance will believe they're on their way to the invitational. That's part of the plan."

He sat back down, disappointed.

"Have you figured out the riddles?" Roman noticed Max's letter amid our plates with only scraps of our breakfast left.

"We figured out the last two were *north* and *west*," Archie answered.

Mrs. Schultz explained our answers to two of the riddles. "But this first one doesn't seem to be like the others," she said.

"What the heck is dry rain?" Archie said.

I picked up my last bite of toast, hoping the goat cheese would work its power to help me think clearly. I stopped, frozen in place, before it reached my mouth. The answer was quite literally under my nose. "This is an ash-rind cheese."

"Yeah. You taught us about Humboldt Fog a while ago," Archie said.

I shook my head. He was misunderstanding. "You asked what a dry rain is."

Comprehension dawned on his face. "Ash!"

"Exactly. I've been approaching this all wrong, concentrating on the riddles and Max, instead of the cheese itself. Ash rinds aren't unusual for blue cheese."

"*My rain dries all the land it touches*," Archie repeated

part of the riddle. "Ash is the rain, so it must be talking about a fire, but where's the land that it touches? That's what we need to figure out, don't we?"

"If it's indeed northwest of here, there are some places that have been devastated by wildfires," Mrs. Schultz said.

Roman tried to work out the rest of the riddle. "*My thunder comes before the lightning. My lightning comes before the clouds.* Thunder means it's loud . . . before the clouds . . . It could be ash from an explosion, not a fire. You know how it rains down ash after a building implodes?"

"Maybe a decrepit building?" Baz threw his guess in.

"The new conference building had to be renovated. Maybe that's what he's talking about," Archie said. He was obviously still clinging onto Mrs. Schultz's initial theory that another clue was to be found somewhere at the cheese invitational.

I thought about Max. "Something's telling me he's leading us to the cheese itself. If this is a clue to where it's aged, then we have to consider the best environment for the cheese. Blue cheese needs a stable temperature for aging. Like some creameries in Oregon use caves to age their cheese.

"An explosive cave!" Archie said triumphantly, meshing Roman's theory with mine.

Baz laughed. "That would be a volcano, Arch."

I stared at Baz. "A volcano!"

We read the clue again.

My thunder comes before the lightning.
My lightning comes before the clouds.
My rain dries all the land it touches.
What am I?

"That's it!" I said, grabbing Max's letter. "Thunder is the noise it makes, lightning must be the lava that it spews before the clouds of ash, and then the dry ash rains down. It's a volcano!"

"Wouldn't that be kind of dangerous?" Baz asked.

"Not an active volcano. Cooled lava can make tubes and caves once it dries and hardens over time. If the caves were formed from an old lava flow, it could explain the unique flavor Max's blue cheese gets from it."

"Where do we look for lava caves?" Baz asked.

Archie spoke up. "There's a national park that has them. My mom took me there when I was little. Lava Beds National Monument, I think it's called. It's north of here."

"I know about that place, but it's northeast of here, not northwest," Roman said. "Besides, how could he get away with aging it at a public park?"

"He couldn't, but maybe there's another one that nobody knows about," I said.

"How do we find out where it is? Northwest of here isn't much to go on," Mrs. Schultz said.

I read Max's letter again. "There aren't any more riddles."

"Maybe he's gonna send you another letter," Baz said.

I wasn't so sure. "It says *Finally, return to Rebecca.* That means there must be something more in the book that we'll understand now that we have these clues figured out."

"Then we need to get the book back," Archie said.

"Should we head over?" Roman suggested.

"I think so," I said, bringing our plates to the sink.

Everyone stood from the table.

"Does everyone remember their part?" Mrs. Schultz asked.

We quickly went over it one last time and then left the shop. We walked up the street together, Baz with his tool-box and Roman behind us, rolling his hand truck with the fake case of mead. We approached the inn.

"Is everybody ready?" I asked one last time.

They nodded.

I was the first to enter.

CHAPTER 27

Constance was at the desk. I hated to do this to her, but better she wasn't aware of any plan so her job wouldn't be jeopardized.

I shook off my nerves. "Hi, Constance."

She wiggled her fingers in a wave. "If you're here for your friends, you missed them. They've already left for the invitational."

"I know. They texted me because they knew I was running late. They forgot their speech. They were practicing it this morning and left it in one of the rooms. They want me to get it real quick so I can bring it to them."

"Okay. We can run up and take a look," she said.

I knew it wouldn't be as easy as her letting me go up by myself, but I'd still hoped for it.

She put her BE RIGHT BACK placard on the reception desk next to the bell, took the old-fashioned skeleton master key, and double-checked their room numbers. "Rooms four through seven," she said to herself.

She made her way around the desk as Roman walked in pulling his hand truck with the fake case of mead. *Right on time.*

"Who's getting the mead?" he asked Constance before we made it to the stairs.

"Excuse me?" she asked. Her forehead creased between her eyebrows, almost forming a question mark.

"Gia took an order for a case of mead, and they said it had to be delivered by ten o'clock. I got the credit card number but no name. They've already paid for it," he said.

"Oh. Hmmm. Let me see if there's a note about it that I missed. Willa, can you wait here a second?" Constance trotted back behind the reception desk. She tapped at her computer keyboard and peered at the screen. She flipped through the guest book and opened drawers to no avail. There was no note, of course. "I may have to call the guests in their rooms to find out who ordered it, because they didn't mention it to me."

"I can run up on my own so that you can make the phone calls," I suggested, crossing my fingers behind my back.

"I couldn't let you do that."

Drats.

Mrs. Schultz waltzed in right on cue, but Constance only gave her a passing smile and focused on Roman.

"Roman, are you able to wait for a minute while I go upstairs with Willa?" she said, coming back around the desk.

"Sure, I'll just move this over here." He swung around with the heavy hand truck and collided with Mrs. Schultz.

"Ow!" Mrs. Schultz cried out and fell to the floor with a thud.

"Mrs. Schultz!" I ran over to her, thinking Roman hadn't been careful enough, but a quick wink from her let me know she was in acting mode. She hadn't been a drama teacher for nothing.

"Oh, my ankle!" she cried.

Constance came running over to us.

"I'm so sorry, Mrs. Schultz," Roman said.

"Are you okay?" Constance asked her, worried.

Roman helped Mrs. Schultz up and she hopped on one foot over to the chair by the unused fireplace.

While we were all fussing over Mrs. Schultz, Archie snuck in and quickly made his way up the stairs and out of sight.

"Let's make sure your ankle's all right," Roman said.

"I think I'll be fine." She lifted her jeans to show a bruise on her ankle. Mrs. Schultz's stage makeup skills were on target.

"It's bruising already. I'd better get an ice pack from the first aid kit in the office," Constance said, leaving Mrs. Schultz's side.

Baz entered next with his toolbox. "Where's the flood?"

"What?" Constance halted in front of Baz.

"I got a call that there was a plumbing leak you needed help with?"

"Oh no. I wasn't told, but I just clocked in. We're trying to take care of Mrs. Schultz."

Everyone was playing their parts perfectly. Our anxiety came from a real place, as I knew we all felt bad for causing Constance stress. *We promise, Constance, it's for a higher purpose.*

"What happened here?" Lou had entered the lobby without us noticing. He was right behind us, holding a market bag. We hadn't counted on him having a part in this. I worried how much of a crimp Lou would put into our plan.

"I had a little accident," Mrs. Schultz said.

"Are you okay? Can I help?"

"I think Constance has it under control," Mrs. Schultz replied.

The last thing we needed was for Lou to help Constance manage the chaos.

"I'll deliver these herbs and go back to my market for some Epsom salts for that ankle."

"Thank you, but you don't need to go to the trouble," Mrs. Schultz assured him.

"No trouble. I've got bags of 'em at the market. Put 'em in a bath, your ankle will be as good as new in no time. Let me deliver this and I'll be back with the salts."

"Thanks, Lou," Mrs. Schultz called as he headed toward The Cellar. Without missing a beat, she returned to delivering her lines convincingly. "Willa, shouldn't you be at the invitational? I know how important it is for all of you to be there at the closing ceremonies to give your speeches."

"I feel terrible leaving you, Mrs. Schultz, but you're right, I only have a few minutes to spare," I said.

"Oh, Willa, I forgot." Constance handed me the master key surreptitiously and whispered, "Here. But be quick about it and don't forget to lock the room door on your way out. And please don't tell anybody I let you in on your own."

"Thanks. I won't tell. I'll be back in a flash." I raced up the stairs with the key, where Archie awaited me.

The first part of *Bauer's Five* was a success. Now to find the book.

We hurried down the hall, passing rooms one through three. Rooms four through six faced the patio at the back of the inn. I stuck the skeleton key into the lock underneath the wooden knob to Room Four. We hurried in and shut the door behind us.

"Let's be quick about this."

"Okay. For the record, I don't feel so great about going through people's things," Archie said.

Now that we were in the room, facing what it would take to find the book, I felt the same. "You don't have to do this with me if you don't feel comfortable. I understand."

"No, I want to find the book."

"Okay, so let's keep our eyes peeled for the book and try not to look too closely at anything else."

We walked around the room, scanning it without touching anything at first, hoping the book would be in plain sight. The rooms were in keeping with the aesthetics of the turn-of-the-nineteenth-century inn. No modern decor here. A large wooden dresser with an attached ornate mirror, a four-poster bed, and a curtained claw-foot tub in the bathroom. The only nod to your average hotel room was the luggage rack in the corner and a USB port on one of the antique-looking bedside tables. Also on the table was a magazine on cycling.

"This must be Maxine's room," I said.

Archie nodded and started with the dresser drawers while I searched her suitcase, which was opened on the luggage rack. I moved her clothes around as little as possible, hoping to see or feel the book, whispering as I did so, "I'm sorry about this if you're not a thief and a murderer." Archie got on his hands and knees and looked under the bed. No luck. We lifted the mattress to check under it and came up empty.

"I guess people only stash money under their mattress," Archie said.

We ended with the bathroom. Nothing.

"Not here. Let's go to the next one," I said.

Room Five had two antique brass twin beds. Both quilts were rumpled, making it obvious that two people were staying in the room. It had to be Pepper and Freddie's room.

"We have to be quick," I said, realizing too much time was passing. "Where would *you* keep a book?"

"It depends if one of them was hiding it from the other," Archie said.

"Good point."

Unlike Maxine, they'd unpacked their clothes, which were hanging and folded in the large armoire. After feeling around the clothes and looking in the corners, we checked the beds and found their luggage stored under them, hiding between the bed skirts. I checked the pockets of one empty suitcase and Archie did the same for the other.

"Anything?" I asked.

"Just a pair of winter gloves," he said, sticking them back in the outer pocket.

Archie slid the suitcase back under the bed. I did the same with mine.

I saw the case of mead Freddie had bought stashed in the corner. I opened the box's flaps. Three bottles were missing. Had they drunk that much between then and now, or was one of the bottles used to kill Kendall? There was no way to definitively know.

"Let's try the next room," I said.

Room Six also had two twin beds, although only one was unmade. It was kept much neater than the last room. From the makeup in the bathroom, I could tell it was Claire's room. I didn't see the book out in the open.

"We're taking too long. Here." I gave Archie the key. "Let's split up. You search Hugo's room and I'll finish Claire's. It'll be Room Seven, right around the corner."

Archie nodded and left the room, closing the door behind him.

I once more got on my knees and looked under the furniture and the bed. I turned on my cell phone flashlight to see the dark corners. Nothing. Not even a dust bunny.

My anxiety rose—I not only had to worry about Constance discovering me mid-search, but I realized I'd forgotten to consider the housekeeper.

I stood and checked the bedside table drawers. A Bible, but no *Rebecca*. I hurried over to the armoire when I suddenly heard Archie's voice, loud and oddly not Archie-like. "Hi, Claire!"

I froze.

CHAPTER 28

Fear kept me statue-still with my hand on the armoire.

Archie made loud small talk with Claire. "How's your morning going?"

I didn't hear what she said in return. My mind was buzzing in panic. I ever so carefully opened the armoire, but there was no room for me to hide. It was stuffed with clothes and several suitcases of various sizes. That's right! Kendall had roomed with her. Poor Claire had this extra reminder that her friend was no longer here. I gently closed the armoire. Poor me! I was about to be caught in Claire's room. Should I hide in the tub or under one of the beds? I scootched under the brass bed closest to the door, making sure no part of me was sticking out of the bed skirt. This was one of those times when being short worked in my favor. Maybe if Claire went to the bathroom, I'd be able to sneak out.

I heard her put her key in the lock and turn it. It had already been unlocked, thanks to me, but she didn't comment on it. Maybe she didn't notice with Archie still chatting away, trying to distract her. I could hear them more clearly now—she'd obviously opened the door.

She said all the polite things to extract herself from any further conversation and shut the door on him. I heard her light footsteps nearing. The bed creaked under Claire's weight as she sat on it, the mattress and springs pressing in on me.

I didn't realize I was holding my breath until I had to release it. Yikes. Would she hear me breathing under her bed? I closed my eyes, willing myself to be invisible like I used to do playing hide-and-seek. I hated that game, anxiously waiting to be found, which always coincided with needing to use a bathroom. There was nothing else to think about—only getting caught and needing to pee, just like now, except getting caught would have far more dire consequences than just being "it." I hoped Archie was thinking of a way to get Claire out of here.

"Hello?" Claire's voice broke into my thoughts.

Oh no, she knows someone's in the room.

"Yeah, it's me," she said.

Relief coursed through me. She was on the phone.

She continued, "I've changed my mind." A pause. "No, don't come here. There's a bunch of people in the lobby. I don't want to be seen here together." Another pause. "The park. Behind the big oak tree near where Kendall—well, you know." Her voice hitched, and she cleared her throat. "Five minutes. See you then."

She stood and I heard her shoes pad across the floor. The door opened and closed, and I heard the old-fashioned lock click into place. I laid still and counted to sixty, then squirmed out from under the bed. Who was Claire meeting and what did she change her mind about? The sound of the lock turning again sent me scrambling across the room, but not in time to hide. The door opened.

It was Archie.

"Thank goodness it's you." I held my hand to my rapidly beating heart.

"Sorry. Didn't mean to scare you. I wasn't sure what

to do when I heard someone coming. I panicked when I saw her at the door. Should I have stayed hidden and not said anything?" he asked, still holding the skeleton key.

"You did the right thing by warning me. I was able to hide. She's meeting someone in the park in secret. We have to follow her."

I took the key back from Archie as we left her room, locked her door, and hustled downstairs. Roman was still pretending to attend to Mrs. Schultz, who was on the couch with her leg propped up and an ice pack on her ankle. I heard Constance laugh. Baz was at the reception desk, chatting with her.

I quickly returned the key to her.

"I must be losing my touch. I didn't even know you were here," Constance said to Archie. She must've been enjoying her conversation with Baz, as any stress we'd inflicted on her was no longer apparent. "And I didn't even notice Claire, either, until I saw her racing out of here."

"She came back for the speech. We got our signals crossed. Thanks, anyway," I said.

She brightened even more. "It looks like everything worked out, then. There was no leaky plumbing after all, Claire got her speech, and we got ice on Mrs. Schultz's ankle in time to stop it from swelling. We couldn't figure out who ordered the mead, though."

Roman joined us at the reception desk. "I just got a text from Gia. She had the wrong info. It wasn't someone from here who ordered it."

"There we go. Riddle solved!" Constance said.

If only.

Roman opened the box to his fake case of mead and took the two bottles that were in there. He handed them to Constance. "For your troubles."

"You mean it? Thanks!" She accepted the mead and

held the bottles close. "I could use it after the week I've had. This hasn't been an easy group. Not that I blame them after what's happened, although they weren't a happy bunch even before their friend died. I keep telling myself, they'll be gone tomorrow."

Tomorrow. We didn't have much time.

"I'm sorry we added to your bad week, Constance. I hope the mead helps," I said.

"No problem. All in a day's work." And just like that, her chipper personality returned.

We said goodbye, and Archie and I were the first ones out the door. Mrs. Schultz hobbled out with Baz's assistance and Lou's Epsom salts in hand until she was outside and out of Constance's sight. Roman wheeled his hand truck and empty box out behind us.

Once we were all on the porch, Roman said to me, "Sorry about Claire! We were too caught up keeping Constance distracted to see her come in. And then we had to make sure Lou didn't stick around when he came back with the Epsom salts."

"You couldn't have known she'd come back. She was supposed to go to the invitational with the others. Right now, we've got to get to the park," I said, leading the way. Roman left his cart on the inn's side porch as everyone followed me. "Claire's meeting someone there in secret."

"Who?" Baz asked.

"I don't know, but she was afraid for anyone at the inn to see them together."

"Mrs. Schultz, are you sure you're all right? You were really convincing," Baz said.

Mrs. Schultz was keeping up with us just fine. "It was all acting, Basil. And a good bout of makeup."

"I'm glad Lou didn't decide to stick around," I said.

"It was very sweet of him to come back with the salts.

I feel terrible for lying to him," Mrs. Schultz said, her hand going to her scarf.

"If we figure out who killed Kendall, it'll all be worth it," Roman said, giving Mrs. Schultz a consoling pat on the shoulder.

We crossed at the light to Main Street.

Archie was ahead of us, taking long strides, still on a bit of a high that we'd pulled it off without getting caught. At the sidewalk, he slowed to let us catch up. "I can't believe it worked," he said. "Well, almost. It was a close call with Claire."

"It was for the best or otherwise I wouldn't have heard her phone call," I said.

"Lucky I was still around the corner trying to figure out how to get that stupid key to turn in the lock or else I wouldn't have heard her coming."

Mrs. Schultz chuckled. "I guess we have technology to thank for that. Who knew a regular old key could be so tricky?" She winked at Archie to let him know she was teasing him.

Archie laughed along with her. "I got it to work on Claire's door. I just needed some practice."

I saw the security complex just ahead and felt a twinge of guilt. Heath wouldn't like this.

"Let's cross," I said, putting him out of my mind.

We crossed the street to the town hall parking lot.

"She said they're meeting at the tree by the picnic area," I told the others.

"What if they see us?" Archie said.

"It's more important that we see *them*. I want to know who Claire's meeting."

CHAPTER 29

We trod across the parking lot and the park lawns to the big oak tree by the picnic area. I didn't see anyone.

"Did we miss them already?" Mrs. Schultz looked around the park, as did the rest of us.

We began to orbit the old oak, keeping plenty of distance from it. If we were early, I didn't want to scare off Claire. I eventually saw her behind its thick trunk. As we continued around it, I saw who she was with. Tall, dark-haired, an untucked polo over khaki shorts—it was unmistakably the guy pretending to be Nathan Parker!

"You guys stay back here. I don't want her to know we're working together," I said.

"Are you sure you should go over there alone?" Roman said.

"I've got this," I assured him.

"We should have a code word in case there's trouble," Baz said.

I nodded. "Okay. How about *Ahhhh*?" I let out a quiet mock-scream.

"Gotcha," Baz replied.

I hurried toward Claire and the guy who wasn't Nathan while the others stayed behind. Claire and the mystery man were too intent on their conversation to notice me until I was almost upon them. Suddenly, his voice got louder.

"So what do you think of Yarrow Glen?" he said to Claire.

"What?" Claire was confused, even more so after she noticed me. "Willa. What are you doing here?"

His journalist act wasn't going to trick me again. "Be careful, Claire. This is the guy I was telling you about and he's not who he says he is."

"You're not really Simon Crowne?" she said to him.

I crossed my arms. "So *that's* your real name."

He punched a fist into his palm and closed his eyes in defeat. Claire had given him away. "Yes, I'm Simon Crowne."

"Why did you tell me you were Nathan Parker?"

I waited while he stared at me, then slid his glance over to Claire, who looked interested in his answer. Was he buying himself more time or deciding how many lies he could get away with telling this time?

He sighed and threw his hands out. "It was the first name that popped into my head. He's a writer friend of my father's. I don't know why I didn't just tell you the truth, but you were accusing me of killing Kendall."

"Why would you think Simon killed Kendall?" Claire asked me.

"I told you he was at the park with Kendall before she died. And I saw him following her around since Friday night," I told Claire.

"I can explain. But, Claire, you have to believe me that I didn't kill Kendall." He put his large hands on her shoulders.

"You should take your hands off her, Simon Crowne, if that's even your real name," I said. I knew with one scream I had backup.

He stepped back, even though Claire said, "It's fine, Willa." Then to him, "It doesn't make sense that you would kill Kendall. I believe you."

I thought she was being naïve . . . unless he wasn't a complete stranger to her. "Do you know him, Claire?"

"Kind of. Kendall and I saw him one day when the two of us were closing the shop and he came in for a meeting with Max. It didn't last long—Max threw him out."

"Why? What did you do?" I asked him.

"I offered him money for his Church Bleu. A lot of money. He wouldn't hear of it," he said simply.

Claire picked up the story. "It's true. Max told us as much. Then a few months later, I saw Kendall with Simon at a coffee shop. I asked her why she was with him. She said he was trying to get her to convince Max to sell the secrets of the Church Bleu to him, but that she'd refused. But they were in that coffee shop an awfully long time for someone who said no." She looked off, her thoughts likely drifting back to the memory. "This was after we'd learned that Max's prognosis wasn't very good, and the four of us were making plans to run the shop, because we were all sure Kendall was inheriting the Church Bleu. Even Kendall was sure of it, as much as she'd never say so to Pepper and Freddie." Claire stared at the ground at this next part. "So I sort of kept my eye on her when we weren't hanging out together after work."

"You were spying on her?" I said.

She lifted her chin and threw her shoulders back. "It was lucky I was, because I saw them together again."

I looked at Simon. He was watching her raptly, seeming to hear this for the first time too.

She continued. "I confronted her. And she confessed that she was going to sell the secret to Simon once Max left it to her. She said she needed to help her mom pay for a place that would take care of her when her MS got worse. The Church Bleu is worth more in the long run—for all of us—but she didn't want to wait. I didn't think it was a good idea for her to give up owning the shop and the lion's share of the profits to the Church Bleu just to make some money right now. I told her I'd give up more of my share of the shop for her. And I thought if she asked, Pepper and Freddie would too."

"She must've agreed?"

"Eventually. She said I was right and that she didn't want to ruin it for us. But she asked me not to talk to Pepper and Freddie about it until she actually inherited the cheese, that she'd renegotiate with them then. So I never said anything to them about Simon, because I believed her. Until you told me you saw him here with Kendall." Her rigid frame weakened in defeat. "That's when I knew she'd lied to me. I still can't believe she planned to betray me like that."

Claire was clearly hurt. I couldn't help but wonder if she had really only learned of Kendall's betrayal last night, or if she had also seen Kendall and Simon together at the park and had decided she couldn't abide such a betrayal from her best friend.

"Did she really plan to betray Claire?" I asked Simon.

Simon cleared his throat. "I don't know anything about all that. I do know she wanted to keep it quiet and that there were people from the shop she didn't want to tell until after the deal was finalized. Look, it went down like this. Kendall got in touch with me a few months after I had that meeting with Max. She said he was ill, and she would be inheriting the secret cheese I wanted. She wanted to know how much she could get for it. I told her and she agreed to it. I said we should meet up here in Yarrow Glen right after the reading of Max's will.

You know, to make sure she wouldn't change her mind. But she didn't want me coming here. I couldn't help but come." He lifted a shoulder like it was no big deal, even though showing his face here in Yarrow Glen might've caused Kendall's death.

I tried to take all of this in. Right now, I was feeling like both of them were super sketchy.

"So why are you two here together?" I asked.

"Simon contacted me yesterday and said he wanted to ask me about some book," Claire said.

"What?" Would Simon confess to stealing my book?

"I didn't know what he was talking about until A. J.'s podcast came on later that day and we heard what he said about *Rebecca* being a book instead of a person."

"You knew about *Rebecca* before the podcast? How?" I asked him.

Simon put his hands on his hips and was suddenly interested in the tree's canopy. His annoyed expression told me he'd wished he hadn't confided in Claire. His attention finally returned to us. "I was just trying to find someone who knew something about the cheese. I was waiting around for Kendall after the will was read on Saturday morning, and when she was finally alone, I asked her about it. I wanted to follow through with our deal. That's when she told me—Max didn't leave it to her. But she said she was still going to get it, because she had a way to find out where it was. At this point, I didn't believe her, so she started to explain that Max left a clue in some book that her friend had, and she was going to get it."

That must've been when I saw him follow her past my shop right before she snuck into my apartment.

He continued. "She told me I should just trust her and leave town, but I wasn't about to do that. So when she saw me in the park, she was mad I was still here. She said she had the book, and we'd meet later. But then next thing I knew, I hear people screaming and I see her on the ground, gasping for air." He put his hands to his head, seeming to relive the moment in his mind. "When the paramedics came and nobody seemed to be paying attention to anything else, I got a little closer and saw the book she was talking about lying right there on the picnic blanket."

"Kendall's dying, and you think to grab the book?" I said, incredulous. Even if he wasn't a murderer, he was a lousy human being.

"I didn't know she was dying! People were screaming for EpiPens. I thought it was an allergic reaction and they'd take her to the hospital, and she'd be okay. They were putting her on the stretcher, and I couldn't do anything to help her, so I took the book. She'd told me it would tell us the secrets to Church Bleu." He gave me the one-shoulder shrug again.

Claire looked at him with disgust. I was certain my face read the same. Oddly, any fear I'd had about this man left me. I just wanted him to fess up to his crime.

"How do we know you didn't kill her for it? Maybe you didn't want to pay Kendall, and that's why you followed her here to Yarrow Glen," I said.

He didn't match my outrage. In fact, he seemed fatigued at having to explain himself again. "I come from a very wealthy family. Money's not an issue, but I'm passionate about cheese. I want to make one great cheese."

"But Church Bleu is *Max's* cheese. *He* created it," I said.

"I would tweak it and make it my own. It would be even better," he said confidently.

He wanted the glory of taking credit for someone else's

creation, dispensing with the heart and soul that went into it. There were so many reasons to loathe this guy: Liar. Opportunist. Murderer?

"Come on, don't look at me like that," he said, making eye contact and smiling for the first time, as if he were charming his way out of a spat with an unreasonable girlfriend. "Why would I kill her before she told me where the cheese was? She said something about Max and a clue and a book. I had no idea what it all meant. I still don't know what any of it means. Here, look." He reached around to his back pocket and took out a tattered book and held it out for me. It was a paperback copy of *Rebecca*.

I grabbed it and looked inside. There was no note from Max, no circled numbers. It wasn't my stolen book. Flipping back to the cover, I realized even though the purple cover was similar to mine, it wasn't the same one. It must've been the one Kendall had bought from Sharice, thinking it was mine. Simon was telling the truth about the book, at least.

Claire stepped closer to me to see it. "So that's the book." She didn't know the difference.

"When Kendall first told me about it, she said her friend had it. I knew Claire was her friend, so after I got the book and couldn't figure it out on my own, I went to her next," Simon explained.

I must've been the friend Kendall was referring to, but I didn't let on.

"This one didn't want anything to do with me yesterday, but she changed her tune this morning," he said about Claire.

Claire shook her head. "Only because of Kendall. I'd started to think after this weekend that Pepper and Freddie were in it for themselves. I actually wondered if one of them had tried to break into that bookstore, especially after all those questions this morning from Detective Heath. Why would he be questioning *us* about it if he didn't think it was related to finding *Rebecca*? And then I couldn't get out of my head what you said about Kendall meeting up with Simon. I knew who he was the minute you started describing him. Sorry I lied to you about it." A flash of an apologetic grin came and went. "It made me realize I was the only stupid one who believed we were all going to share Max's cheese and run Church Cheese Shop together. I told the others I didn't feel up to going to the closing ceremonies with them. I was just going to stay in my room, but the more I thought about it, the more I thought, why not? Why should I be the only loyal one? So I called Simon. I wanted to hear what he had to say. Maybe I *could* help him find the Church Bleu and make some money. Maybe I could even help Kendall's mom with the money too. That's what Kendall would want . . . even though she betrayed me too." Claire brushed at a tear on her cheek.

I handed the book to Claire, knowing it would do her no good. "You can try, but I think everyone might be on a wild-goose chase. I'd keep the book out of sight, though. I don't want you to be in danger." I glanced at Simon. "And I don't know how much you should trust this guy." I gave Claire a quick hug and walked away.

I returned to the group, who were waiting for me under the shade of another tree.

"What happened?" Baz asked.

"Let's go back to Curds and Whey. We need to have a Team Cheese meeting."

CHAPTER 30

We filed into Curds & Whey, and I locked the door behind us.

I brought Archie the laptop from my office so he could look up Simon Crowne. This time I was going to make sure the guy was who he said he was. I relayed the conversation in the park as we sat around the hand-hewn picnic table with waters from the fridge. Archie and Baz sat across from me. Roman sat in between me and Mrs. Schultz.

"Simon Crowne. Here he is," Archie said, pointing to the computer screen in satisfaction.

"Photo?" I asked.

Archie turned the laptop screen toward me so I could see the picture. Yup, it was him. I was relieved not to have messed that up a second time. Archie turned it back so he could read on.

"What does it say about him?" I asked.

I saw Archie's eyes scanning the page as he summarized, "He's thirty-four. His family's super wealthy—they own and breed Thoroughbreds. They've had winning horses in the Kentucky Derby and Belmont." He sounded impressed.

"If he's got a bunch of money, what does he want with the cheese?" Baz asked, reading the screen for himself.

"He said he has a passion for cheese," I told him.

"That's his current hobby. Before that, he owned race-horses, he climbed Mount Everest, and he's written a book." Archie ticked off the list from the internet article.

"Wow. A regular Forrest Gump," Roman commented with a hint of sarcasm.

"I bet he got those recognitions the way he's trying to get this one, by paying someone to do most of the work," I said. I knew how deep Max's passion had run, which was why he was able to create a unique cheese like Church Bleu. I didn't appreciate Simon Crowne trying to buy his way in and act like it was his own.

"It says here he's been a cheese hobbyist for the last two years," Archie said, still reading off the computer.

I rolled my eyes in disgust. "Two whole years, huh? And he wants to fiddle with one of the best cheeses in the country? No wonder I'd never heard of him."

"He might be looking for something to fulfill him if he's had it easy all his life. The problem with that is, if you haven't worked hard for something, you're usually not fulfilled by it, at least not for long," Roman said. "I felt like that about the winery. I worked hard, don't get me wrong, but it's my family's business. It didn't come from me."

Mrs. Schultz patted Roman on the back. "You started from scratch learning to make mead and starting your business. You should be very proud of yourself."

Roman lowered his eyes. He was confident, but not one to brag about himself.

"Mrs. Schultz is right. Baz too—you both took your own path and followed your passion," I said. Having left my family's dairy farm, I knew how hard it must've been for them to break from family tradition.

"Are toilets really my passion?" Baz asked, stroking his chin in exaggerated contemplation.

We all laughed.

"You know what I mean. You could've followed in your family's footsteps building homes, which is a perfectly fine choice. But you struck out on your own as a handyman and carpenter. Everyone in town counts on you. And you're an excellent woodworker."

"Aw, shucks. Tell me more," Baz kidded.

It felt good to instill some levity into the conversation, if only for a few moments.

Mrs. Schultz returned to the subject of Simon. "Do you believe him, Willa? That he wasn't involved in Kendall's murder?"

I thought about it some more. "I kind of do," I said. "I *really* dislike the guy, but unless there's a trail of unsolved murders leading to his other accomplishments, his MO seems to be to pay for his triumphs. I don't think there's enough at stake for him to start killing for them, do you?"

They all agreed. Archie closed the laptop.

"What about Claire?" Mrs. Schultz asked. I think she was still feeling the endorphins from the *Bauer's Five* outing. She was in full detective mode.

"One minute I suspect her and the next, I think she's the biggest victim in all of this—outside of Kendall." I shook my head slowly. "I really don't know."

"Do you think any of the others know who Simon is, and saw him and Kendall talking? Maybe Claire's not the only one who felt betrayed," Roman said.

"That's a real possibility," I responded.

"Assuming he and Claire are telling the whole truth, that does leave Freddie, Pepper, Maxine, and Hugo," Baz said. "Archie told us you didn't find the book in any of their rooms."

"Yup," I confirmed. "Although I didn't finish Claire's room."

"And I didn't get a chance to search Hugo's because that's when Claire came back," Archie said.

"You didn't find *any* evidence?" Roman asked.

"Like what? A bottle of honey? The rock someone threw at the bookstore window?" I said sarcastically, and then immediately regretted it. "Sorry, I'm just frustrated. We executed that whole plan perfectly just to come up empty."

"I think confronting Simon and Claire isn't exactly coming up empty," Roman said, giving me a squeeze on the shoulder.

"I know, I meant with my book." I didn't need consoling—I needed that book.

Roman folded his arms on the table. "Maybe Heath has found something we haven't. Did he dust your place for fingerprints?"

"No. The book was right there on the kitchen counter—it was probably the only thing they touched other than the doorknob, which I touched when I came home."

"The bookstore diversion was obviously planned out. I'm certain they would've worn latex gloves anyway. That's what thieves do," Mrs. Schultz noted. She'd gone back to rubbing her scarf.

Archie's mouth snapped open, forming an O. "Gloves!"

"You found latex gloves?" Baz said, surprised.

"Not latex ones, winter gloves," he said with a grin.

I picked up Archie's excitement. "That's right. And why would anyone pack gloves in May? They were in one of the suitcases in Pepper and Freddie's room. I wish I knew which one of their suitcases it was," I said.

"The gloves could've been left in the luggage by accident from a prior trip," Roman pointed out.

"Or they could've been bought somewhere to use for the book heist. A purchase like that would be less damning than buying latex gloves."

"Who sells winter gloves this time of year?" Baz asked.

"The thrift shop might," Mrs. Schultz said. "I go in often to see what new scarves are in and they sell whatever someone brings in for consignment."

"We should ask them about it when they open tomorrow," Roman said.

"But we need answers now." Patience was not my strong suit.

"Without the book, what can we do?" Baz said.

Baz was right. "Nothing. We're at a dead end." My whole body drooped in disappointment. I laid my head on my forearms on the table.

"You do have one more resource," Mrs. Schultz, ever the optimist, said.

I lifted my head. "What's that?"

"The police."

They wouldn't have the book either, but at this point, I had no other choice. We were running out of time. "I have to copy Max's second letter, then bring the original to Detective Heath. I can't tell him about the gloves, because then I'd have to tell him about sneaking into the rooms, but I have to convince him to do something. If everyone leaves tomorrow, we won't ever find out who killed Kendall."

CHAPTER 31

The security officer I'd dubbed Bruce allowed me in after a brief confirmation call to Detective Heath and accompanied me as far as his office door. Heath was waiting for me and shut the door behind us. I still wasn't very optimistic about this meeting, but getting to be in close quarters with Heath lifted my spirits. He said hi and smiled at me, activating a fluttering I had to put my hand on my stomach to tame. He'd never allowed his detective mask to slip at the station before with a hello and a smile. By the time he sat across from me at his desk, he was business, as usual. I ignored how good his broad shoulders looked without his suit jacket on as I handed him Max's letter.

He unfolded it. "Another clue?"

"Yes. It arrived today." He didn't have to know I'd been holding onto it since this morning.

He read it. "Do you know what any of this means?"

"We figured out that two of the riddles are north and west."

"Who is *we*?"

"My friends and I—Archie, Mrs. Schultz, Baz, and Roman. They can all be trusted to keep a secret."

He said "Okay," but his look told me it wasn't really.

"We think the first riddle answer is *volcano*, which might indicate the cheese is aged in a lava cave somewhere northwest of here."

"Okay," he said again, just as doubtfully. He scribbled some notes and then folded Max's letter again.

"Did you find out anything from talking to the group this morning?" I asked.

"Nothing concrete. We're checking out their alibis."

"They leave tomorrow morning," I reminded him.

"I know."

"If they leave, Kendall's murder will end up a cold case. We have to do something today. Like now."

"I agree with you."

This halted my next plea. "You do?" He was full of surprises today.

"Someone went after Kendall and was in your apartment. We need to find out who it was, so you're no longer targeted."

"Okay, so what can we do?"

"*We*? No. Leave this up to me."

"It won't work without me. I've got a plan." I'd thought one up before coming to the station.

"Of course, you do." He looked mildly amused.

I ignored him and barreled ahead. "I'm the one receiving Max's clues, and whoever took the book knows it, and all of them probably suspect it. So, my plan is to come up with a fake clue to lead whoever has the book somewhere, so we can catch them."

Heath interrupted my grand scheme. "I'm not putting you in danger."

"I won't be. I don't even need to be there after we set the trap, but the only way they'll believe it is if the clue comes from me."

Heath tossed his pen on the desk blotter. "Entrapment isn't something I can sign off on."

"It's a trap, not entrapment. We're not planting anything on them. It's just to catch the guilty one in the act."

"Catch them in the act of doing what?" he asked.

"Looking for another clue!" *Isn't it obvious?*

"That's not a criminal activity."

"No, but they'll have the book. We'll know who stole it, and in turn, who murdered Kendall."

"We can't assume that whoever stole the book also killed Kendall."

I knew that too, but plowed on ahead, still hopeful I could convince him. "That's what you think, though, isn't it?"

"We can't assume," he repeated.

With each idea that he squashed, I was more determined to make him believe in my plan. "At least it would be one step closer—it flushes *somebody* out. Can't you just go on faith?"

He leaned forward and caught my gaze. "I go on procedure and evidence. I have to."

I gnawed on my bottom lip, trying to come up with a retort, but I didn't have one. He was right.

"What?" he said, obviously seeing that I was internally tortured.

"I hate when you're right." I pouted.

He chortled in surprise. "Listen, we all hoped we'd have it settled before they left. We've got some time, and we're still on it. It's a lot trickier with the murder weapon being as innocuous as honey."

I leaned forward again. I wasn't giving up completely. "What about Max's death? Is there anything to A. J.'s assertions that it might not have been an accident?"

"It's another thing about this case that's impossible to be one hundred percent certain. Max died from a heart attack, but he also had bad contusions from the crash. Whether the heart attack caused the crash, or the crash caused his heart attack, we can't say for sure."

"And the anonymous nine-one-one call? Are you looking into that? Why would someone call in the accident but then leave him there all alone?"

Heath didn't answer me right away. He seemed to be contemplating something.

"You know something, don't you?" I said.

He'd made up his mind. "The department in charge of the crash ran DNA tests on Max's cell phone. They didn't come up with a match until Kendall's death."

"What do you mean? I don't understand."

"Kendall's DNA was on Max's phone. Coupled with the nine-one-one recording, we think she was the one who made the anonymous call from Max's phone after his crash."

For the first time, I was at a loss for words. But only for a few moments. "Kendall? She killed Max?"

"There's still no proof that she ran him off the road. The absence of skid marks suggest he never tried to brake and that he had his medical emergency while driving."

"I can't believe she would've left him there to die." I swallowed down the sting of grief that threatened to escape with my words.

"He was almost certainly gone immediately."

"Still, that's . . . heartless." My eyes welled as I pictured the scene in my mind.

"Hey," Heath said gently, as he rose from his chair and came over to my side with a tissue.

I blotted away my tears. "I'm okay."

He returned to his desk, but his look of concern remained.

I made an effort to leave the horrible image behind. "Now it makes more sense why Kendall was killed before she had the secret. It was revenge. She must've followed Max out there without telling the others. Somehow one of them found out and wanted to wait for her to inherit and share the secret to the Church Bleu before they killed her."

"Betrayal could be a motive," Heath agreed.

Betrayal. "Claire felt betrayed by Kendall. She told me so." Leaving out the part about hiding under her bed and overhearing her phone call, I told Heath about my conversation with Claire and Simon Crowne. I thought about everything that had transpired. "I don't know why Max involved me with his Church Bleu. He knew the others were salivating to get their hands on it. I just wanted my own shop. I never gave him any indication that I wanted that cheese."

"Maybe that's why. He saw your authenticity when it comes to your passion. Didn't you say he had the same?"

I thought of how willing Max was to teach me everything he knew about his shop, but the nuts and bolts of it were dispensed with quickly. For Max, running a successful shop started and ended with a commitment to the cheese. He was always testing me—not on my knowledge, but my passion. Was he testing me now, by giving me guardianship of his beloved Church Bleu?

"I guess you're right," I said to Heath. I felt better about Max putting me in the middle now, and even protective of his Church Bleu. "I'll let you get back to work on it."

At the office door, he said, "Let me know if you get any more letters from Max."

"I will," I said, sullenly.

He placed his hands on my shoulders and it was all I could do not to fall into him so he'd wrap his arms around me. "Unfinished business never feels good, but it's going to be okay. We haven't given up," he said.

I nodded. I didn't want to give up either.

CHAPTER 32

Regrettably, the comfort and confidence of Heath dissipated with each step that I took back to my apartment building. I was surprised to see Roman sitting at the foot of my stairs. Baz's truck wasn't in the parking lot, so he wasn't here for Baz.

He rose when he saw me. "How'd it go with Detective Heath?"

"Not great. He appreciated that I shared Max's letters with him, but he didn't go for my plan to trap Kendall's killer."

"What do we do now?"

"Nothing, I guess. What *can* we do?"

"Didn't you just say you had a plan?"

I looked around. "We shouldn't be talking about this out here."

He followed me up the steps and into my apartment. It felt odd for him to be here again. He used to come over regularly, but our last heart-to-heart here three months ago put the final nail into the coffin of our budding relationship.

He waved hello to Loretta on her island. She wiggled back at him flirtatiously. He made himself comfortable on my love seat. "So tell me your plan."

I sat in the chair next to him, glad to at least be able to tell someone about it, since I thought it was pretty clever. "Whoever stole my book has looked through it for the clue. I'm sure they saw all the letters that were circled and figured they meant something, but it would be almost impossible to figure out unless they had the numbers from the first note that Max sent to me to know which letters belonged to the clue."

"Go on."

"They'll all be coming back from the cheese invitational soon, so the first part of the plan would be to invite them over here. You know, for one last toast to Max and Kendall. Whoever stole the book would jump at the chance to be back in my apartment so they could look for the clue to go with it. So if I were to leave those page numbers somewhere here in the apartment where they'd see them, only the person who stole the book would know their significance. They'd take the numbers and solve the word scramble from the book like we did—*Here lies the secret.*"

"And then what?"

"Let me back up. On the paper with the numbers, I'd have added a fake clue—a location where they'd believe the next clue is hidden. I'd make it somewhere that wouldn't be obvious if the others happened to glance at the paper. Like Jackrabbits Run." I'd thought about the walking trail by the park. "If I didn't capitalize the first letters, it would just look like a weird phrase—jackrabbits run. But if you've solved the first part of the clue and know that you're looking for the location of the next one, you'd try to find out where Jackrabbits Run is. The book thief goes to the trail looking for the next clue, and we catch him . . . or her." I sat back, feeling satisfied with my plan, but not for long. "But Heath nixed it. It was a long shot. I didn't really expect him to agree to it. He had a point—if the plan succeeded, what would we do after we caught the person with my book? It's not the same as catching them red-handed at murder."

Roman thought for a moment. "We get them to confess. That's what happens when a criminal's back is against the wall, right? You've gotten confessions out of people before."

"True, but they're usually trying to kill me at the time, so I don't recommend that strategy." A shiver traced my spine, thinking back to my prior encounters with unsavory people.

Roman let out a frustrated sigh. "We can't just give up."

I'd expect this coming from Archie, but Roman? He was usually one to tell me to stay away from trouble. "This isn't like you, Roman. You've never pushed for me to get more involved. What's going on?"

He rested his forehead on his fingertips for a few moments before he spoke. "The stories that came out that first day said my wine was cross-contaminated with my mead and that's why Kendall died. It's not true. It's not even possible, but now it's been said and the only way to squash it is to prove that someone deliberately put mead in her cup. I don't want people to not trust Golden Glen."

I understood. His reputation was at stake, not to mention his livelihood. I hated that there was so much working against us. "Heath said it might be impossible to prove."

"Then why are we waiting for the police to do something? And what about how this affects *you*? You said yourself, they all suspect you're involved now. Whoever stole the book *knows* you are. I don't want the murderer coming after you like they did Kendall because they think you have something they want."

"I told all this to Heath, but—"

"Forget Heath!" I'd never seen Roman riled like this, even when he'd been suspected of murder. He said more calmly, "You don't need him. You and I can do this together."

"I don't know." I didn't want to give up either, but I also didn't want to defy Heath. How many times had I told him I trusted him, only to keep sticking my nose in a case?

When I didn't say more, Roman said, "You're right. I don't want to put you in harm's way or make you do anything you don't want to do. We'll let it go."

He got up to leave.

"What are you going to do now?" I asked.

With one hand on the doorknob, he said, "Nothing. I'm going back to my apartment."

"You're not going to do nothing," I said.

He turned to face me. "Why do you say that?"

"Because I've done what you're doing now plenty of times before. You're going to try to trap the book thief yourself, aren't you?"

Roman dispensed with the façade. "It's a shame to let a good plan go to waste," he said sheepishly. The dimple in his cheek appeared along with his slight grin.

It wasn't like I didn't want to see this through. If it didn't work out, nothing lost. If we could get something out of the book thief, we had a lot to gain.

I stood. "Don't go. Let's do this."

He smiled and rubbed his palms together. "What's first?"

From my pocket, I pulled out the paper Archie had copied the numbers on. I wanted to keep them on me at all times, which was ironic seeing as how we would now be purposely leaving them out for our suspects to see. I got a second piece of paper.

"We have to copy these numbers exactly as they are," I said.

Roman wrote down the numbers in the first word-scramble clue I received from Max.

"Now write *jackrabbits run*, all lowercase letters."

"Do you really think they'll know it's a clue?"

"Whoever has my book is going to be looking for the clue to go with it. And if they don't? Well, it was worth a shot." I noticed the time. "They're going to be back soon. I better call Constance."

I called the inn. "Hi, Constance, it's Willa. I wasn't able to get to the closing ceremonies today, after all, so I wanted to have Max's group over for a short goodbye. Do you mind asking them to come to my apartment when they get back? Let them know it's right above my shop. The door's around back."

"No problem, Willa," she said.

"Include Hugo and Maxine too, please."

"Sure. Maxine's already back. Do you want me to ring her room?"

"No, that's okay. Wait for the others to get there unless you see her leave."

"Sure thing." She then spoke in almost a whisper. "She came back with that rude guy we talked about—the preppy Superman."

"From the park?"

"Yup. And he wasn't any nicer this time. He didn't even look my way. Just kept his head down and went upstairs with her."

"Is he still up there?"

"No, he didn't stay long. I don't know if he's a player or what, but I'm sure glad Lonnie and you steered clear of him."

"Thanks for letting me know, Constance."

She returned to her normal chipper voice. "You bet. I'll give the others your message."

"You're the best."

When we ended the call, I said to Roman, "Simon Crowne was with Maxine. What do you think that means?"

"He's still looking for the answers?"

"I wonder." Did he seek her out at the invitational this morning after he left me and Claire at the park, or did they already know each other? I took Simon at his word just because he finally told me who he was. Maybe that was the only thing he was telling me the truth about. "Maybe I shouldn't have dismissed him so readily. Or Maxine. If they've been working together, then her alibi last night means nothing. Come on, let's get everything ready. We've got a trap to set."

CHAPTER 33

Voices streamed in through my open apartment window, alerting me to the group arriving. I crossed my fingers that whoever had my book would search for a clue while they were here, seeing as how they wouldn't have to break in this time.

I opened the door as soon as they knocked. I was glad to see Maxine and Hugo had arrived with Claire, Pepper, and Freddie.

"Thanks for coming," I said as I welcomed them inside.

As soon as I'd closed the door behind them, Hugo uttered, "Do you have something for us?"

"I have some cheese and wine." I stepped into the kitchen to finish cutting the selections for my board. I'd purposely left tasks for myself to make it easier for prying eyes to look around my place.

"I mean *Rebecca*. Do you have the book or a clue to help us find where the Church Bleu is hiding? I thought that's why you asked us to come. We all know by what happened at the *Gazette* that you know something you're still not telling us."

Wow, Hugo wasn't even attempting to be under the

radar. Unless it was all an act because he already had the book.

I stuffed a piece of cheese in my mouth, an instant stress reliever. "Sorry. Like I said yesterday, I don't have anything to help you. I just thought it would be nice to gather one last time for Max's and Kendall's sake."

Hugo let out a frustrated sigh and reached for the bottle of wine on my butcher block island. "Fine, I'll take some wine then."

"The bottle opener is in the top drawer of the antique cabinet in my hallway."

It's where I kept my linens, but today I stuck the wine opener in there too, to give the guilty party a chance to explore. The slender cabinet was in the back of my apartment right across from my bedroom where I'd placed a pile of old mail on my dresser, including the clue, plain as day right on top. Roman had used colored markers to draw a small target on it. I hoped it wasn't too much, but it was something Max might've done.

Hugo left to retrieve the bottle opener, and hopefully snoop.

"How come you missed the closing ceremonies this morning, Willa?" Pepper asked.

Luckily Claire was sauntering around the living room, so we didn't meet each other's gaze. "Mondays are paperwork days for the shop. I couldn't get away after all," I replied, cutting the cheese deliberately slowly. "How was it?" I was almost afraid to ask after Friday evening's fiasco.

"Claire didn't make it either. It was nice. Didn't you think so, Maxine?" Pepper asked.

She shrugged. "Hugo was better behaved," she said, drolly, as Hugo walked back into the room.

"I hold access to the wine. You'd better be nice," he said to her, holding the bottle opener aloft.

"I'm not partaking. I have to get back to training," she said.

"You're going back to cycling? What are your plans for Church Cheese Shop now that it's yours?" Freddie asked her, waiting for Hugo to open the wine.

"She's selling it to us," Pepper said.

"Unless she's not as disinterested in it as she claims to be." Hugo looked down his nose at Maxine, as if challenging her.

It was already getting tense in here. I stopped delaying and placed the cheese board on the kitchen island. I'd decided to serve Oregon cheeses in honor of Max and Kendall, but perhaps my focus on catching the culprits tonight subconsciously led to my choices of Vampire Slayer garlic cheddar and Up in Smoke chevré.

Maxine ignored Hugo's snipe. "May I use your bathroom?" she asked me, obviously wanting to delay the conversation or put the kibosh on it entirely.

"Right down the hall," I replied, pointing the way again.

When she'd gone, Freddie said to Pepper in a lowered voice, "Without the Church Bleu, can we afford to buy the shop?"

"We'll find the secret to the Bleu," Pepper replied, sounding quite confident under the circumstances.

I noticed Claire stayed quiet.

"You sound awfully confident, Pepper." Hugo echoed my thoughts. "What do you know?"

"Like I'd tell you," Pepper shot back, as direct as ever.

"You *should* tell me. I know Max would want me to have it. I'm the president of the board of NWCS. It would be like donating your personal Van Gogh to the Van Gogh museum."

"Good try, Hugo," Freddie said.

"What *do* you know, Pepper? Aren't I supposed to be included?" Claire said. She'd poured herself a glass of wine and gone through half of it—more liquid courage.

"You are! We're buying the shop together, the three of us," Pepper replied.

This time Claire kept quiet and focused on swirling the wine in her glass.

Maxine reentered the room, saying, "Nice place you've got here, Willa."

I was pretty sure she'd overheard the conversation and wanted to steer clear of the topic. The reason for her small talk seemed to register with Pepper and Freddie too—they looked annoyed.

"Thank you," I said.

"You live by yourself?"

"Just me and Loretta, my fish."

Claire looked up from her wine and glanced around the room. "I didn't see Loretta. I remember how much you loved that fish," she said, chuckling.

"Loretta's still kicking and as fabulous as ever. She's in the bedroom. You're welcome to go in and say hi." I pointed the way. Did Claire expect to see Loretta in her usual place because she was in my apartment last night?

"The famous fish. I gotta see this," Pepper said, heading for the bedroom first.

Loretta's sacrifice in leaving her island to help me set the trap was working.

Claire watched Pepper leave the living room and decided to stay put. "Did you know I got a betta fish of my own, thanks to all your Loretta stories? He's a gorgeous blue one. I named him Aoi—it means *blue* in Japanese. He's so peaceful to watch at the end of a hectic day." She sighed and looked off with a wisp of a smile on her lips.

"I think we should discuss the shop since we're all here," Freddie said.

Nobody responded. Without Pepper, the others must've found him easy to ignore.

"I don't care who gets the shop, but I deserve the cheese," Hugo said, sticking his nose into his glass and then taking a long swill.

"I'm not talking to you, Hugo. Maxine?" Freddie stepped directly in her line of sight, so she couldn't keep looking away.

She reached around him for a grape and popped it in her mouth. "I've already found my buyer."

Freddie's mouth fell open.

"What do you mean?" Claire said, quickly forgetting about her relaxing fish.

"Pepper!" Freddie called.

Pepper strode back into the room.

"Maxine says she's selling to someone else," Freddie relayed as if tattling on a sibling.

"You said you'd sell it to us." Pepper's voice had lost its earlier relaxed confidence.

"I said I'd sell it. You assumed it would be to you," Maxine replied.

"Who is it? Is it someone who found the Church Bleu?" Freddie said.

"Great, now there's someone else out for it?" Hugo drained his wine glass and poured himself another.

"Can we just stop? Listen to all of you!" Claire's raised voice silenced everyone. "Willa invited us here to remember Max and Kendall, and you're all just . . . just . . ." She scrunched her reddened face in frustration and ran out of the living room. A door slammed shut within the apartment.

We stared at one another, still silent. Eventually, Maxine said, "Should someone go check on her?"

"Give her a minute to herself," I replied. It might've all been a ruse to search the other rooms and I wanted to let her do it.

"I know how she feels," Maxine said. "And now that the invitational is over, I'm heading home. It was nice to meet you, Willa." Maxine started for the door.

"So that's it?" Freddie said before I could respond to her. "You're not even going to give us a chance to buy Max's business?"

"Give me your highest offer," Maxine said without batting an eye. "I just want to be rid of it."

"Well, that's sentimentality for ya," Hugo remarked.

This shook Maxine out of her composed state. "My father spent his whole life at that shop. His employees saw him more than I did. When he wasn't at the shop, he was like a mad scientist, trying to come up with a perfect cheese. It didn't change after my mother died and it was just the two of us. He never once came to a race of mine. You people didn't deserve his attention. *I* deserved it. I craved it. I've always despised that shop. So yes, I want to be rid of it, but don't question my love for my father."

We were surprised and speechless, even Pepper.

Freddie left the room without a word, passing Claire who was now standing in the wide doorway.

Maxine cleared her throat and gathered herself. "Contact my father's attorney and make me an offer if you want the shop. I doubt it'll be better than the all-cash offer I have already, but go ahead. I couldn't care less who gets Church Cheese Shop or the Church Bleu." Maxine walked out the door, closing it firmly behind her. This time no one stopped her.

Claire left the doorway. "You can all be very insensitive."

Freddie popped his head in, then cautiously walked over to the rest of us. "Why would Max even leave her the shop in the first place?"

"Because she was cozying up to him the last three months of his life," Pepper said. She grabbed a piece of cheese off the board. "I think we have some things to discuss. We'd better go too. Sorry this wasn't the kumbaya you'd hoped for, Willa," Pepper said.

I let them off the hook. "It's been a long weekend."

Claire and I hugged. Pepper and Freddie threw me a parting wave, and they all walked out. Only Hugo remained.

"Anything you want to share with me now that they're gone?" he said conspiratorially.

I splayed my hands. "Sorry, Hugo. I've got nothing to share."

"I'm not giving up," he said, as I walked him to the door.

"I wouldn't expect any less from the president of the NWCS."

He puffed up a little as he walked out the door. I closed it behind him and ran to my bedroom to see if anyone had taken the bait. The clue was gone. The first part of the trap was complete.

CHAPTER 34

Another knock on the door had me hurrying out to the living room as I was riffling through my junk drawer looking for the colored markers that I was sure I'd put there. I peered through the peephole before answering, just in case one of them had returned. To my relief, I saw the distorted faces of Baz and Roman.

When I opened the door, Baz stuck his head in. "They gone?"

"Yeah. Come on in." I ushered them inside.

"I saw Baz's truck pull in, so I went next door. I told him the plan," Roman explained. "How'd it go?"

"The clue's gone. All of them had an opportunity to take it, so I'm still not sure who it is. I want to draw the target that you'd put on the clue and prop it against one of the trees. I think the book thief will be looking for it, then we'll know without a doubt that it's him . . . or her."

"How long are we gonna hang out in the woods?" Baz asked.

"Until whoever it is gets there."

"I better practice my wild-animal call." Baz let out a screech that was part chimpanzee and part cat who'd just gotten his tail stepped on.

I jumped back. "Yowza. Did you learn that from Mrs. Schultz?"

"My brother Nigel."

"We want to catch whoever's looking for the clue, not scare them away," I said.

"It's not to scare people, it's for wild animals. Have you ever been in the woods when it starts to get dark? We gotta watch for mountain lions, bears, foxes . . ."

"Foxes?" Roman said, looking skeptical.

"Don't be fooled by the fluffy tail. I made that mistake with a rabbit once. Bit the tip of my finger almost all the way off when I was ten." Baz showed us his forefinger. It looked no worse for wear.

I went back to searching the drawer. "I think it'll be fine. Everett bikes that trail all the time and walks it with George sometimes."

"Yeah, but Everett's faster and we don't have a dog to protect us."

"If you're worried about it, you don't have to come. It's really okay. Where are those markers?" I slammed the drawer shut and mentally retraced my steps to figure out where I'd put them after Roman had drawn a target on the clue.

"Baz, you can keep a lookout from the town hall parking lot to let us know when one of them comes," Roman suggested.

"That's a good idea," I said. "Unless they get there first . . . Did you keep them, Roman?"

"What are you looking for?" he asked.

"The red and black markers you used."

"I don't think so." Roman patted his jeans pockets just in case, but no markers.

"Forget the target. If we find someone who was here tonight looking around in the woods, that's enough guilt to satisfy me," I said. "So are you going to be our look-out, Baz?"

"Sure, I can do that. I'll need some sustenance. You got any cheddar there?" Baz eyed the cheese board I'd made.

I pointed to the Vampire Slayer. "If you like garlic, you'll like that. If you eat enough of it, no animals will dare come near you. Baggies are in that drawer. I want to put on something darker for camouflage, so they don't see us before we see them."

I left them and headed to my bedroom, where I exchanged my T-shirt for a long-sleeved black shirt and my shorts for jeans—early evening would be buggy on the trail. I stopped in the bathroom for some bug spray and returned to the living room where Roman was waiting. Alone.

"Baz went to get more snacks," he explained.

"You want some bug spray?" I asked. He was wearing jeans and a T-shirt, his usual attire.

"Good idea," he replied.

"I hate putting this stuff on. I feel like it never comes off my fingers no matter how much I wash my hands afterward."

"Let me," he said. He took it from me and spritzed some on his fingertips. He put the bottle down and moved close to me, gently dabbing it on either side of my neck as if it were perfume. I kept my gaze away from his. He ran his hand down my arm and lifted my hand. His fingers slid beneath my sleeve to touch my inner wrist. "You want some here too?"

I pulled my hand out of his, afraid he'd feel my pulse racing. I stretched my sleeve almost to my knuckles. "No, thanks. That's enough." I wasn't just talking about the bug spray.

He rubbed some on himself, then washed and dried his hands.

"Found your markers," he said, pulling them out from where they were hiding behind the roll of paper towels on the counter. "What do you want to use to draw on?"

I went to the spare room and ripped a flap off one of the boxes. "Here. This'll be sturdy enough."

He took it and began to draw a target like the one he drew on the clue. "Are you feeling okay about the plan?"

"I hope I haven't made the clue too hard. What if they can't figure out *Jackrabbits Run*?"

"They'll know to go to Constance. We could make it easy and just ask her if anyone's asked about the trail."

"No. We have to catch them in the act." I looked at the clock anxiously and gnawed at my lip. "As long as we don't miss them." I had no idea how long it would take the culprit to figure out the clues we'd left.

Roman finished coloring in the target. "They've come this far. They'll look until they find it. Don't worry—we're a good team." He looked at me and winked.

I ignored the flirting. The target was done. "Perfect. Let's go." I grabbed the cardboard target and my keys. "You got your phone?"

Roman nodded.

I opened the door. Baz was on the other side of it, holding three bags of food. "You ready?" Now that he was snacked up, he seemed jazzed by his role.

I wasn't as jazzed spending more time alone with Roman, but he was a good ally, and this was a mission.

CHAPTER 35

Baz drove away in his pickup truck with enough snacks and beverages for a two-day stakeout. Roman and I entered the woods at the edge of the narrow parking strip behind my building. It took us several minutes, but we made our way to Jackrabbits Run. Neither of us had been on this loop trail enough to know it well, so we got confused whether we were going the long way or the short way back to the trailhead at the park.

"What if we're walking in the same direction as them? We could be going in circles and never run into them," Roman said.

"That's what the target's for. We're going to plant it and then stay nearby. We just have to find a decent spot where we won't be seen before they notice the target."

We walked in deliberate silence. I kept my ear tuned for any voices or footsteps, but it seemed we were alone on the trail. The trees' shade made it seem darker on the trail than it was. Baz's concerns streamed through my thoughts and made me start at every snap of a branch and flutter of wings.

"Maybe we should use a compass, so we know if we're walking toward the park," Roman suggested. He retrieved

his phone from his pocket and fell behind tapping at it and
pivoting in each direction.

I kept going. Around the next bend, I halted when I saw
a figure kneeling over someone on the ground. I recognized both. It was Freddie kneeling over Pepper who was
lying prone, the way I'd seen Kendall dead at the park.
My *Rebecca* book was lying next to her.

Freddie!

I should've known all along it was Freddie. He'd been
immediately interested in the mead. It was probably right
then that he concocted his plan to kill Kendall with it—
so much easier than having to kill her some other way.
We'd found the winter gloves in his room at the inn,
surely used so he could steal my book without leaving
fingerprints. Befriending Pepper from the get-go, only to
kill her once he thought he had the final clue that would
lead him to the Church Bleu.

In my shock, the cardboard target fell from my hand.

Freddie turned at the sound.

I backed up a step. "You killed her!"

"What? No, I didn't! I-I didn't, I swear." He waved his
hands at me. "We split up to look for—Anyway, when I
came back around, she was here."

I turned at Roman's footsteps behind me.

"Roman, call the police. Pepper is—"

Moaning from Pepper interrupted me. She started to
rouse.

"You're alive! She's alive! She's alive!" Freddie yelled.

"I'm not Frankenstein, Freddie. Stop yelling," Pepper
groused.

Freddie helped her haul herself to a seated position.
She rubbed the back of her head and winced. "Ouch!"

"What happened?" Roman said, his eyes questioning
all three of us.

I wanted to help Pepper, but I was still wary of Freddie and kept my distance.

"I don't know what happened," Pepper said groggily. "I think I was knocked out."

"By Freddie!" I told her.

"Not Freddie. Get real," she said with an annoyance in her voice that I'd suggest it.

"How do you feel?" Freddie asked her.

"How do you think I feel with a knot on the back of my head the size of their freakin' clock tower," she replied angrily.

Freddie was looking worried and pale, but was it because of Pepper or because of what he'd done to Pepper?

I dashed closer, scooped the book off the ground, and returned to Roman. I flipped the cover open to Max's note. "This is my book. You knocked Pepper out to take the book and the clue from her?"

"I told you, I didn't knock her out! We were both in on it," Freddie said.

"Oh really? Then where did you keep the book this morning?"

"In Pepper's car. What does that prove?"

"Freddie!" Pepper admonished weakly.

It took me a few seconds to digest this, but it made absolute sense they'd be working together. "So you both killed Kendall, then stole my book and the clue."

"You've got it all wrong. All we did was steal your stupid book," Freddie insisted.

"What about what happened to the bookstore?" Roman said.

Freddie looked at Pepper for guidance, but she still had her head in her hands. He continued to look panicky. "I threw a rock at it to set off the alarm so Pepper could get into your apartment with no one around. It's not murder."

"Shut up, Freddie," Pepper managed to say. She stopped rubbing her head and looked at her hand. It had traces of blood on it.

"Pepper, you're bleeding," I pointed out unnecessarily.

Freddie tore off the opened button-down shirt he was wearing over his tee. He rolled it up and, before placing it behind Pepper's head, said, "You know how much I love this shirt, Pepper."

"Thanks for your sacrifice," she said with a bit of humor. She winced when he put it to the back of her head. "Ouch!" She held it in place herself.

"How long have you been waiting for the paramedics?" I asked Freddie.

"I can't get a signal to call," he replied.

"You haven't called the paramedics?" And I was just starting to think maybe he wasn't guilty of trying to kill Pepper after all.

"I'll call them," Roman said.

"I'm feeling nauseous," Pepper said, resting her forehead on one bent knee.

I chanced walking over to Pepper, keeping my eyes on Freddie. Still kneeling, he stared back at me and put his hands up as another show of innocence. I didn't see anything near him he might've hit her with, but he could've easily thrown it into the woods. I knelt beside Pepper.

I remained guarded, keeping my eyes on Freddie and Pepper, as Freddie and I attended to her. "Can you get a signal, Roman?"

A sudden cry of pain whipped me around. Roman was writhing on the ground, grasping the back of his head.

Maxine stood over him, clutching a thick tree branch like a bat.

"Maxine!" Freddie squawked.

"Roman!" I started to crawl on all fours toward him, but Maxine swung the branch over her shoulder, ready to strike again, this time at me. Roman took his hands away from the back of his head. They were covered in fresh blood. He tried to sit up.

"Don't even think about it," Maxine warned with her club still high in the air.

"Maxine, what are you doing? He's bleeding!" I cried. I turned at a sound behind me. It was Freddie, scurrying away.

Go, Freddie, go!

"You won't get away with this. He'll get help," I said to her. All we had to do was wait it out. I hoped Roman's injuries could spare the time.

"He won't get far," Maxine said.

What did she mean by that?

"Were you the one who did this to me?" Pepper asked angrily. She tried to stand but woozily fell back to the ground with her head in her hands. "Whoa." She steadied herself in a sitting position, pulling her knees in close.

"Maxine, why are you doing this?"

At my question, the initial adrenaline seemed to seep out of her. She said in a small voice, "It was only going to be Kendall. She killed my father."

Even with Kendall's DNA on Max's phone, I still had a hard time believing she would kill Max, but I wasn't going to challenge Maxine under the circumstances.

Pepper, on the other hand, didn't let the circumstances deter her. "You expect us to believe Kendall killed Max? No way."

Instead of the angry reply I was expecting, Maxine's face crumpled in grief. "She ran him off the road and left him there to die. She wanted him to die before he changed his will to leave *me* the Church Bleu. I know you don't believe this, Pepper, but I loved my father."

This didn't sway her. "None of us even considered that he'd leave you his Church Bleu, Maxine. Kendall didn't feel threatened by you. She knew, just like the rest of us, that you pretended to love him for what you could get."

Oh, Pepper!

I tensed, waiting for Maxine's anger to resurface. Again, it didn't come.

"You're right that I pretended, but only about the cheese, not about him. I had to let go of my anger about his obsession with his shop and his cheesemaking. It was his greatest love. I had to accept it. So for the first time in my life, these last few months, I acted interested. And I saw a difference in my dad and the way he was toward me. I was a stubborn kid—I didn't love the cheese world the way he did, and I wanted him to love me, regardless. I rejected it, almost on principal, and made it a lifelong competition for his love. But it was a competition I always lost. This time was different—I was willing to accept it to finally have a relationship with my father. He told me how happy he was that the daughter he'd tried to mentor as a child had finally come around, so he wanted to change his will to leave me his shop. He said he'd confided it to Kendall. It must've spooked her into thinking he'd do the same with the Church Bleu."

I didn't want to give Pepper another chance to rile Maxine, so I spoke before she could. "Mission accomplished— you avenged your father's death. There's no need for more bloodshed. Roman's done nothing to you." I looked again at Roman and saw his hand feeling around the forest floor. *Oh no, he'd lost his phone.*

Pepper lifted her head from her tucked knees, where it had been resting. "Are you here for more revenge,

Maxine? Or did you come here for the same thing as the rest of us? You don't know any more about Max's Church Bleu than we do."

Maxine allowed a hint of a smile to break through her grief-stricken face. "Don't I?"

Was Maxine saying he *did* leave her the secret? If he'd told Maxine where it was, why would he leave me clues to it? I dared to glance away from her for a second to check for Freddie. Where was he? Maybe keeping her talking was the best thing.

"What do you know?" I asked her.

Maxine looked down at Roman to make sure he was still immobilized. I watched his stomach rise and fall with the deep breaths he must've been taking to deal with the pain. I was thankful that he'd lift his head and look at me every once in a while, so I knew he was still conscious. But he was pale, very pale. For all Maxine's sorrow about Max, there was a ruthlessness to her.

"My father had a trusted ally in his brother," she began. "Uncle Milo worshiped him. It wasn't hard for him to keep a secret from everyone like my father told him to. Uncle Milo was sort of a recluse, always happy living in the middle of nowhere, never leaving home except to make the Church Bleu. I knew from the beginning— Uncle Milo told me, of course. I was closer to him than I was to my dad. There was no childhood resentment with Uncle Milo. I knew the money from the Church Bleu helped support him, and that's all I cared about, not its secrets. I knew where he made it but not where he took it to be aged, because I never bothered to ask." She planted herself between me and Roman—so she could club either of us in one swing. "When Uncle Milo told me Dad was dying too, he wanted me to make up with him before it was too late. I decided he was right. I didn't do it for the Church Bleu. I didn't care about that until he died and none of *them* could stop talking about the stupid cheese." She sneered at Pepper, who stayed silent. "That memorial on Friday night was a farce. They didn't care about my father. I'd be damned if I'd let any of them profit off him. I just needed that last piece of information I would've gotten from the will if Kendall hadn't killed my father before he could change it a second time and leave me his Church Bleu. Uncle Milo was gone. Dad was gone. And the will only had a cryptic message about Rebecca."

Maxine's gaze stopped darting at the three of us and stayed on me. "Then it seemed *you* might have the answers. I hadn't considered you because you weren't at the reading of my father's will. He sent you the clue, didn't he? It was a clever move on his part. No one would suspect you of having it. I didn't, even after you told me you used to work for him. And then you showed up at the *Gazette* and made it pretty obvious you were the one who figured out *Rebecca* was the book. The questions this morning from that detective told me someone was in your apartment looking for it. Someone was after the clue from my father. I had to hope you either still had it or you had solved it before the book was taken. The invitation to your apartment was my chance to try to find out."

"But Freddie admitted he and Pepper stole my book last night. And they must've taken the clue from my bedroom, or they wouldn't be here." In confusion, I looked to Pepper, who decided *now* was the time to stay quiet.

Freddie, where are you?

I just had to hold her off a little bit longer until he came back with help. I focused on Maxine again. "How did you know to come here?"

"I found the clue in your apartment, but I couldn't

find your book to decipher the numbers, so I left the clue where it was," Maxine said to me. "Jackrabbits Run was all I needed for now—Everett took me biking here. All I had to do was find the target, but I've been walking around these woods for quite some time now without any luck. I spotted Pepper with the book in her hand, so I knocked her out—just to take what she had found, not to kill her. I figured since she had the book, she'd also found the target and the next clue. But she didn't have anything except for that useless book. I was about to give up until I heard you and him." She gestured to Roman, still lying at her feet. "I hid and watched you walk past, carrying the target, proving you were the one who found it. So where is it, Willa? Where's the next clue?"

Oh, huckleberry.

CHAPTER 36

"The clue? I have no idea," I said. This plan was really backfiring on me. *Come on, Freddie.* Maxine was back to looking at all of us. None of us could make a move without a great chance of getting clubbed by the heavy branch.

"You had the target in your hand—one just like it was on the clue in your room. So you must've found whatever clue or information was in the woods before any of us," she said.

Pepper tried sitting up more, interested in my answer.

I stared at the target I'd dropped on the ground when I saw Freddie and thought he'd killed Pepper. There was nothing to do now but tell the truth. "I made a target. I made the clue too."

Maxine's eyebrows stitched together in confusion.

"But Freddie and I had the book, and we deciphered the clue we took from your room," Pepper said. "*Here lies the secret.* There's no way it could've been made up unless you staged everything from the beginning."

I shot a nasty look at Pepper. *Not helping, Pepper! Who's the one with the club here?*

"*That* clue was real—it was Max's. I added *Jackrabbits Run* to it after I knew one of you stole the book. This was the only way to find out who stole it and killed Kendall. I never wanted Max's cheese," I said truthfully. "I don't know why he sent me that clue and I don't know what it means."

I was beginning to think I should make a desperate run for it when I heard rustling behind Pepper. Finally! Help was here.

But it wasn't help. It was Simon, one large hand gripped onto poor Freddie's thin arm, marching him back to us.

"He's a wily little fella, but I've wrangled worse horses," Simon said with amusement.

"It's about time," Maxine said.

I swallowed down the weepiness I felt coming over me now that my hope of Freddie coming back with the police was dashed. "You two are in on this together?"

"Simon's been a big help. He was the one who told me Kendall killed my father."

"Whoa, I never said *that*." Simon suddenly noticed Roman and Pepper on the ground, and a shadow of confusion crossed his face. "What's going on here?"

Maxine ignored his question. "You told me Kendall secretly followed my father on his last trip, because she didn't want to wait anymore."

"She wanted him to lead her to its secret location, that's all. She didn't want to wait any longer to find out the secret to Church Bleu," he explained.

Maxine scoffed. "What she really meant was that she didn't want to wait for him to die."

"Are you saying Kendall killed Max?" Freddie said in a squeaky voice.

"Then Maxine and Simon killed Kendall," I informed him, so he'd know who he was dealing with here.

"Hold on a minute. We didn't kill anybody," Simon said. He looked at Maxine, who didn't speak up. "Y-You didn't kill Kendall, Maxine. Did you?" He'd now totally lost that confident swagger he'd arrived with.

"The joke's on Kendall. My father was never going to leave her the cheese. He apparently left it to Willa." She steeled me with a look that made me break out in goosebumps.

"He didn't leave me the secrets to the cheese. Just a clue I can't figure out," I insisted. No reason to tell them about the riddles.

"You can stop pretending now. All I need is the location where the cheese is aged. I have the rest of the information I need to sell to Simon."

"And then what?" I demanded.

"And then he can buy the shop and the Church Bleu from me, and I can retire from racing. Do you know how little cyclists earn, especially women? Unless you win the big races, you make barely enough to just keep cycling. And that's pretty much over for me too. I could use this money and it's rightfully my inheritance."

"How do you know Simon won't kill you for what you know?" I asked Maxine, hoping to turn them against each other so we could get away.

"Hey, I told you, I didn't kill anyone!" Simon insisted, raising his voice.

"Well, Maxine did. She's already killed Kendall. And look what she's done to Roman and Pepper."

He once again took in the scene before him, and I could see him internally wrestling with what to believe.

"How do you know you're not next?" I poked.

Come on, Superman, get on the side of truth and justice.

"Is she lying, Maxine?" Simon asked, now agitated. Freddie winced as the grip on his arm tightened.

"You know they'll say anything to keep you from

getting the Church Bleu," she replied. "Hand over what you have, Willa."

"Go on. Give it to them!" Freddie said.

"Do you need more incentive?" Maxine lifted the branch as if she was going to come down on Roman again.

"Stop!" I yelled, rearing up from the ground and advancing on Maxine.

A piercing hyena-like sound came from behind her. She turned, startled, and I went for the branch. Roman kicked the side of her knee and she went down hard, holding onto it and screaming in pain. I wrested the branch away and held it in front of me, ready to duel with her and Simon. Roman unsteadily got to his feet.

"Three against one, Simon," I said, as Pepper also managed to stand. "You might as well let Freddie go."

"Four against one." Baz appeared from the woods.

I thought I recognized that hyena.

"I saw Simon in the park, heading to the trail when Freddie came out. Then they went back in together. When Roman didn't answer my text, I came," Baz told us.

"Hey, I didn't want to be a part of any of this. Maxine promised me answers, that's all. I didn't know she was going to hurt anybody." Simon realized he was still gripping Freddie and released him. Freddie took off again.

"Don't let them go!" Maxine shouted from the ground. She rocked back and forth, withstanding the pain of her knee.

"I called the police. They're on their way," Baz said.

"I'm outta here." Simon turned and hightailed it out the same way Freddie went.

"We need to get paramedics here." I went to Roman's side so he could lean on me. He put his arm around my shoulders, and I steadied him.

"Help should be here any minute," Baz said. He took the branch from me and held watch over Maxine.

"How are you feeling?" I asked Roman. I touched the back of his head. He winced. "Sorry." A lump had grown where the gash was, but it felt like the blood had stopped flowing.

Swaths of light cut through the darkening woods.

"Over here!" Baz shouted.

Freddie was with the police as they made their way to us. It was over.

CHAPTER 37

Detective Heath led the pack of police. We all pointed to Maxine, still groaning on the ground, and Heath immediately handcuffed her without incident—she was done fighting. Shep stood watch over her, and Officer Melman radioed for ambulances. Heath checked on Pepper, who was once again being taken care of by Freddie. Heath directed Officer Ferguson to stay with them while he came over to me, Baz, and Roman.

"He needs an ambulance," I said to Heath.

"They're coming," he said. "We weren't sure what we were walking into, so we kept them on standby. Roman, you should sit down. Do you know where you are?"

Roman nodded. "I'm okay."

Baz and I helped Roman to the ground.

"Are either of you hurt?" Heath asked us.

Baz and I shook our heads.

Hurried footsteps were followed by more lights and EMTs rushing toward us. Melman directed them to Maxine, Pepper, and Roman. With a hand on my back, Heath guided me out of their way. Baz followed us but hung back.

Now that everyone was being taken care of and Maxine

was in handcuffs, the tension in my body relaxed. I smiled at Heath. There was no smile in return this time.

"Can you tell me what happened?" Heath said in total detective mode, retrieving his mini notepad and pen from inside his suit jacket.

Okay, right. We *were* at a crime scene. "Where do you want me to start?"

He snapped his head up from his notepad to look at me. Even with the shadows cutting across his sharp features, I could tell he was angry. "How far back do you need to go?"

I swallowed hard. "Well . . ."

Baz came over and, together, we summarized how it all went down. Baz to the rescue again. Heath wasn't impressed by the relatively happy ending.

The EMTs had carried Roman, Pepper, and Maxine to the awaiting ambulances when Shep called for Heath. "Detective."

Heath put up a hand to keep us in place before conversing with Shep for several minutes.

Baz leaned toward me to keep his voice lowered. "He's not too happy with us, is he?"

"I think it's me he's mad at." Tired, I rubbed my hands over my face, wanting to wash away the last few hours, heck, the last few days. He had every right to be upset with me.

Heath returned to us, his stern look no softer.

"Can we go to the hospital to see Roman?" Baz asked him.

"We still need formal statements. You'll both need to come to the station afterward," he said, looking only at Baz.

"I'll follow you in a second," I said to Baz.

He nodded and started down the trail.

I spoke quickly. "I know you're not happy with me right now, but—"

"We'll take your statement at the station," he said. He finally looked at me before he walked away.

By the anger in his eyes, I wished he hadn't.

CHAPTER 38

I paced in the waiting area of the Glen District Hospital, where they'd taken Roman and Pepper. Baz sat in a chair, jiggling his leg. The medical center was a one-story building that serviced Yarrow Glen and three more surrounding small towns. I'd spent a few hours here a few months ago getting a shoulder injury checked out. Heath had stayed with me and had even brought me soggy truffle fries. It pained me to know I'd upset him so much. I closed my eyes for a moment and pushed thoughts of Heath aside. One awful feeling at a time—right now, I was worried about Roman and the extent of his injuries.

A nurse in cat-themed scrubs and lavender Crocs approached us. "You're here with Mr. Massey?" he asked.

"Yes."

"The doctor's through with him. Follow me."

We passed Pepper and Freddie as they were leaving in the custody of Officer Ferguson. They didn't make eye contact. I was glad Pepper was okay.

The nurse stopped at Roman's room and gave the door a quick rap before opening it. "I have your friends," he said in a bright, singsong voice. He allowed us in and left with a smile.

Roman was sitting on the exam table wearing a hospital gown and jeans. His shoes were off.

"Nice look," Baz remarked, giving him a handshake.

"One more test result and I'll be out of here."

"How are you?" I looked him over. He had a gauze bandage wrapped around his head.

"A few stitches and a headache. Nothing to write home about," he replied, back to his usual chill attitude.

I was relieved to hear it, but it only made me feel slightly better. "I'm so sorry you got hurt."

"Better me than you. Thanks for not leaving me with Maxine. I wouldn't have blamed you if you'd made a run for it." He smiled.

"Of course, I wasn't going to leave you! Besides, I didn't think I could outrun an athlete."

We laughed together.

"Baz is the real hero here," I said, giving Baz a love-punch on the arm.

"I knew that call of the wild would come in handy," Baz said.

Roman gave him another bro handshake.

"This is the second time you've saved my reputation. I owe you, Willa," Roman said.

"Just get better. That'll be payment enough." I squeezed his hand. He didn't let go. He caught me in his gaze and his eyes asked for more.

Baz cleared his throat as he started toward the door. "I'm gonna stand outside."

I waited to say anything to Roman until we were alone. "I care about you, Roman. You're a good friend."

"Why do I feel a *but* coming on?"

I gave him a weak smile. He recognized what was coming from the last time I had to make the difficult choice to reject him. Nothing had changed since then. He was still a great guy, but his track record of being transparent with me and past girlfriends told me he wasn't the one to continue to risk my heart on. Plus, I couldn't deny the real feelings I was developing for Heath.

I didn't want to rehash anything. I said honestly, "I'm glad this case brought us together again because I think we do better as friends. Don't you?"

He loosened his grip on my hand. "You're probably right. I'm glad we can still be friends."

"Always."

"Roman!" Gia strode into the room and over to Roman's side. I slipped my hand out of his. She threw me a venomous glance, then focused her attention on him. "Are you okay?"

"The doctor says I'm going to be fine. I'll be sprung from here in no time."

"I can drive you to your apartment." She threw another quick glare at me to make sure I wouldn't suggest otherwise. She needn't have worried. For the first time, I was glad she was here.

"Looks like you're all set then. Baz and I have to go to the station for our second interview," I said.

"Thanks for everything, Willa," Roman said.

"I'll check on you tomorrow," I replied, and walked out to where Baz was waiting.

Baz stayed in the police station's common area until his turn while Shep led me into one of the interview rooms I was unfortunately familiar with. I crossed to the other side of the table and sat in the hard plastic chair. I was surprised when he closed the door and remained in the room, sitting across from me.

"Heath's not interviewing me himself?" I asked. My heart sank.

"He's still with Maxine," Shep explained.

I had hoped Heath and I would be here alone, so I could explain more about why I'd gone ahead with the trap even though he'd told me not to.

I swallowed my disappointment and went over everything again with Shep, explaining my plan to catch the person who stole my book, which sounded worse in hindsight. Maybe it was a good thing Heath *wasn't* here. I finished and Shep turned off the recording device.

"Can I ask you something?" I said.

"You can ask. I might not be able to answer," Shep replied. He grinned, a reminder I was in friendly territory, nonetheless.

"Fair enough. Do you think Kendall purposely caused Max's car crash?"

He was serious again. "There's no way to know for certain."

"That's what Heath said when I asked him. But what do you think? Off the record?"

Shep thought about it for a moment. "The evidence doesn't point to it. He could've thought someone was following him and taken the turn too fast and didn't have time to brake. Or he could've had a heart attack and fallen unconscious. I think it's the latter."

"If she did nothing wrong, why did she make the nine-one-one call anonymously? Why didn't she stay with him?"

"There could be several reasons. She was scared. Maybe she thought it was her fault. She didn't want to have to fess up to the others that she'd followed him. This is all conjecture. I know you want to know who your friend was, Willa, but you might never have concrete answers. You said Kendall wanted to help her mother with the money from Max's cheese. Did she go as far as

Maxine had and kill someone in the name of loving a parent?" He shrugged.

I didn't have an answer either. I guess I'd have to accept that I never would. "What about Simon? Has he been caught?"

"He turned himself in. I just finished with him. He insists he didn't know what Maxine had done until tonight. He was betting on both horses—Kendall and Maxine—for getting Max's cheese. He'd attached himself to Kendall when he thought she was inheriting the cheese. But he also introduced himself to Maxine at Friday's invitational. He wanted to be the first to know, no matter who got the secret to the Church Bleu. But he made the mistake of telling Maxine that Kendall followed Max on the night he had the car crash. Maxine apparently jumped to the conclusion that Kendall must've deliberately caused it, even though Simon denied implying that. According to him, he had no idea Maxine would think that or that she would take revenge on Kendall. Simon was still hoping Kendall might come up with the location before Maxine, so it wouldn't have benefited him to kill her. We believe at this time that Simon had no knowledge of Maxine's crimes. However, he was willing to hold you, Freddie, and Pepper against your will tonight, so he's not off the hook entirely," Shep said.

I thought of everything that had happened this weekend. "After all of that—Kendall sneaking into my apartment, Pepper and Freddie stealing the book, Claire meeting up with Simon, and Hugo stalking everybody—Maxine, alone, was the culprit."

"It seems so," Shep replied.

"And still, nobody knows how to find the last of the Church Bleu." It looked like Max's cheese would forever remain a secret.

I asked to wait in the station instead of the security complex lobby while Baz completed his interview. I was hoping to catch Heath after he was finished with Maxine, but Baz came out first.

"You didn't have to wait," Baz said.

"I was hoping to see Heath, but he hasn't come out yet. I'm going to keep waiting."

"You want me to stay?"

"That's okay. It's best if I talk to him on my own. Thanks for everything, Baz. You really were a hero tonight."

"You think I can put that on my dating profile?"

"Handyman. Carpenter. Hero. I think it works."

"Catch you later." Baz was still chuckling at the thought as he left the station.

I sat back down and kept an eye on the hallway to watch for Heath. Twenty minutes later, he finally walked by with Shep.

I sprang out of the chair. "Excuse me? Detective Heath?" I caught up to them when they were almost at Heath's office. They stopped.

"Baz's interview was over a while ago. You must've missed him," Shep said to me.

"I didn't miss him. I stayed behind to talk to Heath." I dared to look at the detective. As usual, his poker face gave nothing away, but his silence was an indicator his anger hadn't dissipated as I'd hoped.

Shep's gaze swiveled back and forth between us. "I'll start writing this up," he finally said to Heath. He headed to his desk.

Heath continued into his office, and I followed. This time he didn't close the door behind us. He sat at his desk as I awkwardly stood on the other side of it.

"I have a lot of paperwork to do, Willa," he finally said,

shuffling the files on his desk rather than looking at me. "You'll get the rest of the information with everyone else when I give my statement to the press."

"I'm not here for more information."

This seemed to surprise him enough to look at me. I sat down without being asked.

"I wanted to explain why I went ahead with my plan," I said.

"Even though you told me you wouldn't."

"Well . . ." There was no way around it. "Yes."

"Will you answer me one thing?"

"Of course."

"Did you leave my office planning to do it anyway?"

"No. I swear. I was going to leave it be, I really was. But Roman really wanted answers and his reputation was at stake, so—"

"So it didn't take much to change your mind."

"He made some good points."

"Which good points were those? Like you shouldn't be messing with murderers? Like you could get hurt or killed? Like other people could get hurt, which they did? Actually, those were *my* points, which you obviously didn't think were valid."

"No, of course I did. I feel horrible that Pepper and Roman got hurt. I guess I just . . . I thought it would go our way."

Heath stared at me another few seconds. What I saw in his eyes was so much worse than anger—it was hurt and disappointment. He went back to shuffling files.

"I'm sorry. I'm really sorry. It wasn't my intention to lie to you or mess up your investigation or get anybody hurt."

Heath began tapping at his keyboard.

"We did solve the case," I shakily pointed out.

His eyes left the screen to give me a stony stare. "Yes, you did."

Usually by now he'd have warmed up, but not this time. I really didn't want to leave with him feeling this way.

"Maybe we could go for a drink and talk about this some more? Or *not* talk about this at all? Jay?"

He closed the file, which allowed me a sliver of hope he'd stand up, throw his suit jacket over his broad shoulders, and take me to The Cellar where we could work this out.

But he stayed put. "I have a lot of work to do." He stared at the closed file on his desk, tapping his pen on it.

I was only making it worse. I sat for a moment more, until all hope he'd say something nicer trickled away completely. I stood from the chair and silently left his office.

I saw Shep on my way out of the station and gave him a faint wave, unable to offer even a polite smile.

"Don't get too down. He'll cool off and be fine," he said. Somehow, Shep read the situation. I could see why he was counted on to diffuse heated arguments.

I thanked him and walked home. I appreciated Shep's kindness, but I wasn't so sure I believed his reassurance.

I went straight into my apartment and skipped rapping on Baz's door when I got home, as we often did just to tell each other we were home and free for a chat. I planned on sulking on the love seat by myself, perhaps letting the guilt of Roman and Pepper getting hurt seep in even more. I was feeding Loretta when Baz came barreling in like Kramer in an old *Seinfeld* episode.

"Willa!" he said, slamming the door shut behind him.

"What is it?" I asked just seconds before I saw the large mailer envelope in Baz's hand.

We stared at each other, feeling like we'd just gotten

the fifth correct number to a lottery ticket with only one to go.

"It came when you were gone," he said.

This could be it! I grabbed it from him and tore it open. Inside was a business-sized envelope, same as the others. My hands were shaking.

"I gotta sit down for this," I said.

We sat side by side on the love seat as I opened it and read the letter aloud.

Willa,

This is the final clue. I trust when all is said and done, you will understand everything.

With love,
Max

Beneath his signature were numbers:

41.58.20
-121.58.46

"More page numbers?" Baz guessed.

"If they are, they won't do me much good. The police have my book."

"That one-twenty-one looks like a negative number."

"It could be a stray mark."

"The book that Pepper and Freddie stole belonged to you. Can you ask Heath for it back?"

I burst out laughing, releasing my pent-up emotions. "I'm in no position to ask Heath for anything." I tossed the paper on the coffee table bench and let out a big sigh.

"Hey, you'll eventually get the book back, right? We're all curious to solve this thing, but now that Maxine's been caught, there's no rush anymore. Unless you *do* want the cheese, after all?"

"No, I really don't. It was the cause of Kendall's death and possibly Max's. And it's not what I want my shop to be known for. I'm building my shop's reputation on my own dreams, not Max's. But he entrusted me with it, so I do feel an obligation to him. I want to protect the one thing that was more important to him than anything, for better or worse. Plus, curiosity—if I'm going to be completely honest. You know patience isn't my strong suit."

"When you get the book back, we'll figure it out."

I nodded and leaned back against the cushion.

"Is there something else bothering you?" he asked.

"It's Heath. I don't think our relationship's going to be the same after this. He's really upset with me, Baz."

"I got that feeling when he was questioning us at the park. It wasn't any better when you saw him at the station?"

"Worse. I don't blame him. He thinks I dismissed everything he'd said to me and trusted Roman over him."

"Roman told me it was his idea and he had to talk you into it, so it kind of sounds like you did trust him over Heath."

"I went through with it because I wanted to do it. All Roman had to do was nudge me. I do trust Heath, but I also trust myself. I have to go with my instincts. Maxine had figured out that her father had sent me a clue. Who knows what she would've done if left to her own devices? How long was I supposed to be worried about someone coming for me? Maybe I don't always see every dangerous scenario that Heath sees, but in the end, the case gets solved."

Baz considered that. "Maybe that's why Heath's mad."

"No, that's not it. Heath's not like that. He's glad for

the cases to be closed. He just worries about me, and I don't make it easy on him."

Baz regarded me for a moment. "You really like the guy, don't you?"

I looked at Baz and guffawed. "No. I just don't like anybody being mad at me."

Okay that was a lie, but how was I supposed to admit my feelings for Heath to my best friend when I could hardly admit them to myself?

Baz shrugged at my reply and didn't push—a best-friend quality. "At least you and Roman are good again, right?"

"That's true."

He grabbed my wrist and pulled me off the love seat. "Come on, let's go to The Cellar. They extended Jimmy Buffett Weekend through tonight."

"I don't think I'm in the mood." I extracted my wrist and slumped back down on the love seat.

"That's why you gotta go. Get some Buffett vibes!" He started dancing to a slow rhythm only he could hear.

"I don't know . . ."

"After the weekend you've had? Let's kick back and waste away in Margaritaville."

I snorted. He had a way of wearing me down. "I'll take the Cheeseburger in Paradise, but you're not going to convince me to listen to Jimmy Buffett music for an hour. I've had a rough enough weekend."

"You *are* uptight. Who doesn't like Jimmy Buffett music?"

"I'm just not in the mood."

"You'll feel different once we get there. Changes in latitudes, changes in attitudes." He kept on speaking in Buffett song titles.

I laughed and was about to give in when that last song title hit me. "Changes in latitudes . . ."

"Yeah, you know that one." He began to sing it.

I looked at Max's letter again and put my hand up to stop Baz's singing.

"What is it?" he asked, coming back to the love seat.

I pointed to the paper. "What if these numbers are GPS coordinates—longitude and latitude? If we combine them with the *north* and *west* answers to the riddles, it might take us to the lava caves. Max told us to go back to *Rebecca*. Remember the clue in the book? The one that didn't seem like a clue at all?

"*Here lies the secret.*"

"Right. *Here* lies the secret." I pointed to the numbers.

"Wil, I think you just figured out how to find the Church Bleu."

I stared at the GPS numbers again.

"So when are we going?" Baz said, popping up from the love seat like he was ready to leave right this minute.

I didn't know how to answer him. Once we located the cheese, everything would be different, and I wasn't sure I wanted things to be different. In fact, I was quite certain I didn't. I loved the way my little cheese shop was thriving and the plans Mrs. Schultz, Archie, and I had been making for it. Taking responsibility for Max's Church Bleu would change all that.

"Wil?" Baz stood over me with a questioning brow.

"I'll need some time to put some things in order so I can close the shop for a few days," I replied. I'd had harder things in life I'd managed to deal with. Max trusted me with his beloved cheese. I was determined to see this through.

EPILOGUE

We were into the first hour of an expected six-hour drive north in my old CR-V, which Ron's Old-Fashioned Service Station made sure was up to the task. Mrs. Schultz sat next to me in the passenger seat, and Archie and Baz were settled in the back. I took two weeks to get things sorted at the shop, so I could close it for a few days for this trip. I also went to the station to talk things out with Heath, but he'd told the security officer, *Die Hard* Bruce, that he was too busy, and I should see Shep if I needed to add to my statement. I didn't think I could take it if this coolness from him was going to be permanent. All I could do was hope things would be different by the time I returned.

We'd inserted the true north GPS coordinates, and it seemed to be leading us to a deserted area, which was promising for our expedition. There could be a lava cave.

"I hope I'm not dragging you all on a long drive for nothing," I said.

"Who's being dragged? I begged you to let me come," Archie said. "I wouldn't have been able to stand the anticipation if I had to stay back in Yarrow Glen."

"We deserve these four days away no matter how this

turns out," I said. "Besides, we solved the riddles together. We all deserve to be in on this."

"Too bad Roman couldn't take the time away from his meadery," Baz said.

I nodded but kept silent. I was relieved, actually. Some space from him would give time for those sparks of chemistry to dull between us, so we could, hopefully, move on to being just friends.

"It won't be a wasted trip. I bet we'll find where the cheese is. I can't believe after all this, Max pulled a Glinda the Good Witch," Baz said.

I laughed. "What do you mean?"

"Glinda could've just told Dorothy in the beginning to tap her shoes to get home, so she wouldn't have had to go through all that. Just like Max could've just given you these coordinates without all the riddle stuff. We probably could've figured it out."

"Dorothy needed to appreciate home before it would work," Mrs. Schultz said from the front seat.

"Willa already appreciates the cheese," Baz said. "Isn't that why he left it to her in the first place?"

"I do appreciate it. I just don't want it. Everything that's happened makes that even clearer to me. I feel honored that he entrusted me with where his Bleu is, but I'm still not quite sure what I'll do with the information once I have it." I could feel the anxiety over it already forming a pit in my stomach. "I'd have to oversee the cheesemaking aspect, but Curds and Whey is barely a year old. I'm not ready to take time away from my shop. Besides, I want my shop to be known for everything *I've* always wanted it to be, not Max's creation. Being the successor to the Church Bleu would overshadow that."

"You could let other shops start carrying it. Or you

could sell it and use the money for Curds and Whey," Archie suggested.

"But is that what Max would want? He must've left it to me for a reason. I just don't know the right thing to do."

Mrs. Schultz patted my arm. "Maybe you'll know how you feel about it once you have it."

"Does Detective Heath know we're driving up there for it?" Baz asked.

"I left Max's note with the police, but I haven't gotten a chance to talk to Heath about the trip." I stared straight ahead at the road, so as not to see the concern I knew would be on Mrs. Schultz's face. She knew I was upset about the current state of affairs between me and Heath. The truth was, he hadn't returned any of my calls.

Luckily, the others seemed to sense I didn't want to talk about it and let the subject drop. Baz began rustling around the bag of snacks that were between him and Archie in the back seat.

"Anyone want something?" he asked.

"We just got on the road," Mrs. Schultz said, chuckling.

"I can't help it. You rocked these snacks, Mrs. Schultz."

"You can thank Lou. Once I told him I needed snacks for a road trip, he gathered everything for me."

"Lou is very nice to you, Mrs. Schultz," I said, hoping that stating it plainly would finally awaken her to his apparent interest.

"I still feel terrible for having lied to him about my ankle. He thinks his Epsom salts healed it."

"Nothing wrong with letting him think he did something good for you," Baz said.

"He *did* do something good for me—he offered to help. I didn't really expect that from Lou. I don't know why. He's helped Trace and he's good to the Melon sisters, not to mention his father, even though he complains about it. Maybe I haven't really known him all that well. He's always just been grumpy Lou."

Mrs. Schultz looked out the passenger window in silence. Was she giving Lou a little more thought?

"You want some, Arch?" Baz said, holding out a package of beef jerky he'd just opened.

"Nah, not hungry," Archie replied.

Archie had sounded down since we packed the car this morning. He'd been anxious to go on the trip, but I wondered whether it was the excitement of finding the cheese or some other reason. Maybe he was having second thoughts about moving out of Hope's.

"Are you all moved into your new apartment?" I asked, glancing at him through my rearview mirror.

"Thanks to Baz and Everett," Archie answered. He and Baz fist-bumped.

"How is it living with a new roommate?" Mrs. Schultz asked.

"Everett's cool and I like George being there. He's not Batman, but it's fun to live with a dog again." Batman was Archie's family Chihuahua, so named for his oversized pointy ears and his mask of black fur.

"You decided to keep the dog at your mom's for good?" I asked.

"He doesn't like other dogs, and I don't think my mom wants to give him up, anyway. I go over to the house a lot to see him, which she's happy about. I didn't go over as much when I lived with Hope." He sort of mumbled the last part and looked out the window.

Mrs. Schultz and I glanced at each other.

"Are things still okay between you and Hope?" she asked gingerly. "You said you'd both decided to keep dating?"

"She's not mad at you for moving in with Everett so soon, is she? Wasn't *she* the one who suggested you move out before you got up the nerve to say it?" Baz asked.

As it turned out, the advice Hope had asked me for the night the bookstore was vandalized was about her relationship with Archie. She felt the same way he did—that living together wasn't working out.

"Yeah, it was such a relief when she told me. We talked it out, and she was glad I already had a place to go. Everything was cool. She even said it was fine that I didn't want to work in the bakery anymore. That should've been my red flag that she wasn't telling me everything."

"Did she break up with you?" I asked. My heart already hurt for Archie.

"No. Worse."

"Worse?"

"Dude, she's not pregnant, is she?" Baz said.

"No! She's going to Paris," Archie said.

My hands tightened on the wheel in surprise. "Paris? For good?"

"No, for like five months for some French baking school. She's done with her cake classes at Sadler Culinary and she said this will give Rise and Shine the cachet it needs when she turns it into a cakery."

"A cakery? She's already got a bakery. What does she need to go all the way to Paris for just to change one letter?" Baz said.

Mrs. Schultz turned to look at Archie in the back seat. "That's a long time apart. I can see why you're so down. I'm sorry."

He remained quiet and looked out the window.

Mrs. Schultz faced forward in her seat, giving Archie some time with his emotions. "I wonder what Yarrow

Glen will do without a bread bakery. It's been here for almost twenty-five years."

I counted on it every morning for fresh sampling breads, but I couldn't fault Hope for following her own dreams. I hated that Archie was a casualty of that, but maybe it was for the best.

Archie spoke again, "She's not changing the bakery until she gets back. Her manager, Claude, agreed to run it while she's away."

"I'm sorry, Archie," I added. I wished I wasn't driving so I could give him a big hug.

"Your first broken heart. Welcome to the club," Baz said, raising a fist to bump.

Archie tapped it with his own without enthusiasm.

Mrs. Schultz tried to put a positive spin on the situation. "There are lots of ways to keep in touch long distance."

"I don't want to keep in touch. Why would I?" Archie grumbled.

Archie had always been understanding of everything Hope had been doing to get her footing running the bakery and putting her own stamp on it. It surprised me to hear him say this.

"You might feel differently after she's gone. You wouldn't want her not to follow her dreams, would you?" I said.

"No. Never! That's why I'm mad. She had it all planned out and didn't tell me anything about it until last night. She's leaving in a week. And she lied to me about why she wanted me to move out—she'd already told Claude he could rent her cottage while he's running the bakery. She said she applied late for the classes and didn't hear back, so she thought she didn't get in. That's when she asked me to move in with her. Why wouldn't she even tell me it was a possibility?"

"That stinks. She should've been straight up with you," Baz said. "Hey, I'm single too. We'll tear up the town— me, you, and Everett."

This got a smile out of Archie.

"I'm concentrating on cheese from now on," Archie said.

"Now you sound like me. Cheese will always be there for you, but don't let one broken heart sway you from love forever," I said, not that I listened to my own advice.

"All right, not forever. Just for today. I want to find that Church Bleu!"

"I'm on it," I said. I pressed the gas pedal a little harder.

Almost seven hours into the drive, with a stop for lunch, the GPS directed us to our final turn down a lonely road only a few miles from the Oregon border. I parked the car on the shoulder.

I took a deep breath. Only my curiosity about the cheese's location outweighed my anxiety about what it would mean for me to hold its secret. Max knew I didn't want it. As honored as I was that he'd entrusted it to me, I still wished he'd chosen someone else. One person's gift is another person's burden. I inhaled deeply again and reminded myself to take it one step at a time. Literally. According to the directions, we'd have to go the rest of the way on foot.

"You're in charge of the GPS directions from here," I said to Baz, unlatching my phone from its holder on top of the dashboard. I handed out water bottles before we exited the car. Luckily, there was no rain forecasted and it was in the low seventies, but the blazing sun would make it feel hotter.

"I hope this isn't someone's private property," Mrs. Schultz remarked, staring out at the expanse of land before us in her oversized sunglasses.

"You think there's a cave out there?" Archie said, sticking a cap on his head.

"We're gonna find out," I said. "Lead on, Baz."

The terrain was dry and rocky at first, but about two hundred yards in, it flattened out to a green field of cheatgrass that tickled our shins.

"You doing okay, Mrs. Schultz?" I asked.

"You bet. I used to help out with the marching band, leading them up and down the football field during practices. Granted, it's been a few years."

Baz was the one who stopped. He handed me the phone so he could open his water bottle. We all took a water break.

"Are we close?" Archie asked.

I looked at the dot on the phone's screen, then looked ahead of us. I was terrible with maps.

"The last time that thing spoke, she said it was a half mile ahead," Baz said, referring to the voice navigator.

"That close? I don't see anything." Archie said, looking ahead.

"Caves are underground, so there's not much to see from here." Baz closed the cap on his water and handed it to me in return for the phone.

"Let's just keep going and see if we find anything," I said.

Baz kept his eye on our progress on the phone to ensure we were walking in the right direction. Ahead, the field gave way to several clusters of Oregon white oaks above perfectly mown grass.

"Is that something?" Archie said, pointing in the direction of the trees.

There was something near one of the trees, but we couldn't make it out. The discovery raised our hopes and quickened our pace.

The voice navigation kept us apprised as we neared it. "You are nine hundred feet. You are eight hundred feet."

"It looks like a wrought-iron fence in the middle of nowhere," Baz said.

"You are seven hundred feet."

As we approached, it became clearer what was enclosed within the fence's square perimeter, which was no bigger than a few living rooms.

"You have reached your destination."

"It's a cemetery," Mrs. Schultz said.

"Why didn't it show up as one on the map?" Baz said

I perused the headstones. Almost all had the same surname: Dumas.

"It's a family plot," I said. "Private." I continued to walk through and found *Milo Dumas, loving son, brother, uncle* and *Joyce Dumas, loving wife and mother.* Then I came across the headstone I was looking for.

Here lies
Max Dumas
Forever in eternity
with all he loved

The dates of his birth and death were etched beneath it.

"I don't get it," Archie said. "Why would he bring us here?"

"Maybe there's another clue?" Baz wondered, still searching.

"We're not digging up his grave, are we?" Archie asked, horrified.

"No," I said, understanding it all now and feeling overcome with relief. "This is exactly what Max wanted me to find. Remember he told us to return to the first clue from *Rebecca* once we got here? *Here lies the secret.* And here lies Max Dumas. He wants me to know that the secret to his Church Bleu died with him." A smile broadened my face. "Oh Max, you devil."

RECIPES

Ham and Blue Cheese Tart

Mrs. Schultz's rich, savory tart was the brain food we needed for our first Team Cheese meeting.

Start-to-Finish Time: Appr. 40 minutes

Serves: 4

Ingredients
- 6 large sheets phyllo dough
- 1 tablespoon olive oil or spray oil
- 2 eggs
- 8–10 oz. cream cheese, room temperature
- 1 cup ham, chopped
- ½ cup scallions, chopped
- 2 cups fresh baby spinach
- ¾ cup blue cheese, crumbled, plus ¼ cup for topping
- 3 tablespoons pine nuts

Instructions
1. Preheat oven to 350°.
2. Brush (or spray) each phyllo dough sheet lightly with oil, and layer into a tart or springform pan, overlapping each sheet at a different angle around the pan so the corners fan out. (Think blooming flower.) Trim phyllo sheets so they only hang over the edges slightly.
3. Lightly beat eggs and mix in cream cheese until combined.
4. Add ham, scallions, spinach, and blue cheese until just combined.
5. Pour into your phyllo "flower."

6. Sprinkle with pine nuts and remaining blue cheese.
7. Bake for 30 minutes until just set and phyllo is lightly browned.
8. Cool for about 10 minutes before removing from pan.

Gorgonzola Garlic Bread

When I wanted some quick comfort food, this cheesy garlic bread did the trick. How many it serves depends on whether you're willing to share.

Start-to-Finish Time: 10 minutes
Makes: 1 loaf

Ingredients
- ¼ cup butter, softened
- ½ cup gorgonzola cheese
- 1 garlic clove, minced
- ½ teaspoon dried parsley
- 1 (16-oz) loaf crusty bread (French, Italian, sourdough, etc.)
- 3 tablespoons Parmesan cheese
- Salt and pepper

Instructions
1. Set oven broiler to high.
2. Cream the butter with the gorgonzola cheese. Add minced garlic, parsley, salt and pepper.
3. Slice bread in half lengthwise and spread cheese mixture on each half.
4. Sprinkle the top of the bread with the Parmesan cheese.
5. Place bread under the broiler until cheese is melted and bubbly.
6. Cut into generous slices and serve.

Cool and Creamy Dolce Dip

I recommended this cool, creamy dip to a customer and then used it later to satiate my own blue cheese cravings when I needed an easy and delicious snack.

Start-to-Finish Time: 5 minutes
Serves: a crowd

Ingredients
- 1 cup sour cream
- 1 cup mayonnaise
- ¼ cup scallions, chopped
- 4 oz. Gorgonzola Dolce (or blue cheese of your choice), crumbled
- 1 teaspoon lemon juice
- pepper to taste

Instructions
1. Combine sour cream, mayonnaise, scallions, blue cheese, and lemon juice.
2. Add fresh cracked pepper to taste.
3. Refrigerate until serving.
4. Serve with your favorite dipping snacks.